P9-CMK-718

Now You See It

Books by Jane Tesh

The Grace Street Mysteries
Stolen Hearts
Mixed Signals
Now You See It

The Madeline Maclin Mysteries
A Case of Imagination
A Hard Bargain
A Little Learning

Now You See It

A Grace Street Mystery

Jane Tesh

Poisoned Pen Press

Poisoned Pen Press

Copyright © 2013 by Jane Tesh

First Edition 2013

10 9 8 7 6 5 4 3 2 1

Library of Congress Catalog Card Number: 2013933203

ISBN: 9781464201967   Hardcover
      9781464201981   Trade Paperback

Poisoned Pen Press
6962 E. First Ave., Ste. 103
Scottsdale, AZ 85251
www.poisonedpenpress.com
info@poisonedpenpress.com

Printed in the United States of America

This one is for Orion, my oldest friend.

Acknowledgments

Once again, thanks to Annette Rogers and everyone at Poisoned Pen Press, and a special thanks to Ellen Larson for suffering through the first draft.

Chapter One

Do You Believe in Magic?

Monday morning, I stood at the back bay window of our dining room and watched the wind bend and crackle the ice-covered limbs of the oak trees. March in North Carolina. Spring or winter? You never knew. Camden staggered past, heading to the adjoining kitchen. He was still in his pajamas, pale hair in his eyes. He reached in the cabinet for the box of brown sugar Pop-Tarts, his major food source. His voice sounded wheezy.

"Another client coming your way, Randall."

"Thanks."

"A magician."

Great. I was doomed to deal with the screwier side of Parkland. "Lost his rabbit?"

"Not that I can see."

Having a psychic friend can be useful sometimes, and ordinarily, news of a client for my struggling detective agency would have me turning cartwheels. I'd been hired by local socialite Sandy Olaf to track down her stolen diamond bracelet. I could easily take on another client, even a magician. However, something had happened to put an added chill on my day. I'd been cleaning out my desk, and in among all the envelopes, erasers, dried up pens, stamps, and labels there'd been a picture of Lindsey. I'd caught only a glimpse, enough to realize it was one of her last school pictures and I didn't want to see it. I'd shoved the desk drawer in so hard, it clipped my knees.

How did that picture get in there? It must have been in one of the envelopes. I don't have any of her pictures or her toys or her books. I don't even know what Barbara has done with all her things. It isn't worth the searing pain that always shoots through me.

So I concentrated hard on the scene outside—the big trees, the hedge, the outline of the neighbors' porch and roof—trying to seal my emotions back in and freeze them as solid as the ice on the branches. People who have no idea what they're talking about are always telling me, to give it time. Give it time. There isn't enough time in the world. A part of me would always be at the scene of the crash, searching desperately through clouds of black smoke for the one thing I could not find.

The one thing that keeps me from going completely over the edge is, believe it or not, a dream I had of Lindsey. In the dream, she was on a beautiful playground with other children, all well and happy. I even heard her voice and saw that heartbreakingly sweet smile. Now, I'm not much on dreams. That's Camden's department. But every time I feel I can't stand the loneliness, I hang on to that dream. I knew Lindsey had forgiven me. The problem was forgiving myself.

While Camden waited for his Pop-Tarts to pop up, he poured a plastic cup full of Coke. His large blue eyes were sympathetic, but he didn't say anything. He didn't have to. We'd been round this mountain many times.

I refilled my coffee cup and took it to the counter that separates the kitchen from the dining room. Cindy, our gray house cat, wound about my legs until I refilled her food dish. Then I sat down on one of the stools. "Is Kary going to forgive me?"

Kary and I had had our first real argument yesterday, a rip-roaring quarrel in the Camden/Ellin style. As much as I love her help on my cases, I can't put Kary in any sort of danger, and when I found out she'd been to Murry's bar and strip club by herself one night to ask questions about a deadbeat dad I was trailing, I lost it.

"She'll forgive you," Camden replied. "She just got caught up in the thrill of the chase."

"My chase, not hers." This past Christmas, Kary had joined the Super Hero Society, a group of ordinary citizens who liked to dress up and patrol the streets. The SHS had actually helped me catch a killer, and although Kary enjoyed the drama, the late night patrols didn't fit with her busy schedule of classes and student teaching, and to my relief, she quit the group. "We're not going to see the return of Wonder Star, are we?"

"It'll work out." He winced. "Uh, oh."

I put my cup down. "What? What is it? Is she down at the docks wandering through abandoned warehouses?"

"Ellie's on her way."

About that time, Ellin Belton, Camden's girlfriend, arrived in a flurry of squealing tires, slammed doors, and hard footsteps stalking to the kitchen. She stood in front of us, hands on hips, golden curls trembling, blue eyes flashing like emergency lights.

"Cam, there is a crisis! Another woman has been hired to host 'Ready To Believe'!"

"What happened to Bonnie and Teresa?"

"They've been sent back to 'Horoscopes.' I can't believe this! They were excellent hosts. Now we've got this Sheila Kirk, and all because her husband is paying for the show. He said he'd underwrite the season, but only if his wife gets to be host of the program, which the president of the company agreed to without even asking me, and I'm the producer!"

"I thought you needed money," I said.

She cut her eyes around to me so sharply I'm surprised my stool didn't rock back. "But I don't know a thing about this woman! She could be terrible."

It was useless to point out that the Psychic Service Network's show isn't "Masterpiece Theater," and the audience applauds whenever they're told to, no matter who hosts.

"I've got to get over there right away, Cam, and I want you to come with me."

"Ellie. What for?"

"To see about this Sheila Kirk! You can tell what sort of person she is and what she'll do to the show."

"Why don't you try it for a while and see? She could be good."

"It's the least you can do." She frowned at him. "Did you just get up?"

Most women find Camden's rolled-over-in-bed sloppiness attractive, but Ellin had no time for that today.

"I wasn't needed at the boutique."

"Why do you insist on being a salesclerk? I could get you a much better job at the Service."

"No thanks."

Ellin still can't understand that Camden enjoys working at a dull job that has no bad vibes.

"Well, get dressed and come with me." She yanked her cell phone from her pocketbook and marched to the front door.

I watched her go because she does look good going away. "Not even a hello kiss. She loves you, all right."

In a few minutes, we could hear Ellin's rising voice. "But that's ridiculous! What does she expect me to do?" A long dark pause, and then: "What do you mean, share my office?"

Camden pushed his hair out of his eyes. "Oh, lord."

Ellin steamed back to the kitchen so fast, the coupons on the counter jumped. Her eyes gleamed like twin blowtorches. "This woman says we can share the office! *My* office! Camden, for heaven's sake, get up, get dressed, and come with me now. We've got to take care of this."

"Ellie, would you please calm down?"

"I can't calm down when the future of the PSN is at stake. I have worked for months to get 'Ready To Believe' on the air, and now this Sheila comes along with all these ideas—get some clothes on and come help me."

"All right, all right. Don't panic."

Don't panic. She'd already blasted off and orbited the Earth three times. He went up the stairs, leaving me alone with Ellin, a situation I try to avoid. I decided not to say anything, although I agreed with Camden that this new woman might not be so bad if given a chance. Ellin fumed and paced and finally glared me.

"Don't you have a client or something?"

"Any minute now."

"Haven't you found a better office somewhere?"

"Nope."

More glaring. She isn't happy the Randall Detective Agency takes up the first-floor parlor of what might be her future home. She isn't happy the owner and operator of said agency occupies the same planet.

Camden returned, dressed in his usual cold weather attire: jeans, sneakers, and overlarge sweatshirt. Ellin sighed but didn't comment. He owns one suit, and that's for Sundays.

"Let's go."

Camden took his jean jacket and the blue muffler Kary had knitted for him for Christmas off the hall tree. "The magician will call in about a half hour, Randall."

"Okay, thanks. You kids have fun."

◇◇◇

In exactly half an hour, the phone rang, and a man's voice said, "Mister Randall? Lucas Finch. I understand you can find missing items?"

"I'll do my best. What have you lost?" Deck of cards? Couple of pigeons?

"I don't want to discuss it over the phone, but I don't like driving in this weather—traffic is horrible."

"Why don't I come to you?"

"Can you? I'm in Friendly Shopping Center. Box-It."

I first thought this was his way of saying "Roger" or "Ten-Four." Box-It?

"We're in between Gremlin Cleaners and Weigh To Go."

"I'll be right over."

◇◇◇

I put on my coat and went out to my white '67 Plymouth Fury. After three tries, she started and chugged down the driveway. Even though ice still glistened on the trees, the roads were clear, and I had no trouble driving to Friendly Shopping Center, a couple of miles from home, accompanied by my favorite jazz band, the New Black Eagles, stomping through "Old Fashioned Swing." The shopping center started as one main road with shops on either side and has grown to become its own city, including three roads and side streets, plus a sprawl down the hill to a huge bookstore and Wal-Mart Super Store. Box-It was on the far end of road number three, signs in the windows proclaiming: If It Can Be Boxed, We'll Box-It, and No Item Too Large Or Small.

Lucas Finch met me at the door. He was a tall, elegant-looking man with a short beard and round glasses. He wore a brown suit, a white shirt with thin brown stripes, and a tie patterned in little brown and gold squares. I guess I had expected a cape and a top hat.

"Come in, come in."

I stepped inside. Boxes of all sizes and colors crowded the small shop. Large crates were stacked in one corner. Tiny boxes only a few inches long were lined up on glass shelves. There were even triangular shaped boxes and mailing tubes, wooden, plastic, and cardboard.

Lucas Finch wiped his glasses on a silky brown handkerchief and replaced them, his brown eyes looming large. "Thanks so much for coming over. You didn't have any trouble, did you?"

"No trouble. What can I do for you?"

"I've lost a box."

I resisted the urge to ask: How can you tell?

"A very important box. In fact, I can't believe it's missing. I've always taken such good care of it."

I shrugged out of my coat. I took out my notebook and pen. "If you'll start at the beginning."

Finch cleared a stack of yellow cardboard boxes off a chair and motioned for me to sit down. On the wall behind the counter were several framed photographs. All of the pictures were of two well-dressed men, identical down to their expensive-looking shoes, posing at the pyramids, at the Leaning Tower of Pisa, and in front of an ornate theater, the marquee proclaiming: The Fabulous Finch Brothers. Finch saw my interest. "My brother Taft and I on our latest world tour."

"You're both magicians, then."

"Yes. We belong to a group called WOW."

"Wow?"

"Wizards of Wonder. We're a brotherhood of magicians. The missing box was going to be used for a special trick called the Vanishing Ruby. After working on this trick for months, Taft and I finally found the perfect box. We paid a lot of money for it. This box was once owned by none other than the great Harry Houdini himself. It's irreplaceable."

"Could you describe this box?"

He held out his hands. "It's about a foot long and seven inches wide, four inches deep, a rich golden color with a large fancy letter H carved on the top, surrounded by rabbits, hoops, and stars. The inside is lined with red velvet."

"Anything else inside?"

"The key to a cabinet in my house that's filled with my collection of magic memorabilia."

"Oh, so that's your only key, and you can't get your cabinet open?"

"No, I have another key. It's all part of a bet I made with some of the other magicians. There's a trick to opening the box. If someone finds the box and gets it open, they can have whatever they like out of the cabinet."

"Don't you figure one of your fellow wizards already found the box?"

"I thought so at first, but no one's come forward to claim the prize."

"Maybe they're still trying to get the box open."

"I've talked to all of them, and no one has found the box yet." Before I could say, well, someone might be lying about that, he said, "I know these people. We're all friends. They were all excited about the contest. I'm sure if anyone one of them found the box, they'd tell the others."

"How many people know about the box?"

"All the members know. Six people."

Well, that was a relief. I could see myself hunting all over Parkland for rogue magicians. "Let me have their names."

"Well, besides Taft and myself, there's Rahnee Nevis, owner of the club; WizBoy, her assistant; Jilly, the bartender; and Jolly Bob, who owns a magic shop called Transformation and Company."

I wrote down the names. "These are the only people who know about the bet?"

"Yes."

"Where was the box last seen?"

"At our club, the headquarters for WOW. The Magic Club."

I'd heard of the Magic Club, a nightclub downtown that specialized in magic acts for entertainment. "The one on Freer Street?"

"Yes. We meet once a week, all the magicians in town, to talk shop and share some tricks. I hid the box in a secret place in the club. When I went to check on Thursday, the box wasn't there."

"Who was the last one to see it?"

"I showed it to Rahnee right before I hid it. She says she doesn't know what happened to it."

I turned another page on my notebook. "Where did you hide it?"

He looked around as if someone might be hiding in one of the boxes around us, listening, and lowered his voice. "There's a fake cinder block in the back wall of the storage room. I discovered it quite by accident. You can push it in, and there's a hollow place in the wall just big enough for the box. It's the seventh block up from the floor."

"Why didn't you call the police, Mr. Finch?"

"I didn't want word getting out that this sacred item was missing. Besides the fact that Taft is extremely upset, WAM might very well take advantage of the situation."

"WHAM? I thought they broke up a long time ago."

Finch did not appreciate my humor, rolling his eyes. "Not the British pop group. W-A-M. Wizards and Amazing Mages, our competition in Charlotte."

"Would WAM go so far as to steal this special box?"

"I would imagine they'd try anything to discredit WOW."

I had no idea the magic world was so treacherous. I wrote "WAM" in my notebook. "Besides the evil wizards of Charlotte, is there anyone else in particular who wanted the box?"

"Talk to Rahnee. She knows who comes in and out of the club. I wouldn't trouble with anyone else unless it becomes absolutely necessary. As I said, I don't want everyone in town to know the box is missing. Please consider taking this case. I have to get that box back."

"I'll be happy to take your case," I told him my fee.

"That's fine. Thank you."

He wrote me a check, and I told him I'd get started right away.

Chapter Two

That Old Black Magic

The Magic Club was located right in the middle of downtown, which means parking's impossible. I finally drove around to Coronation Street and found one of my old parking places near Morton's Detective Agency where I used to work. Seeing the drab building with its gray alley and even grayer prospects made me extremely pleased with myself for striking out on my own. Even though finding Finch's magic box was a goofy case likely to be solved in a couple of hours, it was still a hell of lot better than working for Mort.

The front of the Magic Club was dark, but when I pushed open the glass door, I entered a sparkly world of neon signs and glitter balls. Glow-in-the-dark stars and moons decorated the ceiling. A polished wooden bar ran the length of one side of the room, the mirror behind it reflecting all the colors and lights. Round tables and chairs filled the space in front of a large stage complete with red velvet curtains and a spotlight where a large man in shiny black clothes was trying to coax doves out of a tube. Music was playing. I recognized the tune. "That Old Black Magic." No one was at the bar. No one paid me any attention, so I wandered up a few dark stairs and found myself in the wings of the stage.

The magician was having trouble with his old black magic. He gave up on the tube and spun theatrically, his traditional cape billowing with a glint of red satin lining. He spread his hands in a big "ta-dah!" gesture, but nothing happened except a few tiny feathers that drifted to the floor. The music stopped, and a firm female voice said, "Thank you." The large man came off, shaking more white feathers from his hands.

"I can't believe this," he said. "That trick always works. Betty, you stupid bird, get out here."

A dove peered from his pocket. The man sighed and pulled it out. "I'm going back to rabbits, I swear I am." A small white terrier of indeterminate breed poked its head out of another pocket and whined. "That includes you, Binky."

On stage, the man had looked younger and more confident. Now I could see he was closer to fifty with a thick waist and bags under his small brown eyes.

"Do you know where I can find Rahnee Nevis?" I asked.

"She's out front, of course, running the auditions."

"She?" I'd heard the name as "Ronnie."

"Rahnee the Magnificent, and she is, too, friend. Are you here for the auditions?"

"I'm here to see Ms. Nevis."

"What a pity. You have a remarkable presence, a natural for the stage."

"The Remarkable Randall, that's me." I went back down the stairs and looked out across the rows of tables. A woman sat down front, a truly magnificent woman with a long, thick mane of red hair pulled back with a gold band, blue eyes gleaming in glitter ball light, a full figure all in black, with a Viking attitude.

She gave me a quick, critical glance. "Well, auditions are closed for today, but I suppose we could fit you in. I like your look: straightforward, no flash. Could work very nicely. What's your act?"

"I'm David Randall. Lucas Finch hired me. It's about a box."

Her expression changed. "I see. We should talk in my office. This way, please."

She led me to a small office and indicated a black leather chair. I sat, admiring the posters on the walls. Each one highlighted a different magician and his specialty. The Amazing Andre and His Cabinet of Death. The Mysterious Mage of Morocco and the Mists of Memory. Lu Fang and the Oriental Fire of Fate.

Ms. Nevis saw my interest. "Some of our most successful members of Wizards of Wonder."

"So Lucas and Taft are up next with their Vanishing Ruby?"

"A useless trick without the box." There were some small brightly colored balls on her desk, and while she talked, she fiddled with them, making them disappear in one hand and reappear in the other. I couldn't tell if this was her way of keeping in practice, or if she was nervous about something. "What did Lucas say?"

"That he came here to check on it and it was gone."

"Most unfortunate. The Finch brothers have been working on that trick for some time."

"Do you know where he hid the box?"

Somehow the pink ball had hopped from her left hand to her right. "No, it's all part of this contest he wanted to have for the members of WOW. I know he hid it somewhere in the club, but I've really been too busy to hunt for it."

Now the pink ball was back to her left hand, and the green ball was in her right. "Excuse me, but how are you doing that?"

"This?" She spread her fingers, and there was a different colored ball between each one. "Simple sleight of hand."

"Doesn't look simple to me. Are you practicing for an act?"

"Always." She still seemed on edge.

"So you're not interested in the bet?"

"I know about the bet, but I'm not a collector. There isn't anything in the Finches' collection I would want. It's hard for me to believe anyone took the box. It's highly unethical for a magician to steal another magician's trick."

"But it happens, doesn't it? Didn't some guy go on TV, giving away secrets?"

Rahnee Nevis' face darkened. "A disgrace. No one would do that here."

"Who else knows the box is missing?"

"My assistant, WizBoy. We're trying to keep it quiet. We wouldn't want others to know their possessions aren't safe."

WizBoy. Now that conjured up a picture. "Is WizBoy here now?"

"Yes, he should be around somewhere."

"Is Taft here?"

"He was here last night for a performance. I haven't seen him today." One of the little balls slipped from her fingers and bounced on the floor. I caught it and handed it back to her. "Thanks. You see why I practice."

You are definitely nervous about something, I thought. *Even more so when I asked about Taft.*

Rahnee put the little balls in a glass dish on her desk. "Let's talk to WizBoy. He should be backstage getting things ready for tonight's show."

WizBoy—what an unfortunate nickname—was thin and scrawny. He'd shaved his head except for an orange cowlick dangling over one eye. A silver hoop eyebrow ring dangled over the other. He had on a skintight lime tank top and tight jeans. The tattoo on his arm had the word "abracadabra" coming out of a skull's top hat. The perfect thing for your punk magician. He was on the floor taping down an extension cord and stood when Rahnee called him. Rahnee introduced us, and he shook my hand.

"Got a lot of work to do here, man. Hope this won't take long."

"Just a few questions. Did you ever see the Houdini box?"

"Yeah, Lucas showed it to me."

"When was that?"

He hesitated. "I don't remember the exact day. Sometime after he and Taft got it."

Like Rahnee, WizBoy seemed nervous about something. "But you're in on this bet, right? Do you have any idea who would want to steal the box?"

WizBoy tugged on his eyebrow ring, which made me wince. "Don't know who'd want it. I know some magicians are doing things with rings and ropes but not boxes, and I don't ever use anything but cards. It's too bad for Lucas and Taft, it really is. They been working hard on that ruby trick. Now if you'll excuse me, I gotta get this done."

"I told the Finches if the box was that important they should insure it and put it in a safer place and not play games with it," Rahnee said. "I can't imagine who'd steal it. Hey, don't put that there!"

This last command was addressed to the large magician with the tube full of doves. He was attempting to put a cage of birds on a trunk. Binky whined and scratched at the trunk. Rahnee strode forward.

"That belongs to Taft. You don't ever mess with someone else's props. You ought to know that."

The magician backed off. "Sorry. I was just going to set the cages on top."

"And what's wrong with your dog?" She shooed the terrier away. "Stop that."

Binky continued to whine and scratch.

WizBoy laughed. "Does he think he's a drug dog or something? Is he sniffing out cocaine?"

"What's in this trunk?" I asked.

"As I said, it belongs to Taft," Rahnee said. "He and Lucas are working on an escape act. As far as I know, it's empty."

Binky and I had other ideas. "Can you open it?"

Rahnee tried the latch. The trunk was locked. "We keep the key behind the bar." When she came back, she unlocked and opened the trunk. Inside lay a tall body, folded neatly to fit.

Rahnee shuddered and recoiled. "It's Taft!"

I looked at the white face. Taft, like Lucas, was elegantly dressed in a suit and tie, now unfortunately crumpled.

Rahnee looked as if she might faint. "Oh, my God, is he dead? I can't believe he's dead."

WizBoy grabbed his cell phone. The bird magician started to reach into the trunk. I caught his hand.

"Don't touch anything."

"I wanted to see if he's alive."

I'd never seen anyone more dead. "I don't think so. Let the police handle it." I turned to Rahnee. "Who's been in here today?"

Rahnee looked like a Viking whose last ship has sailed. "Dozens of people. We held auditions all morning."

"When did you last see Taft?"

"Saturday night. He performed during the nine o'clock show."

"What about Lucas? Was he here?"

She was trembling. "No. He had another engagement. We should call—" Her voice quit.

I sat her down on one of the metal folding chairs. "Take it easy. I'll call him." I took another look at Taft Finch, being careful not to touch anything. He was curled up, a sickly shade of white, and he wasn't breathing. If he wasn't dead, he was doing an excellent illusion.

I called Lucas and told him to come to the club right away. "There's been an accident. I'm afraid your brother's dead."

I heard him gasp. "I'm on my way."

The bird magician came up beside me. "What the hell's going on?"

"Not much of an escape trick. When did you last see him?"

"I missed the auditions Saturday, so Rahnee let me try out today. Bart, Binky, and His Baffling Birds."

"You notice anyone around this trunk today?"

"No, not really."

"Nobody used this trunk?"

"You heard what Rahnee said. Nobody messes with the props."

The police and the ambulance arrived, and we stood back while they worked. The policeman in charge was an old friend of mine, Jordan Finley. When he saw me, he sighed and shook his head. Jordan is large and square with sharp blue eyes that miss very little. I tend to get in his way.

Jordan moved everyone into the main room of the club. Rahnee and Bart sat down at one of the tables. Rahnee was sobbing. Binky curled up under Bart's chair. WizBoy and I stood. "All right, Randall. What's the connection this time?"

"Taft's brother Lucas hired me to find a missing box. I came over to talk to Ms. Nevis. The dog started scratching at the trunk, so she opened it and we found Taft inside. The last time anybody saw Taft Finch was Saturday night around nine when he performed in the club."

"You know Taft Finch?"

"This is the first time we've met."

Lucas Finch arrived, and when he saw his brother's body, he broke down completely, choking on tears. "What was he thinking? Why did he try this by himself?"

"When was the last time you saw your brother, sir?" Jordan asked.

"Saturday."

"This trunk is part of his act?"

"No, we were supposed to do this together."

"This box you hired Randall to find. Does it have anything to do with the trunk?"

Lucas was unable to reply. Rahnee gulped back another sob and answered for him. "The box is a small box for another magic trick. We think it's been stolen."

"Was it a valuable box? Would someone kill to have it?"

Apparently so, I thought. *Unless Taft climbed in the trunk for a nap and couldn't get out.* "It was valuable to Lucas and Taft. It was going to be the centerpiece for their new act." I turned to Lucas. "But what about the act you and Taft planned using this trunk?"

Lucas managed to speak. "We were working on an escape act, but Taft never would've tried it without me. We were always very careful. Besides, there's a way to get out."

"You can unlock the trunk from the inside?"

"It's a special latch that doesn't need a key. Most magicians' trunks have more than one way to open them. This one is hidden in the lining. All Taft would've had to have done was pull back the lining and slide the bolt over."

Jordan turned another page in his notebook. "What about the value of the smaller box, sir?"

"It's very valuable to a collector of magical memorabilia. It supposedly belonged to Houdini. Taft and I paid several thousand dollars for it."

"Is this trunk always kept backstage? Who else has access to the backstage area?"

Anyone who walks up those steps, I thought. *No one questioned me.*

Rahnee said, "We auditioned new acts Saturday, so there've been many people backstage."

"How about last night, ma'am? Do you lock up?"

"Yes, and I set the alarm."

"Anyone else have keys to the club?"

"WizBoy and Jilly have keys. WizBoy's my assistant and stage manager. Jilly's our bartender."

Jordan asked Lucas to come to the station for some more questions. He talked to WizBoy for a while and then thanked us for our cooperation and reminded us to stay in town. He gave me a long stare. "Consider yourself off this case, Randall. We'll handle things from now on."

The police worked a while longer, collecting what they hoped might be evidence, taking photographs, writing notes, and talking in low voices. Finally they allowed the EMTs to take Taft Finch's body from the trunk an carry it off on a stretcher. The trunk was hauled out by two of the larger policemen. When everyone had gone, Rahnee, Bart, and I sat down at the bar. WizBoy went around to the other side of the bar and poured everyone a drink.

Rahnee put her head down on one hand. "I can't believe this." Her voice shook. "Taft was such a kind man. Do you think someone meant to kill him?"

"Did Taft have any enemies? Any rivals? Who'd benefit from his death?"

"No, this is crazy. He didn't have an enemy in the world."

WizBoy passed me a beer. "I guess you're out of a job now, Randall."

"Oh, no, he isn't." Rahnee straightened and gave her face one last wipe to clear the tears from her eyes. "Randall, I want you to find out who did this."

Bart looked at her askance. "The policeman told him to back off."

She fixed me with a fierce stare. "That won't stop you, will it?"

"It never has before."

"All right." She was back in command mode now. "Give me some time. I'll have a list of everyone who was here Saturday for the auditions. Jilly should be in by then, too."

WizBoy looked alarmed. "She wouldn't have anything to do with this."

I could tell Rahnee was trying to be patient. "She might remember something useful. She was at the bar all night."

He relaxed. "Oh."

I looked around the club. "Anyone else? Waitresses? Backstage help? Cleanup crew?"

"There's only WizBoy, Jilly, and myself. When I bought the club, it was losing money. I've managed to turn it around, but I'm still working on keeping expenses down."

"Were there any delivery men today? Repairmen?"

"I do most the repairs myself. WizBoy helps me."

If he'd had a chest, WizBoy would've puffed it out. "I can fix most things around here. I help run the bar, too. Anything I can do now, Rahnee?"

"Go make a sign for the door, will you? Let our customers know what's happened. We'll need to have some sort of memorial service for Taft." She shuddered and sat down at one of the tables. "Poor Lucas. I can't imagine what he's going through."

"So they were close?"

"Oh, yes. They did everything together."

"No rivalry between them? Some professional jealousy?"

"Not at all, and believe me, I know that when I see it. They're great guys, real gentlemen. You don't see that much these days. Taft would always—" Her voice threatened to quit again.

"I'll do my best to find out what happened."

She squeezed my hand. "Thanks."

Bart looked worried. "Do you suppose I could go now?"

"Give me your phone number and address," I said. "I'd like to talk to you later."

"Yeah, sure." He handed me a card decorated with birds. "No problem."

I thanked him and he left. "I'd like to look around backstage," I said to Rahnee.

"Of course."

The area behind the stage was narrow and empty. One side of the stage had a stack of folding chairs in one corner, a couple of card tables, and several large empty wooden boxes. On the other side, where the trunk holding Taft's body had been, were several stools and a large stack of flat boards. I looked through this stack, finding posters for past events and signs announcing special acts, or informing patrons that the club would be closed for the holidays. There was also a rack of costumes, shiny black jackets, shirts in red and blue satin, sparkly tights, and capes. On top of the rack was a box of hats, gloves, and scarves.

I came back to Rahnee. "Do any of those costumes belong to Taft? Did Taft or Lucas have any other props stored here?"

"No."

"I'd like to look in the storage room."

She pointed toward the front door. "To your right, past the bar."

The storage room was bigger than I expected, lined with shelves filled with supplies for the bar, paper towels, toilet tissue, boxes of envelopes, and crates of beer. I had to move several boxes of napkins to get to the back wall. I counted seven cinder blocks up from the floor and gave the seventh block a push. It slid back, revealing an empty hole. When I put the block back in place, I noticed that unlike its neighboring blocks, number seven had a small dark splotch. Mold? A mark Lucas had made to find it? I couldn't tell, but it was possibly blood.

I put the boxes of napkins back and returned to Rahnee. She'd remembered something. "Taft's coat is in my office. He left it at the club one night. I kept forgetting to tell him."

I followed her to her office. She took a long brown coat out of the closet. I thought I might find cards, or rabbits, or long strings of colored scarves in the pockets, but all I found was a wad of tissue, a paper clip, and several blue pills.

"Any idea what these pills are?"

"I'm not sure. I know occasionally Taft had a problem with insomnia. Maybe that's some sort of sleep medication."

It wasn't much, but it could be a clue. I put the pills in my pocket.

Rahnee took the coat from me. "Lucas should have this, or maybe the police need to see it. You have to prove this was an accident, Randall."

"I'll do my best."

As she wrote a check, I couldn't help but think back to this morning and Camden's prediction of another client. Well, now I had three clients: Lucas Finch, Sandy Olaf, and Rahnee. A box, a bracelet, and a body. Maybe that old black magic was really working.

Chapter Three

Semi-Charmed Life

While I waited to hear from Rahnee, I checked in with Sandy Olaf. She lived in Deer Point Estates, Parkland's ritziest neighborhood, and not only did she live in Deer Point Estates, she lived in Barrington Trace, a gated community within the Estates. I wasn't sure I'd be allowed to breathe such rarefied air, but the gateman checked his list and let me in. Sandy's house was built along the lines of a Ramada Inn, with enough columns for a Greek temple. She was on the front steps, waving and smiling.

You'd never guess Sandy Olaf's one of the wealthiest women in Parkland. She has blonde hair and blue eyes and the pleasant addled look of a caterer who isn't sure she has enough hors d'oeuvres. She wears very little makeup and dresses in plain-looking but very expensive blouses and slacks, like the navy blue outfit she had on today.

"Good morning, David. What a chilly day! Come in."

I followed her down a couple of acres of foyer to a huge living room decorated in vertigo-inducing patterns of stripes and flowers, all pink and blue. There wasn't a bare spot in the room. Everything had a matching pattern, from the wallpaper to the rugs to the cushions on the sofas. On one of the tables, Sandy had an array of papers and several telephones.

"Sit where you like. I'm in the middle of organizing the Arts Council Auction, so the phones are going to be ringing. I'm sorry, but I have to get it done. The Salvation Army fund-raiser is next week, and this has to be finished."

I sat down on a striped sofa. "That's all right."

"I had the most fun setting up the Cancer Relay. Do you know we raised over fifty thousand dollars? I was so tickled." One of the phones rang. "What did I tell you? Please excuse me."

She picked up the phone and chatted excitedly about a painting someone was donating to the auction. I looked around the room, being careful not to turn my head too fast. Huge ugly vases posed on little marble-topped tables. Pictures of foxhunts and flowers in heavy gold frames clashed with the striped and flowered wallpaper. Even the ceiling had flowers and stripes.

Sandy hung up. "Now then, where were we?"

"Your missing piece of jewelry."

"Oh, yes! My diamond tennis bracelet. David, I'm embarrassed to say I have several, but this one was given to me by my dearest friend, Bertie, who passed away from AIDS last year. You can't imagine the sentimental value. I mean, I do my best for the AIDS Foundation here in town, all in Bertie's memory, but that bracelet meant so much to me. Our initials are engraved on the clasp, mine and Bertie's. I'm devastated."

"When did you last see it?"

"Well, that's the trouble. I run around town all day, and I can't remember." Another phone rang. "Excuse me again. Hello? Kennedy, sweetheart, how are you?" She listened a moment, and then gave a sigh of exasperation. "But I told Andre you needed those ice sculptures by Saturday. He doesn't have any of them done? All right, dear, just leave it to me. No, it's no trouble. Give my love to Boots." She hung up. "You'd think getting a few ice sculptures for the Debutantes' Ball would be a snap in this town, but everything is such a production. Let me call Andre and sort this out."

While she made her call, I got up and wandered the room. If the whole house was this busy, I was going to have to get some

Dramamine before I began my search. I came back to the table and looked at her calendar, hoping for a clue. It was as scrambled as the room, dates and appointments marked out, rewritten, and squeezed in, with a bright confetti of Post-It notes on top.

Sandy hung up. "It's a mess, isn't it?"

"Can you recall the last time you wore your bracelet?"

She pointed to last week. "I think it was sometime here. I'm pretty sure I had it on when I hosted the PETA Banquet—I almost wore my mink—can you imagine? Yes, I think I had the bracelet on that night."

"And you remember having it when you came home?"

"Yes, I'm pretty sure."

I looked at the appointments for the rest of that week. Sandy had organized, hosted, or emceed four banquets, a charity ball, a dinner party, and two fund-raisers.

"David, you can eliminate the Garden Club Banquet. I wasn't able to go, and someone else took my place. And the banquet at the Silver Estate has been moved to next month."

"So, counting the PETA banquet, that's two banquets, two fund-raisers, a dinner party, and a charity ball."

"That's right."

I copied down the addresses: The dinner party had been at April Meadows, the ball at the Parkland Country Club, the other banquet at the Parkland Hilton, and the fund-raisers had been at First Methodist Church and the Lutheran Church of the Redeemer. "I'll check out these places first. I assume you've searched everywhere here?"

"Everywhere."

"Well, if I don't have any luck at these places, I'll come search your house. You may have overlooked your bracelet."

Her gesture took in the scramble on the table. "Around here, that's possible." She unearthed a checkbook from the piles of paper. "Let me write you a check."

"Does anyone else know the bracelet's missing?"

"The housekeeper helped me look."

"Anyone else?"

"No." As she tore off the check and handed it to me, the phone rang again. "Oh, my goodness."

"That's okay," I said. "I have enough to get started. Could I talk to your housekeeper?"

"Yes, she should be in the kitchen. That's down the hall and to your left."

"All right. I'll check with you later today."

"Thanks, David."

As I went out, I heard her say into the phone, "Ann, dear, I'm so glad you called. I need you to check on the car. Didn't you say you could donate an Infiniti? Wonderful! Well, could you get two? Oh, that would be fabulous! Can you get a black one and a silver one? That way, they'd match the decorations."

Down the hall and to my left took me about thirty minutes. I must have passed twenty-five rooms, parlors, and other hallways. The kitchen stretched the length of the house, a gleaming array of appliances, pots and pans hanging above like copper balloons. A small woman stood at a vast cutting board in the center of the room, chopping carrots and celery.

She glanced up. Her prominent lower teeth made her look like a cheerful little bulldog. "Good morning."

"Good morning. I'm David Randall. Mrs. Olaf hired me to find her diamond bracelet. May I ask you a few questions?"

"I assure you, we've searched every inch of this house," she said. I almost expected her to say, And I sniffed every corner! "Not an easy task, as you can imagine."

"Do you remember the last time you saw her wearing the bracelet?"

She continued to chop vegetables. "She had it on the night she went to the animal rights banquet, and she had it on when she came home, because she came down here and wanted a hamburger. She said she felt bad, but after all the salad at the banquet, what she really wanted was a juicy steak. We made a joke about the rights of cows." She looked at me with an anxious expression. I resisted the urge to pat her head. "I'm paid extremely well, Mister Randall. I'd never take any of her things."

"I'm not accusing anyone. I'm retracing Mrs. Olaf's steps."
I checked my notes. "So, she had it on the night of the PETA
banquet, and you noticed she still had it on when she came
home and wanted a steak."

"Yes, I am almost certain."

"Does she always come down here for a snack after these
social functions?"

"Not always."

"How about Monday night?"

For a moment, the housekeeper's little tongue stuck out as
she tried to remember, and I had to turn a sudden laugh into a
cough. "I can't recall."

I looked at my list. "She had a dinner party, a charity ball,
and a banquet at the Hilton. Okay, how about after the Lutheran
Church fund raiser?"

"That was the one with all the chickens." Chickens! Woof!
"There were quite a few left over, so I helped her pack them."

I really needed to rein myself in. "Did you notice the bracelet
then?"

"I'm sorry to say I don't remember."

"And the First Methodist Church?"

"That was the one with the yard sale and all the baby clothes.
I remember because Mrs. Olaf brought home a big box for my
sister's little girl."

"Any chance the bracelet fell off into the box?"

"No, no. My sister and I emptied the box at her home. I
would have seen the bracelet."

It was hard not to envision the housekeeper and her sister
frolicking like puppies in the clothes. "This may seem like an
odd question, but does Mrs. Olaf have any enemies? I know she
does lots of charitable work in town. Is there anyone jealous of
her success? Anyone who feels replaced or slighted? Sometimes
these country club women try to top each other doing things
for the less fortunate."

She paused in her chopping. "I have never heard anyone say
anything bad about her."

"Okay, thanks. I might check with you again later."

Her teeth jutted out even further. "You check any time you like. If someone stole that bracelet, they need to be caught."

I couldn't imagine a thief getting past this tough little woman.

Outside, I patted the Fury's hood. "Now wouldn't it be nice to find Lucas Finch's missing box with Sandy's bracelet inside?"

Chapter Four

We've Got Magic To Do

My next stop was the Parkland Hilton. The manager gushed over Sandy's generosity and organizational skills and sent a young man in an official-looking blue jacket to show me to the banquet hall and kitchen.

The young man's gold nameplate read "Guest Coordinator." He was thin with a crest of hair that I'm sure took him all morning to perfect. If Sandy's housekeeper reminded me of a bulldog, this anxious fellow reminded me of a nervous yet very particular bird. "We've looked everywhere, Mister Randall. I'm afraid something as nice as a diamond tennis bracelet might have been stolen. As I recall, there were over three hundred people at that banquet."

"But they paid to attend, right? How much?"

"Five hundred dollars."

"Doesn't sound like a thieving kind of crowd."

He cocked his head exactly like a cockatiel. "You'd be surprised. We've had very wealthy guests steal small tables and light fixtures, and one man actually attempted to haul out an ice machine."

In the kitchen, we looked into cabinets, air vents, and drains. The tablecloths had fringe, so even though they had been washed since the banquet, we checked them all to see if the bracelet had gotten snagged. Then we went down to the laundry and looked in the washers and dryers. Back in the banquet hall, the young man found a corner of carpet coming loose, so we checked under that.

"I don't know where else to look," he said. "I promise a thorough search was made the first time."

I shook his hand. "Thanks for your help. I've got a few more places to look."

◇◇◇

My next stop was the Lutheran Church of the Redeemer. By now, I was expecting a bear-like man or a cat woman, but I was in for something new. The assistant pastor was an ordinary-looking man, but he had a strange whistling lisp that made me wonder how he got through the church services. His congregation would get a sermon and an anthem all at once. He was equally complimentary about Sandy.

"Mrs. Olaf is a wonderful person. She works tirelessly with all our worthy causes."

"Works tirelessly" and "causes" trilled like little birds.

"Where did you have your chicken dinner?"

"Here in the fellowship hall. We served over seven hundred people. It was a tremendous success. And we had enough chickens left over to take to the homeless shelter. I'd say almost a thousand people were fed, plus we had a lot of leftovers we've frozen for next month's dinner."

The fellowship hall was a wide yellow room about the size of a basketball court with the standard folding tables and chairs. The church kitchen was wall-to-wall stainless steel, with huge refrigerator freezers and sinks as large as bathtubs.

"You must do a lot of dinners."

"Oh, yes," he said. "We believe in feeding the flock. These dinners are surprisingly special experiences."

Flocks of happy birds, I imagined as "surprisingly special experiences" washed over me. The kitchen was spotless. Everything in the cabinets was perfectly arranged.

"Did Mrs. Olaf go anywhere else in the church?"

"No, she stayed right here all evening, serving food." He paused, "Although, at one point, I think she went out for more bread."

"Which way would she have gone?"

He led me out the side door of the kitchen and down a narrow path to the parking lot. Along the way, I searched the grass and behind the line of shiny plastic trash cans. Nothing. The parking lot was a smooth expanse of asphalt. If her bracelet had fallen off here, it would have been instantly noticed.

I thanked the pastor. "I appreciate your time."

"I assure you we shall search ceaselessly," he said, with a flourish of singing "s" sounds.

Two down, three to go. I was only a couple of streets over from Food Row, so I picked up a couple of cheeseburgers at the Quik-Fry. Then I called Rahnee and asked if she had her list ready.

"Not yet." I could tell by her voice she hadn't stopped crying. "I'm sorry. I can't seem to get myself together."

"Don't worry about it. I can stop by tomorrow."

"No, I want you to have all the information you need. It shouldn't be too much longer. Let me call you."

"That's fine. I understand." I wanted to tell her I understood completely the sudden loss, the shock and bewilderment. You think someone is going to be with you forever, and suddenly they're gone. Just gone. And from the way she was reacting, I wondered if there had been something else besides friendship between Rahnee and Taft. I made sure she had my number and closed my phone. Grace Street was around the corner. I told myself it was foolish, but suddenly I wanted to go home and make sure everyone was okay.

◇◇◇

All of Camden's tenants were accounted for. Rufus Jackson had left for his construction job in his bigfoot truck, old Fred had gone back up to his room, and Angie Dawson was taking up most of the green corduroy sofa in our main living area we call the island. She had a large bowl of Sugar Puffs in her lap and a box of doughnuts on the end table beside her. Angie's one of the biggest women I've ever seen, easily three hundred and fifty pounds, all solid rolls. She wears her brown hair short and sticking out from her tiny ears, so her head looks enormous, and I rarely see her little eyes, lost in the mountains of her cheeks. Still in her yellow nightgown, she looked like a giant pudding that had landed on the sofa.

She clicked the remote until she found a talk show. The topic was "Faithless Husbands and the Women Who Love Them."

"Hell." She changed the channel. A group of hyperactive kids jumped around singing, "We've Got Magic To Do Just For You." "Don't need to see that, either." She changed the channel again.

Knowing I could outrun her if I had to, I ventured a personal question. "You and Rufus still on the outs?"

"Durn fool can't make up his mind about getting married." She crunched a mouthful of cereal. "I don't know what he's waiting on. He's never going to find another woman like me, and he knows it."

There was no safe reply to this. "Has Camden said anything to you about a ring?"

She grinned, eyes disappearing. "Why, I'd marry the little cutie pie in a heartbeat."

"I mean for Ellin."

"I know what you mean, Randall. Where have you been? Blondie's decided she wants this fancy engagement ring. Haven't you heard her talking about it?"

"I try to tune her out."

"Well, there's no way Cam can afford it, so it don't matter."

"Where is this ring?"

"At Royalle's, of course. Might as well be at Tiffany's."

If Ellin and Angie were the last two women on earth, I'd choose Angie. "What the hell's wrong with her?"

Angie shrugged, a huge heaving of the continents. "She's scared, I guess."

"Scared? She's the devil's twin sister. What's she got to be scared about?"

"Commitment, the dirty word in this house. You know all about that, don't you, Randall? Rufus don't want to commit to our relationship, Ellin don't want to commit to Cam, you and Kary can't figure out what you want to do. It's a curse." She put a whole doughnut in her mouth, took two chews, and swallowed. "Where you been all morning?"

After all the excitement at the Magic Club, I was ready for a doughnut myself. "Lots of places, all at once."

"Oh, I almost forgot. Some woman brought you a DVD."

"Hello. That sounds promising."

"It's on the table."

I got up and went into the dining room. Incriminating evidence of a foul deed? Blackmail material for some high-ranking city scum? Darling Darlene Does Detroit?

When I saw the label, I put the DVD back down. "Miss Duncan's Dance School Recitals."

"So what is it, Randall?" Angie called over one massive shoulder.

"Was this woman petite with short black hair?"

"Yep."

Lindsey's dance teacher. She'd come by one day after the funeral and said she'd make copies of all Lindsey's dance recitals for me. I'd forgotten.

"It's Lindsey's dance recitals."

"You wanna watch it?"

Yes. Oh, my God, yes. "Not right now."

Angie turned back to her program. I walked away from the table so I couldn't see the DVD. Doughnut clogged in my throat. Lindsey's dance recitals. She started taking dance lessons when she was three, and I never missed a recital. That first year, she'd been all in yellow with a tiny stiff tutu wobbling around her plump tummy. She did something called "Baby Duckling Dance." I remembered the auditorium filled with proud parents, all laughing and smiling and taking pictures as their little girls did their best to follow the music. Some children stood there, transfixed by the lights and sound. Some cried. Some waved.

But Lindsey always danced. No matter what the others did, she always watched her teacher and did her steps. The next year, she was dressed in something patriotic and did a little ballet number. When she was five, she tap danced to "When the Saints Come Marching In." I remember that one because she was so excited about the music.

"Daddy," she'd said, eyes alight, "we're dancing to one of your jazz songs!"

The rest of the years ran together. I couldn't recall her costumes or her music. I wanted to see the DVD. I wanted to see my daughter whirl and pirouette, graceful as a flower. She always loved to dance, and I always loved to watch her. But to watch her now, to watch what I would never see again—I might as well tear my heart from my chest and throw it away.

"Oh. Hi, David."

I took a deep breath to get my emotions back under control and to manage the new feelings that swept through me. "Kary."

We stood looking at each other for a few awkward moments. She was her usual beautiful self, her long corn-silk blonde hair tied back in a ponytail, her brown eyes watching me warily.

I said the first thing that came to mind. "Did you have class today?" *Idiot. Of course she did.* She had class every Monday. She was almost finished with her teaching degree.

She seemed relieved to talk about something ordinary. "Yes. Curriculum Development."

I wasn't sure what she wanted to say next, because old Fred wandered in, muttering. Fred is small and gnarled with hair growing out of his ears. He always reminds me of something that's been left out of the refrigerator too long, a stalk of celery, maybe, or a poor tired carrot. He had his coat on over his pajamas.

"Fred, you want something to eat?" Kary asked.

"I want to go to the bank."

"Cam will be home in a little while if you need some money."

"Don't need no money."

"I have today's paper, if that's what you're looking for."

"Done read the paper."

I wanted to tell Kary not to bother, but she kept on trying. "What can I get for you, Fred?"

"You can't get me nothing." He frowned at me. "*You* can take me to the bank."

"Sure." Humor the old coot. He'd forget all about this tomorrow.

"All right, then." He wandered out.

Kary watched him go. "Poor old fellow. Last week, he wanted to go to the zoo." There was another long uncomfortable pause. "Do you have any white things for the wash? I'm going to start a load of clothes."

"Some socks and t-shirts. I'll get them."

I took the DVD and put it on the bookcase in my office. Then I retrieved my dirty laundry and brought it to the washer and dryer at the end of the first floor hall. There were some clothes in the dryer, so I helped Kary sort and fold them. I tried not to linger over her pretty pink slips and bras. Here, also, were Angie's huge underpants, big enough for a sailboat, Rufus' red and blue bandannas, Camden's vests, and a few ordinary shirts that belonged to me.

Kary retrieved the little fabric softener sheet that had drifted to the floor. "Can you talk about your cases, or is that off limits now?"

The edge to her voice warned me I'd better stay calm. "I went to see a new client about a missing box. Unfortunately, my client's brother was found dead at the Magic Club."

"Did something go wrong with his act?"

"Looks that way."

"I hope it wasn't one of those sawing-in-two tricks."

"No, no. Nothing that graphic. He tried to escape from a locked trunk and either forgot how to get out, or someone meant for him to get stuck. I've actually got three mysteries now: the mystery of the missing bracelet, the mystery of the missing box, and the mystery of the dead magician. The bracelet is a diamond bracelet that belongs to Sandy Olaf, and the box once belonged to Houdini himself, so the legend goes."

She didn't say anything. She folded and stacked the dishcloths and then reached for the detergent on the laundry shelf. "I suppose you want me to find out everything about Houdini."

One of the main points of our argument was Kary's insistence that she not be relegated to researcher. "I don't want you to do anything you don't want to do."

She poured the amount of detergent she wanted into the washer, closed the lid, and turned it on.

"Kary, I said a lot of things I wish I hadn't said. I'm sorry. I was concerned about you. I still want you to help me."

"As long as I stay home, right?"

"I didn't mean it to sound that way. But there's no sense in putting yourself in potentially dangerous situations."

She had to see the truth in this, but I could tell she was still angry. "Is there something I can do that doesn't involve the Internet?"

"There isn't anything at the moment. I'm also trying to find Sandy Olaf's diamond tennis bracelet, if you'd care to get in on that."

"I'll think about it." She looked at her wristwatch. "I have another class. Will you put these in the dryer when they finish?"

There were many more things I wanted to say, but I figured I'd said enough for now. "Sure."

"Thank you." And she left.

◇◇◇

Before the washer had even filled, Ellin brought Camden home. She paced the island, arms waving.

"She's already moved her things into my space. I can't believe it. She wants to make all sorts of changes. She even wants to change the set. She wants to fire half the staff and bring in her own people, including her son. She's demanding her own phone line, her own secretary. This can't be happening."

"Why don't you quit?" I asked. "Why put up with all this aggravation?"

She paused long enough to give me a laser stare. "Because I helped set up the PSN. I've been with it from the very beginning. It wouldn't exist without me. I'm not letting some stranger walk in and take over."

"Maybe corporate's got something better in mind for you."

Angie heaved herself over so Camden could sit down on the sofa. "We've been through this," he said with a sigh.

"They expect me to work with this woman and keep her happy so we'll have the money to run the network."

"If that's what it takes, do it," I said. "I'm guessing you've had a word with the higher-ups?"

Her eyes have that rare ability to either flame on or chill out. Right now, they were arctic blue. "Several words."

"You're not being replaced, right? This is only a temporary setback?"

"I certainly hope so."

"Can't you hold out until this woman's gone?"

"I guess I'm going to have to. But I don't like it."

"We can tell."

She gave me one of her rare smiles. "What gave it away?"

"Relax. I know what it's like to want to be your own boss."

"You need to meet this woman. Then you'd see what I mean."

"I'd love to, but I have three cases going right now."

"Well, when you get a minute, bring Cam back over to the studio later today and you can have the pleasure of her acquaintance." She cut her eyes over to Camden. "Of course, if you would drive, this wouldn't be an issue."

Camden can drive, he just chooses not to. Something about too many signals coming in. "If Randall has time, he can bring me over."

"Why didn't you stay?" I asked him.

"Sheila wanted me to leave. She said I was interfering with her aura."

Ellin rolled her eyes. "See what I have to put up with? And if a certain someone would use his cell phone that would make my life so much easier."

"One thing at a time, honey," Camden said.

She gave him a kiss. "Your voice is getting worse. Are you sure you don't want to see a doctor?"

"I'm hoping it'll clear up on its own."

"I know you have to be careful about what medicines you take, but don't you have some cough syrup or lozenges or something?"

"It doesn't hurt. It just fades in and out."

"Do you have some singing engagements coming up?"

Camden has a very good tenor voice, which was always in demand from various singing groups, his church choir, and the community theaters.

"A few," he said. "If I try not to talk too much, it ought to be all right."

"Well, if it's not better by tomorrow, we'll schedule a visit to the doctor." She brushed back his hair. "I don't think it's something I can erase."

Her tone was surprisingly light. Camden always says holding her hand can block his worst visions, and usually she's annoyed because her lack of psychic talent makes this possible. But today, she didn't seem to mind being a Psychic Eraser. At least it was a psychic something.

She gave him another kiss. "I'd better get back. Oh, and don't worry about the ring. We'll work something out."

As soon as she had gone, I said. "Okay, tell me about the ring."

"She's seen one she likes, and it might as well be on the moon. I wish I could afford it. You heard her say don't worry, but it would be a nice surprise if I could get it for her."

"Has she ever said anything like, 'It doesn't matter if we're poor, as long as we're together'?"

"Not in so many words. She plans to rule the world, you know, so we won't be poor."

Ellin was indeed on her way to world domination, but she'd shown a bit more concern for Camden than she usually let others see. Theirs was a strange opposites-attract relationship. Maybe his calm approach to life appealed to her. Maybe her intensity made him feel a little more alive. God knows Kary had pulled me back from the brink.

Angie's little eyes twinkled. "Give her up, Cam, and marry me. Don't look like Rufus wants to."

"I suppose you want a ring, as well?"

She opened the doughnut box. She took out the last glazed doughnut and shoved it around her sausage-sized finger. "This'll do."

"That kind of ring I can afford." He gave me a look. "What about these three cases of yours?"

"I told you Sandy Olaf hired me to find her bracelet. The magician, Lucas Finch, hired me to find a special box he and his brother wanted to use in their act. Unfortunately, the brother, Taft, was found wadded up nice and neat in a trunk backstage at the Magic Club."

Angie made a face. "That's gross."

"Not only is the special box missing, but there's a possibility Taft's been murdered. The owner of the club has hired me to find out what happened."

"This box made of gold or something?" Angie asked.

"Lucas says it once belonged to Houdini."

"Who what?"

"Harry Houdini, famous magician and escape artist."

"Famous enough to get killed over?"

"Looks that way."

Camden accepted a piece of doughnut from Angie. "Did you see Jordan?"

"Yes. There were only four of us at the club: me; the owner, Rahnee Nevis; a magician named Bart; and the stage manager, WizBoy. Everybody seemed properly horrified. Taft performed Saturday night at nine. That's the last anybody saw of him." I made a mental note to ask Lucas where he was Saturday night and if he had any idea where his brother might have gone.

"And the box?"

"Last seen in its hiding place at the club behind a fake cinder block in the storage room."

He frowned and held out his hands. "Is this box about twelve inches long, kind of gold, with an 'H' on top?"

Even though I've known Camden for years, he still spooks me with this stuff. "Where are you getting this from?"

"From you. Someone described it to you."

"Lucas did."

"I don't know where it is, but I can see it very clearly. Damn. You know what this means."

This kind of prediction means he's involved somehow. Camden never sees his own future, and sometimes his visions are so scrambled I have to figure them out. I made some "Twilight Zone" noises. "It means it's magic."

"It means trouble."

"Come on, then. You know you love trouble."

Angie licked the last traces of sugar from her finger. "Don't think he oughta be tromping around with you when his voice still ain't one hundred percent."

"It'll be okay," Camden said. "I won't talk that much."

"Why don't you go see a doctor?"

Camden must have had some scary hospital experience when he was younger, because he has a borderline phobia.

"No, thanks."

"We'll go see my doctor," Angie said. "He won't stick you with nothing."

"I need to go with Randall, right?"

I'm always glad to help with an escape. "Right."

Chapter Five

Energy Fools the Magician

The Parkland Country Club is the oldest club in town, an imposing white building that looks like the main hall of some Ivy League university. A smooth golf course spread out on all sides, trying to turn green in the uncooperative weather. The fountains hadn't been turned on yet, and there weren't any flowers in bloom, so the place looked a bit desolate. This didn't keep several groups of golfers from their games.

We checked by the office and I spoke with the woman in charge of events. I was relieved to find she did not remind me of an animal or possess an unusual voice. Like everyone else, she was a big fan of Sandy Olaf and all her causes, and agreed to show me the dining room where the country club ball had been held.

We went down several halls carpeted in rich money green; past the bar, which was crowded for early afternoon; past a smaller dining room where a meeting was in session; past the pro shop, full of incredibly expensive golf clubs and golf shirts—hell, you'd have to take out a loan to buy a box of golf balls—until finally we reached the dining hall, a circular room in shades of dark pink and green, complete with chandeliers and a small stage framed by dark green velvet curtains.

"Mrs. Olaf was on stage with the other prominent guests, and I believe she sat at the first table to the left."

I looked on stage, which was bare and polished to a high shine. Around the tables, the pink carpet was immaculate.

"Did you happen to notice if Mrs. Olaf had on her bracelet?"

"The dining room was completely full that night. The only thing I noticed was one of our more prominent member's dresses, which was almost falling off. I'm not sure why she bothers wearing them. She seems to think this makes her more attractive."

"So it's a safe bet to say all eyes were on that woman?"

"That's the way she likes it."

So an enterprising jewel thief could easily make the most of this distraction.

Camden slowly walked around the room and came back to me, shaking his head. Sometimes he can find things just by being in a room, but usually he needs to touch someone's hand or a personal object to get a clear picture. And he's told me that leftover vibrations often cloud the visions. A dining room full of party people would have left plenty of vibrations.

The event planner had been eying Camden. "Now I know who you are."

Camden got that look he gets when someone recognizes him from his infrequent appearances on the PSN. I could tell he was bracing himself to explain that yes, he was psychic, and no, he couldn't give her any winning lottery ticket numbers.

"You sang for a wedding here a few months ago. I have to tell you, I hear a lot of singers, and most of them are good, but your voice is absolutely beautiful."

"Thank you," he said.

"And you're an investigator, too?"

"I guess you could say I'm a consultant of sorts."

"Well, I'm sorry I can't be more help. I honestly don't think Sandy Olaf's bracelet was stolen by anyone at the fund-raiser. She's got so many things going I think she's simply misplaced it."

"That's my theory, too," I said to Camden when we got back into the car, "but I needed to check all leads. Nice of her to mention your other talent."

"My real talent. Now all I have to do is recover it."

"You've got a sore throat. You'll live."

We drove on to the First Methodist Church. Unfortunately, a funeral was in progress. We stayed in the car and listened to the Black Eagles Jazz Band rip through "Original Jelly Roll Blues" followed by "Sweetie Dear." Most of the time, the music helps me forget. This wasn't one of those times. I kept thinking of the dance recital DVD, but what good would it do to see it? I knew I wouldn't cry. I didn't have any tears left. How would I react? I didn't see how looking at it would make me feel any better.

Do you want to feel better? my perverse side asked, *or are you enjoying this everlasting pity party? Do you think you have to punish yourself in some way? Does holding in your grief make you feel more manly?*

I told myself to shut up.

The funeral procession left the church. Seeing the headlights of the cars brought up another unwanted memory. That other dismal gray afternoon, there had been so many cars coming out the winding road to the cemetery the lights had looked like a long moving string of pearls. I remembered thinking, how can anything be beautiful today? But there they were: hundreds of little lights like a living necklace flowing down the road.

"Do you want to go in?" Camden asked.

"Yeah. It's okay."

We went inside the church and found a man gathering up hymnbooks and papers.

"The family has left for the cemetery," he said.

"We've come about something else."

He straightened and wiped his eyes. "Excuse me. We lost one of our younger members to cancer."

"I'm very sorry."

"Only fourteen. Can you believe it? Makes you question the fairness of life."

I tried to ignore the sudden grip in my middle. "Sure does."

"May I help you?"

"David Randall. I'm investigating the disappearance of Sandy Olaf's diamond bracelet. This is my friend Camden."

He shook hands with us. "I know Mrs. Olaf, but I didn't know she'd lost a bracelet."

"She helped organize a yard sale here. Who would know about that?"

"I helped set it up."

"Do you remember if she had it on during the sale?"

He thought a moment. "I honestly don't recall. She helped me put lots of things on tables, and when it was over, we put lots of things back into boxes. I couldn't tell you if she had on a bracelet or earrings or any sort of jewelry. We were so busy."

"Was Mrs. Olaf working with anyone in particular?"

"She did what she always does, run around doing everything. She was all over the place."

"Could you show me where you had your sale?"

He took us outside to a large lawn near the church playground. Ice crunched under our feet. The man shivered in the sudden cold breeze. "What a day for a funeral. Even the weather is mourning."

It had rained the day of Lindsey's funeral and rained every day afterward for a week. Sometimes I felt it would always be raining. Camden and I checked the frozen grass and along the pathway. "Do you have the leftover stuff stored somewhere?"

"We gave it all to Goodwill."

Another dead end. I thanked the man and we started to go when a young girl came up to us, gave the man a nod, and spoke to Camden.

"Your name's Camden, isn't it? Could I ask you something?"

"Of course," he said.

Here it comes, I thought. Is my loved one in heaven? Will I ever see her again? Is there any way to communicate with her and say everything I wish I had said? How many times had I wanted to ask Camden those same things?

Camden readied himself for her question.

"Kimberly's favorite song was 'Be Thou My Vision.' Do you know it?"

I could see he was taken aback, but he smiled. "Yes. It's one of my favorites, too."

"We're planning a special memorial service for her next week here at the church. I know this is sudden, and you probably have lots of other obligations, but if you're free, would you come sing it? I visited your church last month with our youth group, and you sang 'His Eye Is On the Sparrow.' It was so beautiful. Maybe you could sing that, too?" She started to cry.

The man put his arm around her, and Camden patted her hand. "It's okay," he said. "I'll be glad to, but as you can probably tell, I'm having a little problem with my voice. I promise if I can get it back, I'll come sing whatever you think Kimberly would've liked."

I wrote Camden's cell phone number on one of my business cards and handed it to the young woman. "You can reach him through my number, too."

She brushed the tears off her cheeks. "Thanks. Kimberly was my best friend, but I couldn't go to the cemetery, I just couldn't."

You wouldn't believe how well I understand that, I wanted to say.

"You don't have to, dear," the man said. "It's best to remember Kimberly in happier times. Are either of your parents here?"

"They're waiting for me in the car. I told them I wanted to come in the church for a minute, and then I saw Camden. It's kind of neat how that worked out."

She thanked Camden again, and he told her to keep in touch. The man wished us luck on our search for Sandy's bracelet.

"'Kind of neat how that worked out,'" I said as we walked back to the car. "I'll say. That's two affirmations of your singing ability within the space of one hour and not one mention of your spooky power. What more do you want?"

"This singing ability is no good if it doesn't clear up."

"Well, now it has to, doesn't it?" My cell phone rang.

"Randall, it's Rahnee. I've got that list for you."

"I'll be right there."

◇◇◇

The Magic Club was deserted, the glitter balls halted in mid-gleam. As we approached the office door, we could hear voices raised in argument. I recognized Rahnee's voice, and the other sounded like WizBoy's.

"But I thought we had an agreement!"

"I told you I was still thinking about that," she answered.

"But I heard you tell Taft he could run the club. What the hell was that all about? What kind of management skills did he have? You know I'm qualified. You said so yourself."

"Can we discuss this later? I'm expecting Randall to come by."

"I've worked really hard. I've done everything you said. I've never been late for work."

"Yes, and I appreciate that, but—"

"Taft's dead, Rahnee, so whatever grand plans the two of you had are over."

I waited for the sound of Rahnee's hand across WizBoy's face, but she had more control. "You need to leave right now and calm down. We'll talk about this later."

Wiz Boy charged out of the office, slamming the door behind him. He was so angry he didn't notice me or Camden. He stalked across the stage and into the wings. We heard a thump as the back door opened and a crash as it slammed shut.

"All is not well in Magic Land," I said. "When you get a chance, check out that storage room over there. The fake block is the seventh one up from the floor."

I waited a few minutes and then knocked on the office door and we entered. Rahnee was seated behind her desk, her flaming red hair in limp tendrils around her face. She had on a black sweatshirt and dirty jeans. "Hi, fellas, have a seat."

"Rahnee, this is my friend Camden. Camden, Rahnee Nevis."

Rahnee pushed back her hair. "Nice to meet you. You probably heard that little altercation."

"Some of it."

"I think WizBoy might have misunderstood. I was only asking Taft for some advice about the club. I'm not planning to hand it over to anyone yet."

"Sounded as if Wiz feels he's entitled to it."

"I'll take care of it. His little fits of temper don't last long."

Long enough to murder Taft? I wondered. Sounds like he had a grudge.

Rahnee moved a stack of books to one side. "I'm going through Taft's things he kept here. Lucas wasn't up to it."

"What sort of things?"

"A few papers, books, notes about illusions he was planning."

I took a closer look at the books. "Big fan of Houdini, I see."

"Yes, both of them were."

"This Vanishing Ruby trick they were planning. What can you tell me about that?"

Rahnee sat back and rubbed her eyes for a moment. "From what I understood, the box played a major role. The ruby was placed inside, and it would be gone."

"That's it?"

"I'm sure there's more to it, but that was their secret." She sighed. "Now we'll never know. Even if you find the box, I doubt Lucas will want to use it."

"What about the bet Lucas made with the other members of WOW? Anyone crazy enough about getting the cabinet key out of the box?"

"I certainly don't need any more magic things. WizBoy doesn't collect, and neither does Jilly. The only person who would be really interested is Jolly Bob. He has a magic shop out by Commerce Circle Mall. Transformation and Company." She placed all the papers in a large manila envelope and stacked the books on top. "People have been calling all day, asking questions. Everyone's very upset. I wish I knew how it's going to affect business. I'm afraid morbid curiosity will pack them in." Her voice caught. "I don't mean to sound so callous. You wouldn't believe what our competition will make of this."

I couldn't imagine what sort of competition the club could have. "And that would be?"

"The Bombay Club has recently added magic acts. I've worked hard to keep this place in the black. Now another club is siphoning off my talent. But I can't really tell people where to work, can I?"

WizBoy came to the door and stopped when he saw us. "Oh, uh, Rahnee, sorry, I—"

"Come in," she said. "It's okay."

WizBoy turned red. "Yeah, well, I guess I overreacted a little. Sorry, Rahnee. I didn't mean what I said."

"Apology accepted. Was there anything else you needed, Randall? Oh, yes, the list." She pulled a piece of paper from an overstuffed clipboard. "The police needed it, too. I made copies. I think that's everyone. There may have been a few walk-ins."

The list was a daunting twenty names long. I folded the list and put it in my pocket. "I'm going to see Lucas. Would you like for me to take those papers and books to him?"

"Yes, thanks, and tell him everyone here feels terrible and sends him our deepest sympathy."

I wanted to talk to WizBoy, and gave Camden a slight nod.

"Rahnee, I've never been in your club. Would you mind showing me around?" Camden asked.

"I'd be glad to."

She and Camden went out, and WizBoy came in. "Guess you heard me yelling, huh?"

"A little. What's the deal?"

He shrugged and plopped into Rahnee's chair behind the desk. "Well, it's no secret I want to run the club. Then I found out Rahnee was going to give it to Taft, and I got kinda upset about that."

"How upset?"

"Oh, no," he said. "Don't go there."

"Then tell me what happened Saturday night. You last saw Taft at the nine o'clock show?"

"Yeah, only I wasn't paying much attention. Don't get me wrong. I like to see other guys perform, but I'd seen this act a hundred times, and Rahnee needed me to help with some cabinets backstage."

"When did he finish?"

"I'd say quarter to ten. Rahnee don't like the acts to go on too long. Says the audience gets bored."

"Did you come in Sunday?"

"No need to."

"Where were you?"

"That policeman asked me the same thing. I got no alibi, if that's what you mean. I was at home, sleeping in like I always do on Sundays."

"Where's your key?"

WizBoy's key was on a key ring shaped like a skull. Two little silver bones dangled between the keys. "House key, car key, and key to the Magic Club. Most important keys I keep together. And before you ask, no, I don't ever let anybody else have these keys."

"And you didn't notice anything unusual this morning?"

"Man, we must have passed that trunk dozens of times. 'Course, Rahnee's got that rule about not touching anyone else's props. It's a good rule. You don't want to take out your top hat and find somebody's pinched the rabbit." He looked worried. "You don't think he might have still been alive, do you? If we'd known he was in there, maybe we could've done something."

"I don't think so. Who locked up Saturday night?"

"Rahnee takes care of that. We don't close till one."

"You remember seeing Taft after his act?"

Thinking hard required WizBoy to screw up his face until he looked like a punk monkey. "No. He usually has—had a drink afterward."

"Then I need to talk to the bartender. Jilly, is it?"

"Yeah, she's here. She just came in." WizBoy stayed in his seat, apparently liking the view from that side of the desk. "The cops won't close down the club, will they?"

"You'll probably have a bumper crowd tonight. Thrill-seekers."

"Kinda sick, isn't it?"

"That's show biz."

"I mean, I'd hate for the club to get a bad rep. We're on our way up, know what I mean?"

"Rahnee said you had a little competition from the Bombay Club."

WizBoy looked scornful. "Amateurs. We're the best. You have to be really good to get in here."

"What can you tell me about the auditions Saturday?"

"Man, they were all pitiful. People think if they know a few card tricks they can be magicians. This one guy, I swear, he won't take no for an answer. I'll bet he's in here every other day. He can go play the Bombay Club."

"What about the Vanishing Ruby trick?"

"I don't know anything about that. The Finches kept pretty quiet about their trick."

"Would you say the brothers were close, or were they rivals?"

"Close. And they were majorly excited about that box."

"What can you tell me about this bet they had about opening the box?"

"Lucas said whoever found the box and got it open could have something from his collection."

"Any idea where he might have hidden it?"

WizBoy shook his head.

"I'd like to talk to Jilly," I said.

"I'll introduce you."

Jilly Porter was the bartender, a slim, mournful-looking young woman, mournful because Taft didn't stop by Saturday night after his act for his usual drink. She had on a floor-length black dress with long sleeves. Her long straight black hair made a curtain for her small face. She looked like Cher's kid sister.

"I kept waiting for him," she said. "I had his drink all ready and everything. He always had the same thing, a Screwdriver, and he liked the little fish crackers."

"Were you close friends?" I couldn't help notice how WizBoy stiffened at this question and then relaxed at Jilly's answer.

"We were really good friends, and he said I could assist with the new act. I was really looking forward to that. I told Rahnee I could be a magician's assistant easy. I've watched these guys for months. But she keeps interviewing other people."

"I told you I'd put you in my act," WizBoy said.

"Taft was going to teach me some card tricks."

"I can teach you card tricks. Nothing to it. You're already real good with coins."

She showed no interest in WizBoy's offer. She showed no interest in WizBoy at all. I wondered if she and Taft had been really close friends. "Do you have any idea why Taft would hurry out after his act Saturday night? Did he have another show somewhere else?"

WizBoy immediately brought up the enemy camp. "He could've been heading over to the Bombay Club."

"Oh, no," Jilly said. "He was faithful to this club. He wouldn't play anywhere else. He said Rahnee had given him his big break, and he wasn't going to forget it."

"Were you here on Sunday?" I asked her.

"No."

Well, somebody had to let him in, unless Taft used his magic to unlock the door. "Did you give anyone your key?"

Her face was hidden behind that curtain of hair. "I had to go down to the police station and answer all sorts of questions like this."

WizBoy tried to pat her hand, but she withdrew. "Jilly, he's only trying to find out what happened."

She hugged her arms in tight. "I'm sorry. This is really upsetting."

"I can come back later," I said.

She hesitated. "No, that's okay. Give me a minute." I could tell WizBoy wanted to leap over the bar and comfort her. After a while, she pushed back her hair. For the first time, I could see she was wearing a silver chain necklace. She pulled the necklace up to reveal two dangling keys. "Here's where I keep my key, and no, I didn't give it to anyone."

"What about the box he and Lucas were going to use for their new trick?"

"Lucas showed it to me when he made the bet."

"When did he show it to you?"

She shrugged and then rubbed her shoulder as if cold. "I don't remember. When he first got it, I think."

"Do you have any idea where he might have hidden it?"

"No."

"Did anyone come to the club especially to see him? A girlfriend, maybe, or groupies coming around to catch his act every night?"

She gave me a look. Her eyes were very dark. "No."

"Sorry, Jilly. I'm trying to find out who murdered him. If that means some uncomfortable questions, then I have to ask them."

She took a deep breath. "Okay. I guess you have to. But Taft didn't have what you'd call groupies, and if he'd had any, he would've treated them as nicely as he treated everyone. He always made me feel like a lady, you know? Is that all?"

"Yes, thank you."

Jilly walked to the register. WizBoy watched her and then turned to me.

"I'd better make sure she's all right."

"If you remember anyone Taft might have been seeing, let me know," I said, but he was already heading down the bar. As far as WizBoy was concerned, there was only one woman. Too bad she didn't return the feeling.

I had a few more questions for Rahnee. I found her and Camden backstage. She was counting an array of interlocking rings. As she handed them to Camden to put on a pegboard, they continued their conversation.

"Oh, I've always been interested in magic," Rahnee said. "I started doing shows with my girlfriend when we were in our teens. But what about you? Have you ever thought about being on stage? Maybe using your psychic ability in an act?"

"It's too unpredictable for that," Camden said. "And sometimes people aren't happy with the results."

She handed him the last ring. "I'm not afraid of the future. Would you tell me what you see?"

He set the ring in its place and took her hand. I've seen him read people dozens of times with many different reactions. Sometimes his eyes will glaze over, and he's gone for a while, taking a stroll to the Other Side. Other times, his eyes will darken, or even turn gray, which always creeps me out. This time, the spirits must have been cooperating because he smiled and gave her hand a comforting squeeze.

"You've worked hard for everything you've got, Rhonda, and everything is going to be all right." She gave a little start at the mention of what must have been her real name. Camden says if nothing else, a person's real name comes through. "It might be hard to see it now, but the magic is still here. It will always be here."

When the tears began to roll down her cheeks, I searched my pockets and found a handkerchief. Rahnee thanked me and wiped her eyes. "You'd better not tell anyone my name is Rhonda," she said with a slight laugh.

"Your secret's safe with me," Camden said, "and Randall didn't hear a word."

"Not a thing," I said.

Camden kept her hand in his. "You remind me of my girl-friend. Like you, she's from a wealthy family, but she wants to make her way on her own. That's one of the things I really admire about her. I'm afraid I don't have the kind of ambition you ladies have."

"You picked up on the wealthy part, too? My God, you're good. I hope to hell you didn't see me having anything to do with Taft's death."

"I didn't, but a psychic's word doesn't go very far in court."

"Let's hope it never comes to that."

"Rahnee, when Taft left Saturday night, did he say anything to you about where he was going?" I asked. "Jilly says he didn't stop for his favorite snack."

She brushed a few more tears away. "He didn't say anything to me." She motioned to a large panel on the wall filled with switches and toggles. "I was busy keeping everything moving. I run the lights from back here, too, so I had my hands full. I know the Finches' act. They need a pale blue special and a blackout."

"Who performed after them?"

"They were the last act. We had a break and cleared the stage."

"And the trunk was backstage?"

"Yes, where we found it today. That's where the Finches always kept it."

"So Taft performed Saturday night and hurried out. Sometime during Sunday or early Monday, he must have come back to the club, but how did he get in? WizBoy and Jilly both say they weren't here. And why would he be here by himself on Sunday?"

"Sometimes he'd ask if he could come and practice a trick on Sunday or early Monday before he went to work, but he'd always call so I could come unlock the door and stay in case he needed assistance."

"Where do you keep your key?"

She pulled a ring of keys from her pocket. "I always have it with me."

"Do you ever lend your key to anyone?"

"No."

I glanced back at the bar where WizBoy was doing card tricks in a vain attempt to make Jilly smile. Damn it, somebody let Taft Finch in, and that same somebody didn't let him out. WizBoy, jealous of Taft and Jilly? Or someone on my long long list who maybe harbored a grudge against Taft? Maybe Lucas Finch could shed some light on this mystery.

I thanked Rahnee and said I'd be in touch. Camden and I leaned against the Fury and compared notes. I told him everything I'd learned from WizBoy and Jilly. He told me that besides what he'd seen for Rahnee, there was a lot of leftover performance anxiety from backstage.

"See anything particular between Rahnee and Taft?"

"Yes, she's still in shock over his death, but she's also practically running over with concern for her club. It was hard to see anything specific."

"What about the storage room?"

"I found the fake block, but the whole wall's a jumble of impressions. Rahnee, WizBoy, and Jilly are in and out of there all the time."

"So aside from making Rahnee feel better, you're especially useless today. Did the Deadly Sheila usurp your powers?"

"'Usurp.' That has to be worth at least twenty-five points."

"I've been waiting for years to use that one. Did you see the dark spot on the cinder block? Is it blood?"

"Yes, but I couldn't tell whose blood."

I started to say "useless" again, but he held up a hand to forestall my criticism. "I've got my own performance anxiety. Ring or no ring, I'm asking Ellie to marry me."

"Today?"

"No. But soon."

"And you think that's affecting you?"

"I know it is. My own emotions always get in the way. Besides, you're always telling me you want to solve things on your own."

"That's true," I said. "But I'm not against a little help."

"That's me," he said with a wry grin. "A little help."

Chapter Six

Mysterious Ways

Lucas Finch lived on Prospect Avenue in a remodeled apartment complex. I rang the doorbell and tried not to grimace when he opened the door. I've seen what grief can do, how it can alter people. Lucas Finch looked ravaged: haggard, red-eyed, unshaven. His voice was as hoarse as Camden's.

"Mister Randall."

"I hope I'm not disturbing you."

"No, come in."

We stepped inside the small, neat apartment, not surprised by the color scheme of brown and brown and the large framed poster of Houdini. "This is my friend Camden."

Camden shook his hand. "I'm very sorry about your brother."

"Everyone at the club sends their sympathy," I said.

"Thank you. Please have a seat."

It looked like he'd been lying on the sofa, so I chose one of the brown armchairs across from the sofa, and Camden sat down in the other. "I brought Taft's things from Rahnee's office."

He sat down on the sofa and took the stack of papers and books. "I appreciate that."

"Rahnee's hired me to find out what happened to Taft. I know this is a difficult time, but I need to ask you some questions."

"Of course."

"You and Taft performed at nine o'clock Saturday night and then he hurried out. Do you have any idea where he went?"

I thought he wasn't going to answer. He looked at the floor for such a long time, I thought he'd fallen asleep. He rubbed his face. "No."

"Did he have a wife, a girlfriend? Was he going to meet someone?"

"If he was, he didn't tell me."

"Where did you go after the act?"

"I was hired for a friend's birthday party. Sounds corny, but there's not a whole lot of work for magicians these days. Sometimes I take these jobs just to keep in practice."

"This friend can vouch for your whereabouts?"

"Yes. The police have already checked on that. After the party, I came home and didn't get up until late Sunday morning."

"Did you see your brother on Sunday?"

"No. I was still annoyed at him for losing the box. I should've apologized. Well, it's too late now. It's too late for everything."

"Is there anyone else who might have had a grudge against your brother, or against you?"

He lifted his head. "Me?"

"The two of you were planning a terrific new act with a valuable magic box. Maybe one of the other magicians was jealous."

"So they'd steal the box *and* murder Taft? That's insane. No one could use the box. It's one of a kind, instantly recognizable. And what could anyone gain by murdering my brother?" With a trembling hand, he sifted through the papers I'd brought. "Taft had plans for many new acts, not just the Vanishing Ruby."

"Did Taft take anything besides sleeping pills?"

"Why do you ask that?"

"I found some in his coat pocket. Maybe he took too many one night, and that made him too groggy to think clearly the next day."

"No, no. He rarely needed anything like that."

I gave the apartment another look. There were several framed posters and lithographs on the walls similar to the ones I'd seen in Rahnee's office. One showed a man in a black frock coat and top hat and cane surrounded by fancy trees and bright red flowers. The name "Kellar" was written above his head in bold yellow letters.

Lucas saw my interest. "Kellar was considered the Dean of American magicians. Always very tasteful."

Camden got up and went to the beautiful glass-fronted cabinet beside the living room door. The cabinet was filled with books, games, packs of cards, programs, and toys, all having to do with magic. "This is quite a collection."

"Taft and I collect magic memorabilia. I won't feel like doing that any more."

I got up to have a look. "These are the things someone can choose from if he or she opens the box?"

"Yes."

The cabinet was lined with mirrors decorated with little silver stars so everything inside reflected and glittered. I could tell the books were antique by their ornate covers with titles such as *Magick Illusions* and *Houdini's Rope Ties and Escapes*. A grinning skull sat next to a brightly colored box with Asian designs and a metal bank shaped like a magician holding out his top hat for coins. Boxed magic sets in bright red, yellow, and blue featured tricks called "The Floating Wonder" and "The Devil's Delight." There was also a large box trimmed in brass and filled with odd objects that looked like someone's woodworking project, cups and spindles and eggs and something called Pillars of Solomon. A card on the box from Martinka and Company, Museum of Magic and Magic Shop, proclaimed the shop as the "Magicians' Headquarters" and "Formerly Owned by Harry Houdini."

"What's this box?"

"An antique magic set. We found that at Martinka and Company, the oldest magic shop in the country. Every time we visited New York, we'd go there. So much wonderful history. The very first magic society was founded there, the Society of American Magicians in 1902, and Houdini was president of Martinka in 1919." He rattled on about the Martinka brothers coming over from Germany and all the famous magicians who frequented their shop.

"What does 'Pillars of Solomon' mean?" Camden asked. "I know what it means in the Bible, but what's the connection to a magic trick?"

"It's quite a good illusion. A string passes through the pillars, and then the magician appears to cut the string, but the string still goes through."

Talking about his collection seemed to steady Lucas, so Camden asked more questions about the items. "What about those cubes? They look like three-dimensional playing cards."

"Oh, there are hundreds of variations on cube illusions."

"And the skull? What do you use that for?"

"The talking skull is one of the oldest tricks in magic."

As he explained, I checked out the room. While I found all the magic stuff interesting, I couldn't imagine that Taft had been murdered for it. It was too easy for a thief to break in, smash the cabinet doors, and take whatever he wanted.

"Lucas, what's your collection worth?" I asked.

"Taft and I had it appraised at fifty thousand dollars, but it would be worth much more to a collector."

I had expected it to be more, but fifty thousand dollars was still a lot of money. I took another look in the cabinet. Beside small framed photographs of Houdini and a woman I guessed was his wife, a small program card announced: "The Finest Escape Ever Attempted!" and showed a man covered in chains perched on top of a bulky-looking box. "Were you and Taft attempting a trick like this?"

"Oh, no. Nothing that drastic. Something much more simple. We really hadn't worked out the details. Taft wanted to see how quickly he could get out."

"And he could get out?"

"Yes, but it was taking longer than he liked."

"Had you tried it?"

"No, I get claustrophobic. I was always on the outside, in case Taft needed help. My God, I wish we'd never seen that trunk! What were we thinking? We should've stayed with what we knew."

"Would Taft have attempted the trick by himself?"

"I have no idea. Why."

"You said there some sort of latch inside in the lining."

"Yes. I don't know why he didn't use it. It's a little bolt that slides back and releases the lock."

"You haven't heard from the police about the official cause of death, have you?"

"No, not yet."

"Lucas, there's a possibility he was already dead."

"And then put in the trunk?"

"It's better than being locked inside alive and suffocating."

He put his head down in his hands. "I don't want to think about how it must have been. He was all the family I had. You can't imagine how I feel."

My answer wouldn't have helped the situation. "Sometime Saturday night or Sunday, Taft went back to the Magic Club. As far as we know, he didn't have a key to the club, so someone let him borrow their key, or let him in. For some reason, he decided to try to escape from the trunk, which should be easy, since there's a special latch that works from inside. Something went wrong, and he suffocated. If this is what happened, the medical examiner should find signs of his struggle. If someone hit him on the head or choked him and put him in the trunk, there'll be signs of that, too. But when I saw him, it looked as if he'd curled up inside for a nap, which makes me think maybe someone got him to take one or more of his sleeping pills, or got him drunk, or some combination of the two, and said, 'Let's see your new trick,' and closed the lid, hoping he'd run out of air before he woke up."

"But all of that brings me back to why someone would murder him," Lucas said.

"That's what I'm going to find out." I motioned to the stack of books. "Let me borrow some of these books about Houdini.

Maybe there's something about that box that set someone off. Maybe it's more valuable than you thought."

He handed me several books. "I can't get my brother back, but if you could find the box, it would be some small consolation to me."

"I'll do my best. Rahnee said Taft would come by the club on Mondays to practice before work. Where did he work?"

"At Shepherd Missions."

"I'll talk to the people there. Any other friends, acquaintances?"

"Just those of us in the magic community."

"One other question. When you hid the box or when you went to look for it, did you cut or scrape yourself on the cinder block?"

He shook his head. He rubbed the ends of his fingers and held them out. "The block's a little rough, but I didn't cut my hands. I know exactly how to push on it to make it open."

A thief or someone in a hurry might have had more difficulty. "Thanks."

Camden had made a slow circle of the room and came back to Lucas. He shook his hand. "Again, my sympathies, Lucas."

"Please find out what happened."

"Anything?" I asked Camden as we left the house.

"Just grief," he said.

Chapter Seven

In the Morning of the Magicians

Camden and I went by Transformation and Company but the shop wasn't open until Wednesday, and Jolly Bob didn't answer his phone. Tuesday morning, I got on the phone and eliminated several people off Rahnee's list. Half of the auditionees had been from out of town and left Parkland before noon on Saturday. Three more had gone to audition for a club in Fayetteville. The owner could vouch for them. According to their answering machines, Wendle the Wonderful had gone to his beach house in North Myrtle; The Amazing Janica had flown to California to see her mother; Tammy and Her Ten Talented Assistants were performing on a cruise ship in Bermuda; someone named Fancy didn't answer her phone; and The Mystic Maria could be reached at the Richmond Dance and Supper Club, two shows daily, at seven and ten.

Fortunately, halfway through my message, The Mystic Maria picked up her phone. She had a booming voice, which didn't seem very mystic to me, but what do I know about show business? In the background, I heard an old pop song, "We've Got Magic To Do."

"Mister Randall, what can I do for you? I'm booked for two months, but after that, I have some time slots available."

"I'm investigating the death of Taft Finch."

"Don't know him, sorry."

"He performed at the Magic Club Saturday night. You had an audition for Rahnee Nevis that day. I was hoping you might have seen or heard something that could help."

"What did he look like? Was he auditioning, too? There was quite a crowd Saturday. Can't say that I'd remember any of them."

"He was a tall, well-dressed man with a beard."

"Nope. I would've remembered someone like that. Everyone I saw was flashy, you know? Wild costumes, elaborate props."

"He was attempting a locked trunk escape act. Do you remember seeing a large trunk backstage?"

"There were several large trunks backstage. Have you checked with Fancy? She uses one in her act."

I looked down my list. "I left a message on her answering machine. What can you tell me about her?"

"I remember her because she's a juggler. You don't see too many magicians who are good jugglers, too."

"Do you know of any rivalries between magicians, anything that might turn ugly?"

"I'm sure there are plenty of people with personal differences, but most of the time we're too busy scrambling around for jobs to waste time on rivalries. I'd say on the whole, we're a pretty genial group."

"Can you tell me anything about Wendle the Wonderful, the Amazing Janica, or Tammy and Her Ten Talented Assistants?"

"Like I said, there was a crowd. I don't know any of them."

"There must have been a crowd if Tammy had ten assistants."

Her loud burst of laughter almost made me drop my phone. "Those are her fingers! Ten talented assistants? Get it?"

Oh, brother. I should've seen that one. "I'm new to the world of magic." She was still laughing when she hung up. At least I'd made The Mystic Maria's day. Next I called Bart of Bart, Binky, and His Baffling Birds.

"Come on over," he said. "I'm working on a new act and need some input."

Bart had an old blue Toyota in need of a paint job parked in front of his small house, but inside, the house was filled with entertainment centers that held every new gadget on the market and other shiny machines I didn't recognize. Beyond the living room was a large glassed-in room where Bart's baffling birds chirped and squawked in their cages. Binky yapped excitedly and ran around the furniture until Bart got him to stop.

"Good lord, Binky. Where do you get all this energy?" He shooed the small dog out the back door. "What's the latest, Randall? Hear anything from the police?"

"Not yet."

"You suspect foul play? I don't know the Finch brothers real well, but I always thought Taft was a nice guy, harmless. I can't imagine he was a threat to anyone."

"Was it possible he was involved with a woman?"

"Involved with a woman? Sure, women seemed to like his type."

"His type?"

"Yeah, the old-fashioned type. You know, holding doors, bringing flowers. And he and Lucas had been everywhere and had all these adventures, so they had plenty of stories. They were chased out of Egypt, did Lucas tell you? Years ago when they were teenagers, they were out camping in the desert and tried a few tricks on the wrong people. They went down the Amazon, too, doing shows on these little riverboats, and sailed halfway around the world. Really knew how to live." He stopped. "That didn't sound right, did it?"

"I know what you mean. The Finches had some wild times."

"Yeah, which is odd, because Taft was kinda on the shy side, but when he was on stage he'd come alive." He stopped again. "Damn. I keep putting my foot in it, don't I?"

"So you've seen the act?"

"Many times. The Finch brothers look like they stepped out of *Gentleman's Quarterly*, but you get them in a spotlight, and they would bring down the house. Being twins, of course, they knew exactly what the other one was going to do. Hard to compete with an act like theirs."

There was a definite twinge of jealousy in Bart's voice. "Did you see them Saturday night?"

"No, I wasn't there Saturday, but I'm sure they were fabulous as ever. Great with cards." He picked up a deck from the coffee table, and that's when I noticed the large bandage across the back of his right hand. "I've decided I need to change over to the cards, myself. Those birds are driving me crazy."

"How'd you hurt your hand?"

"These stupid birds, I'm telling you. I was trying to teach one of them to stay down in my pocket, and he caught me with his claws."

Hmm. Maybe. "Did Taft ever discuss the trunk escape with you?"

He shuffled the cards and made the ace of spades hop up. "No, but if they had I would've said 'Stick to what you do best.'"

"Was it that difficult a trick?"

"No, not at all. Just an escape from a locked trunk, and they never could get it right." The king of spades hopped out of the deck.

"Who else knew they were planning an escape trick?"

"I don't know. It wasn't a secret. I suppose anyone at the club might have known." The queen of spades peeked up from the deck. "As for this woman angle, why don't you ask Fancy about that?"

"Were she and Taft an item?"

"You'll have to ask her."

"She's on my list."

His fingers paused. "Well, I hope you'll take me off your list. I'm a good enough magician that I don't need to kill off the competition, especially the Finch brothers. They certainly aren't a threat to me."

So Taft was a great guy, a gentleman, an adventurer. I wondered if I could rule out money as a motive. "What about their collection of magic memorabilia. Worth anything?"

"Only to another magician or a student of magic. Some guys get all excited over some limp mildewed book or a crumbling piece of equipment." He looked around at all the gleaming machines. "I never saw the need to clutter my house with junk like that." He stacked the deck of cards on the table. "What do you think about the card tricks? Pretty good, huh?"

"Not bad. What about this special box supposedly owned by Houdini? Did you ever see it?"

"No. I wasn't interested. Just another trinket for their collection."

"And the bet Lucas had about getting the box open? Did you ever hear anyone talking about it?"

"I may have overheard some guys talking about it at the bar. I think they were going to call their new trick the Vanishing Ruby."

"That's right."

Rahnee had said there was no rivalry between the brothers, but I thought I'd try out the idea on Bart. "Any indication that Lucas might be jealous of Taft?"

"No. What would he have to be jealous about? That's ridiculous."

I'd worked on cases where people had been murdered for very ridiculous reasons.

"Well, thanks for your help. If you think of anything else, give me a call. I'm in the book. The Randall Detective Agency."

"The Remarkable Randall Detective Agency?"

"Some days it is."

Binky's insistent barking at the door made Bart sigh and get up to let his dog in. "Know anyone who'd like to buy a dog and six uncooperative birds?"

◇◇◇

My next stop was Shepherd Missions. The people there were sad to hear the news about Taft's death.

"We all thought a lot of Taft," an earnest young woman said. She had a head full of what I call fried hair, as pale and crinkly as packing material. She was extremely plain, but her smile made you want to smile back. "We're in and out all the time taking food and blankets to the needy. Taft kept records for us, typed letters, answered the phone. Very nice guy. Always well-dressed and polite. Remembered everyone's birthday. You don't meet a lot of men like that anymore."

"Did you know he was a magician?"

"Yes, every now and then, he'd do a card trick for us. What happened to him?"

No need to upset her with the details. "There was an accident at the Magic Club. The police are investigating."

"Well, that's a real shame. He was a hard worker for the Missions."

"What exactly do you do here?"

"This is a clearinghouse. We accept all kinds of donations from the community, and then we distribute the canned goods and clothing to our needy families."

"Did Taft have a work station?"

"That's his desk by the window."

"Do you mind if I have a look?"

"Go right ahead."

The fried hair woman sorted canned food into cardboard boxes while another worker looked through a pile of used toys. I sat down at Taft's desk. A stack of stamped envelopes, a glass jar full of pencils, and a telephone flanked the computer. I hesitated before opening the top drawer. Idiot. You're not going to find a picture of Lindsey in there. I found paper clips, rubber bands, a stapler, and a ruler. The larger drawers had more envelopes, paper, and some forms thanking donors and showing them how to take their donations off their taxes. No angry letter from a rival magician. No incriminating photo of Taft with the Other Woman. There was, however, a birthday card showing a white rabbit peeking out of a top hat saying, "The Trick is Remembering Your Birthday!" Inside, the card said, "Sorry I'm Late!" A note written in red ink said, "I love you as a friend. Let's keep it friendly." The note was signed, "Rahnee."

Keep it friendly. A Dear John birthday card.

The woman peered over my shoulder. "What are you looking for?"

I held up the card. "Do you mind if I take this?"

"Take whatever you need. I wish we could help you more, but Taft never said anything about himself. I don't even know about his family."

"He has a brother."

"Really?"

"He's a magician, too." I closed the desk drawers and put the card in my pocket. "Do you know if Taft had a girlfriend? Anyone come to see him at work?"

"They may have. Like I said, the other workers and I are in and out all day long. Taft could've had visitors, and we'd never see them."

I checked my wallet and found a twenty-dollar bill I wasn't using. "I'd like to make a donation. Thanks for your help."

"Thank you," she said with her infectious smile. "Sorry we couldn't be more helpful."

My smile faded when I saw what was in her hand. A little pink teddy bear exactly like the one Lindsey used to carry everywhere. I had a sudden memory of Lindsey laughing as she refused to believe that "The Teddy Bears' Picnic" was a jazz song. Even after I played the 1907 version with men growling in the background, she remained unconvinced.

"Mister Randall?" The woman's concerned voice brought me back to the present. "Are you all right?"

"Sorry. Just thought of something."

She offered me the bear. "Did you need a toy for someone? Please take this. We have plenty of stuffed animals."

I backed away. "No. No, thank you."

That's the trouble with grief. You never know when it's going to mount a surprise attack. Somehow I made it to the car. I don't have any tears left, so I took a few painful gasps and managed to get control. For a few minutes, I wanted that bear. I wanted to feel the soft plush and remember the countless times I picked it off the floor. I wanted to smell the baby powder, the fresh smell that was Lindsey. But of course, it couldn't be the same bear. And I couldn't have the same life.

◇◇◇

My cell phone ringing startled me, but I wasn't surprised to see it was Camden. Our connection, psychic or not, comes in handy when I need a distraction.

"Can you give me a ride to the studio?"

"Yeah, sure."

I swung by Grace Street. Camden was waiting on the porch. When he got into the car, he gave me a look, but didn't say anything about photographs or teddy bears or the overwhelming sadness I battle almost every day.

"How about Sandy's bracelet? Any leads?"

"No luck. There's one more place on her list, and then I thought I'd check the pawn shops, ask around. Do you know where it is?"

"No."

"You're a sorry excuse for a sidekick, I'll say that."

"I'd have to meet Sandy. Do you want me to?"

While it's true many of Camden's predictions and insights have been helpful in past cases, I know my own deductive powers are damn good, and those are the only powers I want to rely on. "No, thanks." I turned up Food Row. "You sound like you've been gargling with gravel. You need to see a doctor."

"Think again."

"My doctor's office isn't far from here. I have questions to ask him, and he can have a look at your throat at the same time."

"You don't need me for that."

"Don't you want this cleared up so you can get back to singing?"

He took a deep breath as if resigned. "No needles."

It took me a moment to realize what he was talking about. "Okay, no needles."

◇◇◇

Nick Lamachio shared an office with two other doctors, so the waiting room was full.

Camden started to back out. "We can come another day."

I kept hold of his arm. "Let's see if he can squeeze you in."

When I checked with the receptionist, Nick had a cancellation. We could go in right away. Camden groaned while I hauled him through the door.

Nick came out of another room, saw me, and grinned. "Randall, no matter how many times you come, I can't fix that personality of yours."

"It's not me this time. I want you to have a look at Camden's throat."

Nick's a big friendly man who's obviously dealt with reluctant patients before. "You don't look too happy about that, Camden."

"He's a little nervous around doctors."

"I'm not going to do anything you don't want me to. Come on in and sit down." He must have been giving out good vibes, because Camden relaxed a little in the examining room. I told Nick the problem. He checked Camden's throat and felt along the sides of his neck.

"No lumps or swelling. My guess is you've worn it out. Your vocal cords are okay. You're going to have to not talk a couple more days."

"He's worried about his singing voice," I said.

"I don't see any sort of damage. Has this ever happened before?" Camden shook his head.

"Well, don't push it. Let it rest. If it's not back in two days, come see me again."

"Camden's my excuse to get in here," I said. "Nick, where's the place you can press on someone's neck to knock them out?"

Camden looked at me askance. Nick demonstrated on his own neck, thumbs under his jaw. "Right in here. Pressure on the carotid artery will cause unconsciousness."

"Would it leave a mark?"

"Not necessarily."

So maybe somebody had squeezed Taft Finch's neck and then packed him in the trunk.

"I don't recommend it as a remedy."

"Something else I want you to see." I took the pills out of my pocket.

Nick looked them over. "This is Unisom."

"Sleeping pills, right?"

"Yes, doxylamine succinate, to be exact, one of the most potent you can get without a prescription."

"Powerful enough to kill someone?"

"Depends. How many pills, how they're delivered, if they're mixed with other things. But, yes. Hope you're not planning a murder."

"Something to do with a case. Now, I know you're not supposed to mix your drugs with alcohol or operate heavy machinery. What's the deal with this pill?"

"Definitely not something you want to mix with alcohol. No sleep medication should be used with alcohol, and this one shouldn't be taken with Zyrtec or Benadryl. Both those drugs will enhance the side effects, which include blackouts and seizures."

Blackouts. That's all the murder needed in order to make certain Taft was securely locked away.

"Thanks," I said. "Thanks for fitting us in today."

"No problem. Let me know how things go, Cam."

Camden thanked him. When we got in the car, he said, "Do we know exactly when and how Taft died?"

"That's what I'm going to ask Jordan."

Chapter Eight

Witchy Woman

At the Parkland Police Department, Jordan Finley greeted Camden with a smile and me with a grimace.

"Cam, can't you keep him out of my way? What do you two want?"

"Do you have an official ruling on how Taft Finch died?" I asked.

Jordan checked his computer. "The report's not complete. Looks like he died sometime Sunday morning."

"Did the medical examiner find any marks on his body, signs of a struggle?"

Jordan turned back to the computer and clicked a few more keys. "Sorry. No marks on the body."

"No marks of any kind?" And why didn't the latch work? Maybe it wasn't there. Maybe it was broken. "Did your guys check out the latch?"

"Yep. Works fine."

"Somebody definitely didn't want Taft to get out."

"You know, that's exactly what we thought. Imagine that."

"Any indication he was drugged?"

Jordan's little eyes narrowed. "Do I recall putting you on this case?"

"You never put me on a case, so what's the difference?"

He sat back in his chair. "We're still waiting on the lab report. What's your stake in this, anyway?"

"Rahnee Nevis hired me to find out what happened."

"Well, you need to keep out of our way." He glanced at Camden and lowered his voice. "Do you see anything unusual about this?"

Jordan will use Camden's talent on occasion, but never officially.

"Not yet."

"Then both of you get out of here. I've got real work to do."

As we walked back to the car, I said, "Why aren't you seeing anything? It would be very handy if you knew who killed Taft."

"Aside from the fact that this talent of mine is unpredictable, I'd have to shake hands with Taft to find out who killed him, and I don't think that would work."

"You've had contact with dead people before."

"If Taft starts haunting the Magic Club, and if he wants to talk to me, maybe I could find out. And you know things get really foggy if I'm involved somehow."

"Involved how? You hadn't met the Finches before, had you? Or Rahnee or any of the other magicians?"

"Somewhere along the way there'll be a connection. I can't see it till it gets here."

"Useless, I tell you. Useless."

"I'll buy lunch."

◇◇◇

We drove to the Quik-Fry and I let him buy the cheeseburgers and fries. We sat in the car to eat. There's plenty of room in the front seat of a '67 Plymouth Fury.

I put more salt on my fries. "Maybe Taft took too many pills. Maybe he panicked and passed out. Nick said sleeping pills should never be taken with alcohol. I thought maybe Taft had a few Saturday night, but Jilly said he didn't stop for his usual drink." I ate another fry. "Somebody could've put their hands around his neck and given it enough of a squeeze to knock him out, somebody tall enough and strong enough to fold Taft into the trunk."

Camden unwrapped his cheeseburger. "Any ideas?"

"Looks like Lucas Finch is the only one who fits that description, although Rahnee Nevis is a tall, strong-looking woman."

"Motives?"

"Lucas was not happy about Taft losing the box. Maybe he lost his temper. Rahnee—I don't know."

He took a drink of Coke. "How about the other people at the club?"

"Well, you saw WizBoy, a wispy nerd of a magician and Jilly, the equally wispy bartender. They're in love, only no one's notified Jilly."

"They might have put their wisp together and killed Taft."

"Well, as we heard, WizBoy saw him as a rival for the club, and he's not very happy with Rahnee's restrictions. Is there more ketchup?"

Camden dug in the bag and tossed me another packet. "So he kills Taft to cause bad publicity for Rahnee."

"Maybe." I couldn't see WizBoy making that much effort.

"And Jilly? If Taft wasn't in love with her, she might have been testy."

"Wispy and testy, a deadly combination. She wants to be a magician's assistant, and Taft promised to put her in his act, promised to teach her some card tricks. I think things were going smoothly between them. The last time anyone saw Taft alive was around ten when he finished his act. Rahnee and WizBoy were backstage. Jilly was at the bar, unhappy because he left in such a hurry."

"And the next time anyone sees him, he's dead in the trunk."

"That's right. Maybe this box is more valuable than we thought, and someone killed Taft to get it." I took the card out of my pocket. "The only thing I found in Taft's desk that might be helpful is this birthday card from Rahnee saying she wants to be just friends. Maybe it made him suicidal, so he climbed in the trunk and closed the lid."

Camden set his cheeseburger aside. He held the card for a few moments. "Prepare to be dazzled by my psychic insight."

"I'm ready."

"He kept the card, so maybe being just friends was okay with him."

"Yeah, I guess if he'd been upset about it, he would've put it through the shredder."

"He's had this card for a while. There was more to this relationship."

"It was back on, you mean?"

"I don't think it was ever truly off." He gave me the card. "No other clues in his desk?"

"The usual stuff." No school pictures. No DVDs. No memories that kicked you in the stomach and made you wish you'd died in a car crash, too.

Camden's glance told me he'd tuned in on this useless little bit of soul searching. He picked up his cheeseburger and changed the subject. "I really oughta put in an appearance at the PSN."

"Sure you want to go? I thought you were endangering auras over there."

"Thought I'd be there for moral support."

My cell phone rang. A sultry-sounding woman's voice said, "This is Fancy returning your call."

"Thanks for getting back to me. My name's David Randall, and I'm investigating the death of Taft Finch."

There was a pause. "How about the Bombay Club tomorrow, say, around ten a.m.?"

"That would be fine."

"See you then." She hung up.

I closed my phone. "That was a magician named Fancy. She sounds as fancy as her name. I'm meeting her tomorrow."

"So you have time to meet the Deadly Sheila at the network today."

I started the car. "Can't wait."

◇◇◇

The first thing I noticed about the Deadly Sheila was her two overlong front teeth. The teeth plus the bleached blonde hair in fat old-fashioned curls reminded me strongly of Bugs Bunny in drag. She had on an expensive-looking yellow suit and white blouse, no jewelry except a wide gold bracelet watch, and large glasses in clear frames with gold trim. She was about five feet nine and stout, with pinched features, as if she had only five minutes to solve all the world's problems, and here were two more of them right in front of her.

She crossed her arms over her ample chest. "Who are you?"

"I'm David Randall, friend of Camden's."

She gave us the once-over, and unlike most women, didn't seem impressed by my dashing dark good looks, or by Camden's sloppy charm. "Are you here for some specific purpose?"

I could see why Ellin didn't like her. Two steamrollers have trouble flattening the same road. "No, we just thought we'd come by and get in the way."

I could tell she didn't want to talk to us, but she managed a brief smile. "Very nice to meet you, Mr. Randall, but we're really quite busy. So much to do."

I looked around the studio. It was odd not to see Bonnie or Teresa, the two lovely but vague young women who usually host the PSN's shows.

"Is Ellie here?" Camden asked.

"I believe she's talking with the cameraman. But we really have a lot of work to do, so if you don't mind—"

Ellin saw us and hurried over, followed by Reg Haverson, the last remaining original PSN cast member. Reg is always posing, even when no one's looking, a male model type with perfectly sculptured hair and unnaturally white teeth. Today, he'd lost his sparkle and I knew why. Hired to warm up the audience and occasionally host, he was always scheming in a harmless way to get more airtime, and Sheila was this new threat to his career.

Ellin was working hard to control her temper. "I see you've met Randall and Cam. Everything's ready for the taping, if you'd like to get on set."

Sheila protested. "But I wanted to turn the chairs the teensiest bit to the side."

"We went through this yesterday, Sheila. They're fine."

"I don't think the audience on the left side can really see me."

Both women spoke politely but with undertones of steel. Everyone else in the studio stood quietly, watching the battle. Reg rolled his eyes.

"When the audience comes in, we'll ask them," Ellin said.

Sheila had already turned one chair around. "Let's go ahead and move the chairs and see how it works. We can always move them back."

Ellin started forward and Camden touched her arm. "Ellie, it's just a chair."

I could see her neck muscles tense as she decided what to do. "All right, we'll try it. Anything else?"

"Well, we'd already talked about the flower arrangement. I can have some new ones in here by tomorrow. And didn't I say something yesterday about this picture? Can we do without it?"

Camden kept his hand on Ellin's arm. She took a deep breath. "It was a gift from the National Psychics Association."

"I find it distracting. Can we hang it somewhere else?" She turned to Reg. "Take it down, would you?"

Reg blanched. His idea of physical labor is doing his nails.

"I'll get it," I said.

Ellin's lips were compressed into a tight line. She gave me a brief nod.

"You can hang it in my office," Sheila said.

I saluted. "Yes, ma'am."

She was either oblivious to sarcasm or too busy planning what to change next. I took the large photo of swirling stars off the set wall and carried it offstage to the office Ellin now shared with the Deadly Sheila. Her desk had been pushed over to make room for another larger desk. Two filing cabinets and a large plush swivel chair took up most of the room, along with stacks of boxes. I propped the picture beside one cabinet and came back to find the set completely rearranged to suit Sheila. She was telling Reg where to sit and what to say.

"You can do the commercial announcements and introduce the guests."

Reg looked aghast. "But I told you, Mrs. Kirk, I usually warm up the audience and interact with them all during the program. Didn't you see me do that during yesterday's taping?"

"I don't know about interacting so much, but the warm-up will be fine if you do that before we start."

"That's what 'warm-up' is."

"As long as you're finished when I'm ready."

Camden now had a tight grip on Ellin's arm. "Ellie, you're still the producer. If she wants to change a few things, you can change them back."

Her voice was low and tense. "She's ruining everything."

"She wasn't too bad yesterday, was she? How much is her husband giving the PSN?"

"Enough for the whole season."

"Worth a little irritation?"

"I suppose so."

Sheila waved a plump hand. "Ellin, I'll need you to stand over here and cue me."

"Oh, I'll cue her all right."

As I've said, the PSN isn't high art or even high entertainment, but I've watched enough episodes to know today's show was a disaster. Dispirited by his demotion to straight man, Reg failed to get much warmth out of the audience, and as a result, their reactions were tepid. Sheila's idea of hosting was to keep the camera focused on her the entire hour while she told her life story. Despite Ellin's cues, she rambled through a commercial break and forgot to answer the phones during the call-in segment.

So far, Reg hadn't gotten in a word and had to stand on the sidelines with me and Camden. I expressed my sympathies. "She's pretty bad. You'll have your old job back in no time."

Reg was so upset he ignored a strand of hair that had escaped from his perfect upsweep. "Bad? She's awful. Look at her out there, the old bag. If I turned on my TV right now and saw that face, I'd run screaming from the room. And what's all that crap she's saying about being psychic? Listen to that."

As if sensing an entertainment disaster, the audience had on attentive faces. Ellin stood next to the camera, arms folded, her expression grim.

"So I want all of you out there to call me or come by the station and get on the air with me," Sheila said. "I'm not only a host, you understand. I've been blessed with extraordinary psychic powers. I can solve your problems, big or small. Why worry about the future when you can know all the answers? Why fret over money troubles, troubles of the heart, or petty daily annoyances? Come talk to me, Sheila, reincarnated spirit of the Oracle of Delphi, ancient goddess of prophecy."

I forced my snort of unexpected laughter into a sneeze. The audience sat rapt. Reg groaned. I could read Ellin's lips, and what she said I can't repeat.

"Yes, friends, from now on, the PSN not only stands for Psychic Service Network but for Psychic Sheila Network. Until tomorrow, keep thinking good thoughts."

The audience applauded. Sheila beamed. Reg glanced at the studio clock. "There's still three minutes."

"You're on, Reg."

"She doesn't deserve it, but I'll take care of this."

He stepped on camera and smoothly thanked the audience. "And another round of applause for our special guest, Sheila Kirk. The PSN was brought to you today by our good friends down at Francy's Frame Shoppe, and Candle De-Light."

Sheila acted as if he'd stepped on her toes, but Reg continued until Ellin signaled all clear.

By then, Sheila was radioactive. "What was all that about?"

He explained. "You had three minutes left. It would've been dead air, plus we always plug our sponsors at the end of each show."

She turned her glare to Ellin. "Why didn't you cue me?"

"I did," Ellin said.

"We'll have to work out a better system, then."

Ellin's idea of a better system would be pull the pin and hand Sheila the grenade, but before she could say anything, Sheila flapped one hand to motion someone over.

"I want my son Dirk to help with advertising. We really need more sponsors."

Dirk lumbered up, a hulking blob with a broad dull freckled face and a head too small for his body, covered by a windblown haystack. Despite his expensive white polo shirt and khaki slacks, he looked unkempt and unfinished. Grinning, hands in his pockets, I expected he'd blurt a Goofy "huh-yuck" at any moment.

"Dirk?" His name caught in Ellin's throat.

"Yes, my son Dirk. He's perfect for the job."

Dirk Kirk. Perfect. Ellin quivered to remain calm.

"Does he have any experience?"

"How difficult can it be? You go to businesses and ask for their support."

Ellin had found out the hard way not every business in Parkland wanted to be associated with the Psychic Service Network.

"Will he write the commercials, too? Film them? Edit them? Satisfy the sponsor?"

Sheila waved her words away. "Dirk is a natural. He makes friends so easily. You see, he's an entertainer, too." If she'd been Medusa, she couldn't have done a better job of turning cast and crew to stone. "We'll be featuring him soon. This is going to be an excellent experience for all of us. Show them what you can do, Dirk."

Dirk beamed, took a pack of cards from his pocket, and waddled up to me, fanning them clumsily. The design was a garish paisley swirl of pink and red. Three cards tumbled to the floor, which didn't faze him. "Pick a card. Any card."

Sheila called, "Phil! Come here."

A tall, white-haired, craggy-faced man came over to us. Mister Kirk. Sheila took his arm. "Phil, show them what Dirk can do."

The man obligingly picked a card.

"Don't let me see it." Dirk tried to shuffle the remaining cards. He furrowed his brow, his tongue in one corner of his mouth. "Okay, okay, it's the six of clubs, right?"

The card was the five of spades. "Very close!" Phil Kirk said. "Dirk's going to be a famous magician some day."

I had several replies to this, but to avert open warfare Ellin said, "Cam, Randall, this is Phillip Kirk, Sheila's husband and the man who is responsible for the show."

We shook hands all around. Camden frowned at the handshake, but the man didn't notice his worry. Kirk gave his wife a hug. "What do you think of my little girl, eh? Hosting her own television show! I knew she could do it. You'll see, Ellin, we'll turn this network around."

Like Linda Blair's head in "The Exorcist," I wanted to say, but valiantly held back. Apparently—though this stretched my imagination to its limits—Phil Kirk thought of his wife as a cute, fluffy little blonde who delighted him with her original ideas. I could tell he wasn't going to tolerate any criticism, no matter how well deserved.

"Sheila's always been psychic. Amazingly accurate. Sometimes it scares me."

Despite Ellin's killer glare, I had to reply. "Me, too."

"She's already done wonders for this show. I told her she'd be a natural."

A natural disaster, absolutely. "Nice to meet you. Camden and I were just leaving."

Sheila huffed, "But Dirk knows many more tricks."

I glanced at my watch. "Gosh, sorry, I have to be somewhere in ten minutes. Maybe next time. Come on, Camden."

He kissed Ellin. "Hang in there, sweetheart."

"Thanks for coming by." Her brief smile included me. "We'll have lots to talk about later."

We left the happy Kirk family exclaiming over Dirk's ability to straighten the pack of cards.

"Interesting that Dirk's sort of a magician," I said as we walked down the hallway. "Maybe he's been to the club. Maybe he knows something about the Houdini box. Although it's hard to believe anyone that dull knows anything."

"I'm sure Ellie's heard more about Dirk than she ever wanted to know."

"And what's the deal with Phil? I saw your face when you shook his hand."

"He's got a health problem. Could be serious."

"Think he'll believe you?"

"Probably not."

"Then you'd be wasting valuable voice." I checked my watch. "Let's go by Bilby's and see if he's heard anything about a diamond bracelet or a Houdini box."

"Speaking of jewelry, swing by Royalle's first. I want to show you the impossible ring."

Chapter Nine

Some Enchanted Evening

Royalle's Fine Jewelry was in Old Parkland, the historic part of the city. I found a parking space across the street. We looked in the huge windows of Royalle's like a couple of kids checking out puppies in the pet store.

"Which one is it?"

Camden pointed to a brilliant cluster of diamonds and emeralds. "That little number right there. Take a guess how much it costs."

"More than you and I will ever make in a lifetime."

"Twenty-five thousand dollars."

"Okay, you've had your fun. Get back in the car."

"I really wish I could afford it."

"And I wish Kary would marry me. Come on. Maybe Bilby's got something nice you can afford."

◇◇◇

Unlike the stereotypical dark cluttered hole in an unsavory neighborhood, Bilby Foster's Pawnshop is a clean, modern building with neatly arranged shelves full of electronic gadgets, musical instruments, and appliances. Bilby, a short squat little man, was sitting as usual on a padded stool in the back of the store behind glass cases filled with jewelry and watches.

"Randall," he greeted. "Cam. What do you fellas need today?"

"I need a diamond bracelet, a box that may have belonged to Houdini, and Camden needs an expensive-looking diamond and emerald ring," I said.

Bilby didn't even blink. "Diamond bracelets I got plenty of. Rings, too. What's the box all about?"

"A shiny wooden box about the size of a shoebox with an 'H' on top. Stolen from the Magic Club last Thursday. The bracelet should have Sandy Olaf's and her friend Bertie's initials engraved on the clasp."

Bilby rubbed his nose. "Well, it's interesting you should ask that. I had a fella in here not long ago looking for a magic box."

"You're kidding."

"Nope. Wanted to know if I had any sort of old stuff that might have belonged to a magician. Some sort of collector, looking for any kind of magic stuff, wands, books, those rings that stick together. I told him he'd have better luck at an auction or estate sale."

"But he specifically asked you about a box?"

"Yeah, a wooden box with an 'H' on top. Said it would have stars and some other things carved on top, too."

"What did this guy look like?"

"Kinda stout, dark curly hair and a beard."

"Did he leave an address or a card or anything?"

"Nope. I take it you want to know if he comes back in?"

"Yes, I do."

"Will do." Bilby hopped off his stool. "Okay, let's see." He unlocked the jewelry cases and pulled out the trays of bracelets to put on top of the cases. We checked each one, but none had initials on the clasp. "What kind of ring did you say, Cam? Diamonds and emeralds? Got a few."

He took out the trays of rings. Camden chose one, but after inspecting it, shook his head and put it back. "Not exactly what I'm looking for."

"I'll give you a good deal. Gonna ask Ellin to marry you?"

"Yes, and I want a very special ring for her."

"These don't suit you, I'll keep an eye out and call you if something better comes in." He put the tray of rings back in the case. "Same thing for you, Randall. I'll check any bracelets. Don't know about that box, though. Doesn't sound like something somebody'd pawn."

◇◇◇

Camden and I checked a few more pawnshops in town before heading back home.

He went into the kitchen to start supper. I went into my office and found a stack of paper about Houdini on my desk.

Upstairs, I tapped on Kary's open bedroom door. "Got a minute?" She'd presented me with a peace offering. I was definitely going to return the favor. "Care to visit the Magic Club tonight? Might not be too cheery since they've lost Taft Finch, but the show must go on."

"I'd like that, thanks."

"Thank you for all the Houdini stuff. You're not still looking, are you? I'm sure I have enough."

She turned her laptop so I could see the screen. "Mothers United." Another adoption site. Great.

"I've been reading letters from pregnant women who can't keep their babies and want to find the perfect mothers for them."

She didn't look as thrilled as I thought she'd be. "But?"

"But there's really no way to tell if any of their stories are true."

"The downside of the Internet."

"Anyone can put anything on a website. On Mothers United, you're supposed to email the mothers and tell them about yourself. Then they decide if you're a good match."

"Pick one you like, and they get UPS to deliver?"

"That's another thing that sets off the alarm bells. Nowhere on the site does it mention any sort of fee or price."

"So I gather your search helped you eliminate online baby shopping as an adoption tool."

"Pretty much, yes."

I allowed myself a moment of temporary relief. Due to a difficult unplanned teen pregnancy, Kary is unable to have children.

She was as determined to adopt a baby as I was determined not to. She wouldn't give up.

Did I say temporary relief? Because that's all it was.

"So," Kary said, "I've decided to investigate Mothers United and see what's going on."

"Investigate?"

"Yes. I'm going over to their headquarters and pretend to be a pregnant woman in search of the perfect parents for my unwanted child. I won't use this kind of service, but if they're not legitimate, I don't want anyone to be taken in and lose their money."

Okay. "Do they actually have headquarters? I thought they were only online."

"Ah, yes, but I have skills and a friend who works with the Better Business Bureau. They've had several questions about Baby Love, which is a part of Mothers United, and Baby Love has an office in Parkland. My plan goes into action tomorrow."

I almost said, "Do you want me to come with you?" but I'd learned my lesson. "Is it a secret plan, or can you tell me about it?"

"I'm still working out the details."

What would be the safest thing to say? "We'll leave for the club tonight around seven."

◇◇◇

The only way to deal with Kary's new plan was to shove it out of my mind and concentrate on having a pleasant evening out. Right up until seven, I figured something would happen to spoil things, but at seven o'clock exactly, Kary came down the stairs dressed in tan slacks and a cream-colored sweater. I held her coat. We went out, and I opened the Fury's door for her. She slid in. On the way to the club, she filled the awkward silence by talking about the students she was tutoring at an elementary school.

"There's one little boy that's so cute, I have a hard time scolding him. His name is Ozzie."

"Ozzie? You don't hear that every day. Is he Oswald?"

"Yes, poor thing. I see a hard life ahead for him."

"Nah, his college buddies'll call him Oz. He'll be cool."

"I hadn't thought of that. Okay, no need to worry about his future."

What about our future? I thought. *Have I really screwed it up this time?* Then, as she pushed back her hair, I caught a sparkle of silver and saw she was wearing the bracelet I'd given her for Christmas. I'd found the perfect bracelet with little dangling stars to commemorate Wonder Star, her super hero alter ego, saving the day and me in a dark tunnel under the city.

Okay, so maybe things weren't totally messed up.

News of Taft Finch's death had, as I figured, boosted business. The club was full. Kary and I found a table at the back. WizBoy was on stage, performing card tricks to loud rock music.

I used to date a theater major, and she took me to see a musical called *The Fantasticks.* I didn't remember much about the show except one humorous character, an old actor, who said "Look for me in the light." Just as the light had made Bart appear younger and trimmer, the light transformed WizBoy. Offstage, a scrawny kid with a sad lack of grammar. Onstage, surprisingly engaging and colorful and making those cards dance. Unlike poor Dirk Kirk, who could barely hold onto his cards, WizBoy made them sail up in fountains of red and black and spiral like butterflies. His finale was collapsing a house of cards and making it rebuild. Kary joined the enthusiastic applause. I wedged myself against the bar to order our drinks. Jilly, in her usual basic black, listlessly took orders and filled glasses.

"How are you tonight, Jilly?"

"Oh, okay, I guess. I'm glad it's busy. Takes my mind off things."

She handed the man on my right his beer. As he moved away, WizBoy took his place. He grinned at Jilly. "Hey, great crowd, huh? Did you hear that applause?"

She threw him a frosty look. "I'm very happy for you."

"Well, heck, I'm sorry about Taft, too, but, in a way, it's a tribute that so many people came out tonight. A memorial."

"We're planning a memorial for him. A real one."

She went to get my order. WizBoy gave me a look I recognized from bitter experience: the can't-I-do-anything-right? Look.

"You were great," I said.

"Glad somebody thinks so."

"My friend Kary thinks so, too."

"The blonde you're with? Man, she's gorgeous." Still, his gaze returned to Jilly.

"And she believes in magic. Let me introduce you."

He glanced back at Kary. "Not a bad idea."

Jilly brought my drinks. I paid and led WizBoy to the table.

"Kary, this is WizBoy. Wiz, Kary Ingram."

"Pleased to meet you," he said.

"Your act was wonderful," Kary said. "I really enjoyed it."

He took out a pack of cards. "That was nothing. Watch this."

His close-up sleight of hand tricks brought a crowd around the table and more applause. When he'd finished, I offered to buy him a drink.

"Sure, thanks."

We went to the bar. I got Jilly's attention and ordered. WizBoy gave her a big smile, which she ignored. When she'd brought our drinks and drifted back to the register, he took a big gulp and set his glass down with a thunk. "Can't she see what a hit I am? Why is it I can impress everybody and his brother and not her?"

I found myself saying the thing I hate most. "Give it time. She's still upset about Taft."

"But he wasn't interested in her. He told me one time he thought she was sweet, but too young for him."

"Did he tell Jilly this?"

"Nah, he was too nice. He and Rahnee had something going, though. Couple of times I came by her office, and the two of them were in there, you know, fooling around."

"Did you mention that to Jilly?"

"And upset her? No, I thought I'd let her figure it out on her own. If I told her, she wouldn't believe me. Or maybe she'd kill the messenger." He took another drink. "We've got a lot in common, even if she doesn't see it. My folks wanted me to be a banker like my old man. They thought being a magician was foolish. Jilly's parents didn't want her to be a magician, either, only they thought it was evil."

"Evil? You mean, satanic?"

"Yeah, they thought she was going to be calling up demons or something. They had all kinds of Bible verses they said proved their point, but you can find a verse to fit anything, can't you?"

Camden knows every single Bible verse that relates to the evils of sorcery. He says in his teenage years, he had them flung at him all the time. "But you and Jilly became magicians, anyway."

"Well, my folks still aren't too happy about it, but they've come to see my show, and they sorta grudgingly admit I got skills. Jilly left home before her folks could kick her out. She told me they were planning to, but she didn't care. She really hates them. She says her mom decided she was some kind of bad seed because she likes to wear black and play with cards. But her dad's the real hypocrite. He was a magician once, and since he couldn't make it, he had this complete turnaround."

This explained Jilly's perpetual gloomy mood. Camden had escaped by traveling across the country and working through all the visions until he could control them. He'd had the good fortune to land on Grace Street. Jilly had landed in the Magic Club.

"You'd think this would be the place where she'd be happy," I said.

"You would, wouldn't you?"

The next act was onstage, a wild-haired fellow in a silver jumpsuit making rings jump through hoops. Each ring was a different color, and when the light hit, their sparkle tossed a kaleidoscopic effect all over the room. For the life of me, I couldn't see how the guy was doing it. The audience sat spellbound, except for WizBoy, who checked his watch.

"Gotta go."

"Are you on after this guy?"

"Nope. Rahnee only lets me do one set. I gotta check on the heater. Sometimes it cuts off. Excuse me."

The magician onstage spun the silver hoops around each other like a giant disco ball and then made another series of silver rings dance on a scarf. After the scarf dance, he scooped up all the rings and hoops and bowed to enthusiastic applause.

"WizBoy looks like he should be playing drums in a rock band," Kary said. "Is he a suspect?"

"Right now, anyone in this room could be a suspect. Be right back."

I circled the room, looking for Rahnee. She was seated at a table near the stage, looking splendid in a gold blouse and black skirt.

I sat down next to her. "Looks like a nice turnout for Taft."

Her fiery hair was dusted with gold sparkles. "I'm sorry Lucas isn't here to see this. He said he couldn't manage coming out tonight."

A well-dressed couple offered condolences to Rahnee. She thanked them. After they'd moved on, she said, "Two of our best customers."

"Looks like the club will be okay."

"Yes. I don't want to sound cold-hearted, but I was really afraid Taft's death might have kept people away. It's like Cam saw in his vision. I worked very hard to buy this club, and when I got it, I had to work even harder to get it up to standard. This room was a mess, and I don't think anyone had washed the glasses in years. Chairs and tables needed to be replaced, the ceiling leaked, the heater never worked, and I had to put in a whole new lighting system. A lot of people said it would fail. Taft wasn't one of them. He stood by me the whole way." She swallowed hard and brushed away her tears.

"Would you say the two of you were more than just friends?"

"Just friends, that's all."

Hmm. Did she have some reason to lie, or had WizBoy misinterpreted what he'd seen in her office? Maybe she and Taft had been practicing some fancy dance steps. Maybe WizBoy was lying.

Some of the little gold sparkles stuck on Rahnee's fingers. She wiped them off. "Sometimes all you need is one really good friend."

"That's true. He kept the birthday card."

Her mouth trembled as if she were controlling a sob.

"Rahnee, be honest with me. Did you have a relationship with Taft?"

She briefly put her hand to her mouth. "We didn't want Lucas to know. Lucas had asked me first, and I said I wasn't interested. But I *was* interested in Taft. You wouldn't think identical twin brothers could be so different, but Taft was so dashing and the life of the party and the better magician—don't ever tell Lucas I said that! We were worried that Lucas would take things the wrong way."

"So Lucas never knew about the affair?"

She looked alarmed. "Are you thinking he might have—? Oh, no. No, he's not that kind of man."

"I'm just trying to cover all the bases."

"I like to think he never knew. I didn't want to hurt him."

"So the let's-keep-it-friendly birthday card didn't work?"

"We tried. But we couldn't deny our feelings for each other. And we saw no reason to tell Lucas anything. Why get him upset?" She brushed tears from her cheeks. "Are you any closer to finding out what happened?"

"No." And as long as people lie to me, I won't have much success. "Taft died sometime Sunday morning. The medical examiner didn't find any signs of a struggle, but doesn't know yet if drugs were involved."

"I still can't believe anyone killed him. You'll keep looking, won't you?"

"I'll keep at it." And I'll keep trying to figure out what's going on. "Is Jolly Bob here?"

"No, he couldn't come tonight."

"Is he by any chance a stout man with dark curly hair and a beard?"

"Yes."

"Thanks. That saves me a lot of trouble."

When I got back to my table, the wild-haired magician was in earnest conversation with Kary.

"But, my dear, I could teach you. All you'd have to do is stand there and hand me rings."

"What's up?" I asked.

The magician straightened as if speared from behind. Kary's eyes sparkled. "David, this man is asking me to be his assistant."

Uh, oh.

Out of the light, the magician was a plain middle-aged man, his thin features caked with makeup. Even his spiky hair had a deflated look. "I said I'd be glad to teach her everything she needs to know. I can tell she has exceptional stage presence."

Kary gave me a meaningful glance. "I think it's a great idea. Not only would it be fun, it could be very useful."

I spoke to the magician. "If you could excuse us for a minute."

"Of course." He kept his gaze on Kary. "Here's my card. Or you can contact me through this club."

After he'd gone, Kary held up a hand to forestall my next protest. "I know what you're going to say. 'It's too dangerous.' But honestly, David, it's perfect! I could get all the inside scoop on what's been going on around here."

"Kary, a man was killed here."

"Over a Houdini box. Do I have a Houdini box? No one's likely to pay attention to an assistant."

Except when the assistant looks like you, I wanted to say, but knew better. The magician's card was decorated with glittery rings. "Omar the Ring Master" was printed in silver. "But you're not planning to tour with this guy, are you? What about your classes?"

"I'll tell him up front I can work with him only in Parkland. I'll call him tomorrow. It's decided."

I needed another drink. At the bar, I ran into the Ring Master.

"I didn't mean to intrude," he said, "but your friend is quite attractive and would be an asset to any magician. Any chance she might take me up on my offer?"

"We're discussing it."

"It's impossible to find a good assistant. You hire a pretty one, she can't tell a ring from a card. Hire a smart one, and she's got her own act before you know it, runs off, taking half your supplies, half your tricks."

"Have you thought about asking Jilly?"

"Who?"

I motioned. "That young lady there, the bartender. I understand she wants to be an assistant."

"Oh, her."

"Something wrong?"

"Well, she's too morose."

Looking at Jilly slumped listlessly at the bar, again rubbing her shoulder as if she were cold, I had to agree on his choice of words.

"I need someone with sparkle, with personality, and, quite frankly, I'm looking for a blonde."

Aren't we all? "Did you know Taft Finch?"

"Sure, we all knew Taft. He was a fine man, always willing to help a fellow magician. I owe him a lot. This was a terrible tragedy."

"What's your take on what happened?"

"Well, the Finch boys were good at what they did, but this business with a trunk escape—I don't know. I think it was beyond them. Even the Amazing Randi had to call for help to get out of a safe one time, and he was one of the best. Things can go wrong."

Jilly set his glass down, and he picked up his drink, not even glancing at her. "When can I expect an answer from Miss Ingram?"

"She's taking several classes at PCC. You'd have to work around her schedule."

"That's all right. I have a day job here in Parkland and do magic a few nights a week, sometimes less."

The magician looked harmless, and his act hadn't included knives or swords or fire. "You just want her to stand there and hand you your rings?"

"And the silks, yes. And occasionally I do a variation on the rabbit in a hat trick, only I use kittens."

Gah. I gave up. "She'll call you tomorrow."

"Excellent!"

◇◇◇

Miss Ingram had picked up another fan, but this one was about nine years old, and transfixed that his student teacher had come to the Magic Club.

"David, this is one of the students in Mrs. Parker's class where I'm helping with a reading group, Dana Heit. He's here with his father."

In my book, Dana's a girl's name. "Hi, Dana."

He gave me a similar stare. "Are you here with your father, too, Miss Ingram?"

Ouch. Round one to Dana.

"Mister Randall is a friend of mine."

"This is so cool!" Dana said. "I didn't know you liked magic."

"I love it," Kary said. "Wasn't the man with the rings amazing?"

"I'm going to be a magician," he said. "I've got a kit and everything. Dad gave it to me for Christmas."

"You'll have to show the class some of your tricks."

He beamed at her and then said, "Well, I gotta go. See you later."

I sat down. "You made his day."

"You should see how they react if they see me in McDonald's."

"What? Miss Ingram eats food? Miss Ingram likes fries?"

"And Miss Ingram is having a very good time, thank you." Her eyes narrowed. "I saw you talking with Omar."

"I wanted to find out if he knew anything about Taft Finch. And I told him you'd give him a call tomorrow. I hope that was okay."

"Yes, thank you."

"You know, you don't have to become a superhero or a magician to help on my cases."

"I think I do, David. Besides, it's fun to try new things."

"If one of my clients drowns, are you going to swim with the sharks? If a murder victim is found in a cave, are you going to bungee jump into a volcano?"

"Okay, now you're overreacting."

"I can't help it."

Kary gave me the full force of her big brown eyes. "Look, you're always asking me to marry you. Suppose—just suppose—I say yes. Once I become Mrs. David Randall, are you going to become even more protective? I won't be able to leave the house without a bodyguard and a pack of Dobermans."

"Maybe just one Doberman." She didn't appreciate my joke. "Once we're married, we can work this out."

"No, we're going to work it out now. I managed to make my way before I met you, remember. You need to back off, take it easy, realize that nothing's going to happen."

But things did happen, horrible unexpected things.

"David? Don't go there."

I caught her hand and tried to smile. "Nothing's going to happen."

Chapter Ten

Every Little Thing She Does Is Magic

The next morning, when I came down to breakfast, Kary had already left for class, and Camden was washing the dishes. I often volunteer for this chore, but he says he doesn't mind. It was one way he'd supported himself during his vagrant years—gave him time to think, he said. From the way he was scrubbing the pot, there must have been some serious thinking going on this morning.

I went to the coffee maker. "Ellin didn't drag you along today?"

"She and Reg are meeting here for lunch and battle plans."

"Well, around ten, I'm meeting Fancy at the Bombay Club. I need to talk to the people there, too."

"Come back for lunch. The meeting should be interesting."

I poured myself a cup of coffee. "Speaking of interesting, did Kary tell you what she's up to?"

"She said something about auditioning for a magician's assistant. She's going to call the man today and find out more details."

"Yes. That way, she can be a mole in the world of illusion. From Wonder Star to Magic Mole."

Camden paused, a pan halfway out of the water. "This isn't a magician who likes to put pieces of his assistant in different boxes and then reassemble her, is it?"

"No, this is Omar the Ring Master. He plays with hoops."

"You didn't say anything stupid like, 'Over my dead body,' I hope."

"I like to learn from my mistakes."

He continued scrubbing. "It'll be like that superhero group. She'll have fun, contribute to your case, and then she's back to a normal life."

"Until the next screwy thing that intrigues her. But I promised to back off." And try to keep my dread under control. I sat down at the counter. "She's planning something else, did she tell you that? She's taking on the seedy world of black-market babies."

"She did not mention that little endeavor."

"Apparently there's something called Baby Love, which is a branch of Mothers United, and Kary wants to infiltrate their ranks and discover their secrets. She's going undercover as an unwed mother seeking parents for her unborn child."

"What is she hoping to find out?"

"If either company is legitimate."

Camden rinsed the pan and set it aside to dry. "Sounds like a good idea."

"Yes, but if she finds something illegal, then what?"

"It's Wonder Star to the rescue."

"I shouldn't be surprised. What are we having for lunch?"

He pulled out the stove drawer and reached for a large rectangular glass dish. "Lasagna."

Lasagna's one of the two things Camden makes. Not having a father, he's had to invent himself, and he's decided the less change the better. He eats the same things, wears the same clothes, and has practically the same routine every day. Maybe he thinks these rituals keep change at bay. He's told me several times how he hated all the changes in his early life, being shifted from one foster home to another, then out on his own, bumming rides and food in exchange for carpentry work or odd jobs. When he found the house here in Parkland, he decided to stay. He saw something in the owner's future that saved the man a lot of money, and in return, the man gave him the house. Camden says 302 Grace is his true home. Ellin would just as soon plow it under and salt the ground. I can't wait to see how they resolve this little problem.

He put the glass dish into the suds and scrubbed it until I had to make a remark. "I think that dish is clean."

"Ellie and I discussed the Kirks last night while you were at the club. I actually called Phil and tried to talk to him."

"What did he say?"

"He said I must be joking. His wife would've foreseen any medical problems."

"Okay, so you did your best. Did you ask Ellin about Dirk? I meant to ask Rahnee if a candidate for village idiot auditioned on Saturday."

He rinsed the dish, set it aside, and let the water out of the sink. "Ellie's perfectly willing to spy for you. She wants you to discover Dirk's evil past."

"Anything new on the ring issue?"

"No, she didn't stay very long. Her mother called."

Ellin's mother is the pint-sized version of Ellin. "How does mom feel about you?"

He looked in the refrigerator for a package of hamburger. "Oh, she likes me, but she doesn't think I'm very good husband material."

"A psychic sales clerk whose idea of a square meal is a Pop-Tart? What's wrong with her?"

"She doesn't think I can support Ellie in the style to which she is accustomed. She's right."

"Ellin listens to her mother?"

He put the meat in a frying pan. "No, they argue all the time."

I looked through the stack of mail on the counter. "Is this yesterday's mail? I forgot to check it."

"That big envelope's for you."

There was a large cream-colored envelope addressed to me. "Maybe one of my ex-wives is finally remarrying." I opened the envelope and took out the sheet of paper, realizing what it was. "It's an invitation to the Wright Reunion."

"Is there a wrong one?"

"Wright with a 'W.' Barbara's family. Some of her aunts really like me. They always send me an invitation, but I haven't seen Barbara or any of her family since the funeral. I don't want to see any of them." Thinking of Lindsey's funeral made me think of the dance recital DVD on the bookshelf. I didn't want to see that, either—not yet.

Camden gave me his full attention. "I can sense some of it, Randall, but I won't pretend to know what it's like."

"At least you're not one of those people who tell me time heals, or it was God's will, or I'll get over it."

"Because I don't believe it was God's will."

I hadn't worked my way through that one. "Or, don't worry, David, you'll have another child some day. Or her soul is at peace now. The angels must have wanted another playmate."

He grimaced. "That one's particularly gooey."

We didn't say anything for a moment, and then he said, "You know how desperately Kary wants a child."

"I know. It's that big rock in the middle of the road, the one I can't see over."

His eyes were set on high beam. "But I see you with children."

"Well, I like hanging around the schoolyard with my pockets full of candy."

He gazed off into another realm. "I'm not sure, but I think they're mine."

I sat down at the counter, thinking over what he'd said. It's easier to say I'll never have another child. It's the buffer that keeps back the pain. I'll never go through something like this again. But I'll also never go through a child's delight on Christmas morning again, or the awe of seeing that first snow, the thrill of flying that first homemade kite, the little frilly dresses, the hair ribbons sliding awkwardly through my fingers as I try to tie a bow.

I felt the emotion threatening to choke me. Camden kept his back turned, opening cans of tomato sauce, but I knew, like me, he was seeing the black smoke and twisted metal along the side of the road and feeling my panic as I searched for the one thing I could not find.

After a while, I balled up the invitation and threw it away.

◇◇◇

The Bombay Club was located in a classier part of town and had its own parking lot. Someone must have found a bargain in fake palm trees because they were everywhere, crowding the door, the foyer, and scattered all around the large room. The stage was about the same size as the stage at the Magic Club, but the curtains were new, the floor shiny, the lights a splash of pink and gold. "Every Little Thing She Does is Magic" by the Police was playing softly. The bartender was a woman built along the same lines as the Deadly Sheila, but a hell of a lot friendlier. She had on black with a necklace of gold stars and gold star earrings.

"What'll you have?"

"A little conversation."

"Fine by me." There was a muffled conversation from somewhere behind her in the kitchen. "Excuse me a moment." She turned and yelled, "I know what you're doing back there, and if you don't quit, you're gonna be sorrier than a mustard-eatin' frog on Sunday!" She turned back to me, all smiles. "So what's up with you?"

I was still trying to get my head around "mustard-eatin' frog." Rufus always came up with some strange Southernisms, but this one was bizarre, even by his standards. "My name's David Randall. I'm investigating the death of Taft Finch."

"Oh, yeah. Heard about that. Too bad." The person in the kitchen said something else, and she whipped around. "What did I tell you about sassin' me? Do you want your butt handed to you in a shoebox? Just fill the damn order like I said." Then she was back to me. "Sorry about that. That boy's about as worthless as a tea bag in a coffee maker. Now, what you need to know?"

"Did Taft ever perform here?"

"Not that I know of."

"There seems to be a little friction between your club and the one on Freer Street."

She shrugged. "I don't know why. We only added a few magic acts for variety, a hypnotist, a woman who does the Ouija board. Our customers prefer singers and jazz trios."

"So none of the Magic Club regulars ever played here?"

"I can't say that. Little scrawny guy came over a few times, Whiz Bang, or something."

"WizBoy, maybe?"

I had to wait for her to give the kitchen worker a little more hell. "And don't forget to scrub those trays! I can't have 'em lookin' like last week's lettuce. Yeah, that's it, WizBoy."

The Wiz performed at the hated Bombay Club? Wonder why he didn't mention it. "I'm also looking for a box Taft was going to use in his act." I described the box, but the bartender shook her head.

"Nothing like that around here."

"Are there any other nightclubs in town who hire magicians?"

"Not much call for magic tricks. People want to hear music, drink, dance. That's about it." She turned to glare at a man who came through a door at the end of the bar. He was about the same general build as WizBoy, but he wasn't intimidated by the bartender's size or her attitude. He marched right up to her.

"I'll thank you not to yell at me in front of Marlene," he said.

"Marlene's back there? Why isn't she out here cleaning tables like I asked her?"

"'Cause she don't feel like it. She's got the flu or something. Looks like death suckin' a sponge."

Okay, that was one I had to write down.

The bartender said, "Excuse me, buddy, but I got to go tend to this."

"No problem." I enjoyed the show. "Thanks for your help. I'm supposed to meet a magician named Fancy. Do you know her?"

"Make yourself at home. She'll be late. She's always late."

Fancy was twenty minutes late but worth the wait. She walked in like she owned the place, a short, striking young woman in black and red, her platinum blonde hair cut short and ragged, her full lips a luscious shade of magenta. Her narrow ice blue eyes looked me up and down.

"Hi. You must be David Randall. I'm Fancy."

"You certainly are," I said. She grinned as if she expected me to say that. "Nice to meet you."

"Same here." She sat on the next stool. "Where's the bartender?"

"A little problem with the kitchen workers." From the back, we could hear the rumblings of another scold. "Marlene looks like death sucking a sponge."

Fancy didn't even blink. "That bad, huh? She ought to go home." Why is it everybody knows these sayings? My childhood was sadly lacking. "You don't know how to mix drinks, do you?" she asked. "I sure could use a Screwdriver, easy on the orange juice."

"You like goldfish crackers with that?"

"Yeah. How'd you guess?"

"Taft Finch's favorite snack."

"So what's the deal with that? Was he murdered?"

"That's what I'm trying to find out."

She scratched her wild hair. "Okay, so Taft and I had a few drinks every now and then. I showed him some tricks and he showed me some, but strictly magic. He was always a total gentleman, maybe too much of a gentleman for my taste. Besides, that little bartender Jilly had her eye on him, and who am I to get in the way of true love?"

"Did Taft have any enemies, anybody who'd profit from his death?"

"Not that I know of."

"When you auditioned for the Magic Club on Saturday, what was going on backstage?"

"The usual nonsense. People running around, dropping things and getting in the way. My stuff's valuable, you know? I don't want anybody messing with it."

The bartender returned, shaking her head. "I tell you, I might as well cross a mud bridge in a rainstorm as get anywhere with those two. I'll get your usual, Fancy, and anything for you, sir?"

"No, thanks."

"Fancy juggle anything for you yet?"

"No, she hasn't." Was this another saying I should know?

Fancy smiled. "I juggle and make things disappear, all at once. Two acts for the price of one. That's why it's fancy."

"So you were backstage guarding your stuff. Who else was back there?"

"I can't remember. I only wanted to keep people from playing with my knives."

"Knives?"

"I juggle anything."

"That sounds kind of dangerous. When you make them disappear, where do they go?"

"Hey, I'm not telling my secrets."

"Could you show me exactly what you did for your audition?"

"Sure."

I followed her backstage where she unlocked a large black case. Inside were balls of all colors, including pearl-colored bowling balls, clubs, hoops, sticks, and a set of six fierce-looking knives.

"I also juggle chairs, babies, and whatever the audience tosses to me."

"What did you juggle for your audition?"

"For you, free show."

She pulled the case onstage, chose the balls, and sent them spinning in a bright circle. "I started with something easy. Then I added the hoops and the clubs."

The balls disappeared, replaced by the hoops, and after the hoops had gone a couple of rounds, they disappeared, and the clubs were circling. She was so fast I didn't see what happened to the other items. She stopped the clubs, gave me another grin, and took the balls from her pocket, one by one.

I applauded. "That's great. What about the hoops?"

She turned around. The hoops sat together on a small hook on her belt. "The trick is to get everything going really fast. The audience is so busy looking at the circle they don't notice when

I palm the other stuff. I can get them to look wherever I want." Her ice blue eyes sparkled. "You're looking where I want you to look right now."

It was true she held my gaze. She leaned over and pulled a ball from behind my ear. "See? You weren't watching my hands, at all."

"You're very good," I said. "What about the knives? Did you use them?"

"Sure." She took the six knives from the case and began to juggle them. "They're trickier to get rid of, but it can be done."

I tried to see how she did it, but I couldn't. One by one, the knives disappeared. She caught the last one in her teeth.

"Okay, I give up. Where are they?"

She took the knife from her mouth. "Back in the case."

Five knives sat in the case. "How'd you do that?"

She leaned forward and whispered with that luscious magenta mouth. "Magic."

It was a struggle, but I managed to pull back without offending her. "Who auditioned before you, do you remember?"

She sat back and gave a laugh. "Boy, do I remember. It was some real big goofy kid trying to do card tricks. He was awful. We were all laughing at him, I'm afraid. He even tried some fire effects and nearly set himself on fire. We weren't sure if he meant to be that stupid or not. It would've made a great comic act. Everybody was rolling."

A big goofy kid doing card tricks. Bingo. "Was this guy's name Dirk Kirk, by any chance?"

"How did you know?"

"I've had the pleasure of meeting Mister Kirk."

"'Dirk Kirk.' We thought that was part of the act, too. Then we realized he really was awful."

"So your attention was on the stage and this goofy kid."

"Yeah, but only for a little while. I kept checking on my case. It was still there."

"And who auditioned after you?"

"I didn't stay to watch. I had another show over here at nine."

"Why audition for Rahnee Nevis when you have a pretty good deal over here?"

"I had a bet with Jolly Bob to see if she'd hire me. He said she wouldn't, and I said she would. I won."

"Why would he say she wouldn't hire you?"

"Sour grapes. She won't hire him, 'cause his act is too stale, so he doesn't like her. But I've known her for years. We get along fine. I've got three weeks there. Not bad." Again her icy eyes held mine. "Don't get me wrong. I don't mean to be all happy and everything when Taft's dead. If I were you, I'd check on Jolly Bob. Sometimes I think he'd do anything to get his hands on the Finches' collection. Some of it's worth quite a lot, and Jolly Bob is quite a fanatic collector."

"Thanks. I'll look into it."

"There's something else you could look into." She leaned forward again. Just when I thought she was going to kiss me, she sat back and handed me my wallet. "Open it."

Tucked in with the bills was a silver card with her name, address, and phone number. "Thanks."

She winked and sauntered out.

Chapter Eleven

I Love a Magician

As for Sandy Olaf's case, April Meadows was the one place on my list I hadn't checked. I found out April Meadows wasn't a place, but a person, a very chilly person, who objected to my suggestion that Sandy Olaf's bracelet had gone astray.

"Not in *my* home."

She stood at the door of her gray stone house on Burnley Lane and refused to let me in. She was a tall white-haired woman of about sixty, and she had painted on her eyebrows: two perfect dark brown arches over pale blue eyes. It looked like she'd used a Magic Marker. Somehow I doubted April Meadows would appreciate anything humorous, so I didn't comment on this fanciful use of make-up.

"Mrs. Meadows, I—"

"Miss."

What a surprise. "Miss Meadows, I'm not accusing you of anything. I just want to ask you some questions."

"You may not."

"Very well. I understand. I'm sure a woman with your high standards wouldn't be interested in the reward, anyway."

The eyebrows were painted on, otherwise, they would've gone up. "Reward?"

"Thanks for your time. So long."

"Wait," she said. "What sort of reward?"

Whatever I can make up on the spur of the moment. "Mrs. Olaf is thinking thirty thousand dollars." And she probably was, at some point in the day.

"For that bracelet?"

"It has great sentimental value."

"And she thinks she lost it here?"

"Possibly. What sort of event did you have?"

"A dinner for fifty guests. We used my dining room because I've recently had it decorated in Italian style and wished to show it off."

"I'll bet it's fantastic."

"Well, I am quite proud of it. Come have a look."

"Oh, no. I wouldn't want to impose."

"Nonsense. Come along."

The ceiling of her dining room had been painted to look like a sky full of ridiculously fat cherubs, grinning like Dirk Kirk.

"Wow," I said. "I've never seen anything like this."

"It's an exact copy of a ceiling in Florence. Would you believe my nephew painted it?"

With his very own set of Magic Markers. "No, I wouldn't."

"Everyone was most impressed. A true vision of heaven."

And while everyone was staring up at this, could Sandy's bracelet have fallen off, unnoticed, or slipped off her wrist?

"You had fifty guests, you said?"

"City Council members, the mayor, very important business-men, and a young man who may be running for state senate next year."

I looked all around and then down. In direct contrast to the gaudy ceiling, the carpet was a deep rich blue-green with a pattern of yellow roses. "This is a lovely carpet." Lovely, yes, but not thick enough to hide a bracelet.

"I found it in a bazaar in Turkey. The bargains were so extraor-dinary, I bought three carpets. The silver frame on that mirror is from Venice. You see it matches the candlesticks. And this vase is from Paris. Have you ever been to Paris?"

Once she started showing off her trophies, it was impossible to shut her up, but I let her rattle on. A row of photographs in gold frames decorated the top of some chunky bureau. I got to hear about every single one of them.

"This is my dear cousin Elanor, that's my Uncle John, here I am with my sister, May. This is our lovely little sister June, who died when she was eight, poor thing."

The last thing I wanted to look at was lovely little sister June who died when she was eight.

April Meadows picked up the picture and sighed. "I find it a great comfort to have such a beautiful reminder. Wouldn't you say so?"

She turned the picture my way, and I had to give it a brief glance. "Very nice."

Then she remembered I was the Enemy and got all huffy again. I'm chill-proof. Women can get as cold as they like. Nobody comes close to Ellin for total freeze.

"I really think you should leave now, Mister Randall."

I gave her my best smile. "Thanks so much for your time, Miss Meadows. I enjoyed seeing all your wonderful treasures. I'll tell Mrs. Olaf you're helping search for her bracelet."

"Well," she said, "all right."

◇◇◇

I sat in the car for a long time, listening to the Black Eagles whomp through "Old Fashioned Swing," letting my mind follow first one instrument and then another as the musicians tied complicated patterns together with ferocious rhythm. Somehow all the melodies blended. If only I could make all the pieces of these cases fit as easily. If only I could keep my thoughts from straying to that damned DVD on the bookcase at home.

I gave Sandy a call and told her I hadn't had any luck, but I'd keep looking for her bracelet. I hadn't had any luck finding Lucas Finch's box, either. Maybe Jolly Bob held more than a grudge against Rahnee and the Magic Club for not hiring him and not wanting to sell the club. Maybe he hoped to stir things up between the Finch brothers by stealing their special box.

I had plenty of suspects in my murder investigation, too. Jilly was upset because she didn't have a relationship with Taft and no one would hire her as a magician's assistant. I couldn't rule out Lucas, even if I wanted to, because Rahnee preferred Taft. She said Lucas didn't know this, but I imagined he had some idea what was going on. Then there was WizBoy, who'd made no secret he wanted to run the Magic Club and had hesitated when I asked him when he'd last seen the box. I thought I'd better have another talk with him.

◇◇◇

I went back to the Magic Club, said hello to the still-disconsolate Jilly and asked if WizBoy was around.

She was wiping the bar in slow circles. "He went to Trans-formation and Company. He should be back in a few minutes."

"I understand your dad was a magician."

She stopped wiping and gave me a dark look. "Who told you that?"

I figured WizBoy was already so far in her disdain I'd give him a break. "Somebody at the Bombay Club."

Jilly's voice was scornful. "He was a magician until he got scared he was losing his soul. Have you ever heard of anything so stupid?"

"Is that why he didn't want you to become one?"

"That and the fact I was better than he was. He never got any bookings, even though I kept telling him how he could improve his act. He never appreciated my help. We could've had a really good act, and then he got religion."

She was getting wound up and would have said more, but WizBoy came in carrying two large black and silver bags with a fancy logo depicting a rabbit in a top hat.

"There was a huge selection of bottomless glasses, Jilly. And take a look at this great stuff." As usual, she ignored him, moving her way down the bar, picking up the little snack bowls. He pulled items from the bags, mostly cards and rings, and several things I didn't recognize. I also noticed he had Band-Aids on two of his fingers.

"Why didn't you mention you'd played the Bombay Club?"

He glanced frantically at Jilly and waved for me to be quiet. "Damn it, don't let anyone hear you. It was only one time, and I needed the money bad."

"Well, then, stands to reason some of the other performers might do the same, even Taft."

"I don't know if he ever did."

"What else haven't you told me?"

He tried to pout, but lack of lower lip made the attempt look like Grandpa trying out new teeth. "I don't have to tell you anything."

"No, but maybe Jilly would like to know about your little trip to Bombay."

He clutched the black and silver bags to his scrawny chest. "Man, you play hardball! She'd never speak to me again."

"She doesn't speak to you now."

"Okay, so maybe she's still broken up over Taft. She'll forget him. He was too old for her, anyway."

That would be a magic trick I'd like to see. "If you know something about Taft or Lucas or this box, you'd better tell me. The police will find out eventually. It's called withholding evidence. You're sure you can't remember when you last saw the box?"

He looked at Jilly, apparently weighed his chances, and shrugged. He set the bags down and took a seat on the next stool. Satisfied no one was listening, lowered his voice. "Okay, there's one other thing. The last time I saw the box I borrowed it from Taft to show Jilly."

"Hadn't she already seen it?"

"Yeah, but I thought I'd try and get it open."

"You want something from the Finches' collection?"

"I don't, but, you know, if I could figure out the way to open the box—"

He stopped and I finished. "You'd impress Jilly."

"Hey, whatever it takes."

"When did you borrow the box?"

"It was long before Lucas decided to hide it. He didn't care if I gave it a try."

So this was why he'd hesitated when I first asked him about the box. "I'm guessing you didn't get it open or impress Jilly."

He scrunched up his face. "Nope. She was washing glasses or something and gave me a look like, 'Big deal.' After that, Lucas hid the box. I gave it my best shot, though."

"And you didn't know anything about the hiding place in the storage room?"

"Nope. Not till Lucas told us."

"What did you do to your fingers?"

He held up his hand. "Scraped 'em trying to get some boards out to make a stand for a sign."

"Someone who makes his living doing card tricks might want to be a little more careful with his hands."

"It don't matter. I can still do my act. I'm always getting a cut or bruise around here." He began putting his treasures back into the bags. "Look, about the Bombay Club. You're not going to tell Rahnee, are you? She'll fire me."

"Have you told me everything you know?"

"Yeah, man, that's it."

"I know there's something else. I believe I need a refill." I raised a finger to get Jilly's attention.

WizBoy screwed up his monkey face. "That's all, I swear. As for the Bombay Club, I played it a couple of times, okay? Rahnee don't always let me perform when I want to. Sometimes there's people from out of town she wants to feature, or friends of hers she's promised stage time, or relatives who want to try playing magician. She's got one cousin who thinks he's the next Blackstone. I want to work my way up, so I go where I can be seen, you know?"

Somehow I didn't think talent scouts were frequenting Parkland, looking for the next Blackstone, or even the next Siegfried and Roy. "You're not breaking the law. Why sneak around?"

"These are really the only two good clubs in town for magicians. I don't want to cut myself off."

"What about Charlotte? It's not that far away. That's where WAM lives, isn't it?"

He scowled. "Less said about them, the better. Hey, one of them probably took the box. Talk about sneaking around. They're good at that." He glanced down the bar. During our conversation, Jilly hadn't once looked his way. "I don't know what it's going to take to get her interested in me."

I knew the answer to that one: not enough magic in the world.

WizBoy turned back to me. "As much as I hate to say it, maybe you oughta be looking at Lucas. I know they were brothers and everything, but they could get into some pretty fierce arguments. They argued about the box."

"When was this?"

"Right after it went missing. I went out to mail some things for Rahnee and they were going at it out on the street. Taft was saying where was it, and Lucas was saying where was it. They were both upset."

"Any idea why they didn't call the police?"

"I figured they would. Then Lucas hired you. Now Taft's dead, so what the hell difference does it make?"

That was a very good question.

WizBoy left, and I asked Jilly if she had known about the cinder block hiding place in the storage room. "No," she said. "If anybody had known, Lucas wouldn't have used it, would he?"

"Any idea why it's there?"

She shrugged. "I guess whoever owned this place before put it in there."

"What was this building used for before the Magic Club?"

"It was a bar. Nothing special."

"You and Rahnee and WizBoy are the only ones who go in the storage room, right?"

"Sometimes a delivery man goes in if I need help putting stuff on the shelves. Some of the boxes are too heavy for me." Jilly's slim fingers were unmarked. For a moment, her sad eyes looked into mine. All her earlier anger was gone. "Are you close to finding out who killed Taft?"

"Not as close as I'd like, but I'm getting there."

Chapter Twelve

Magic Trick

I made it home for lunch. The lasagna was ready by the time Ellin and Reg came in, but they were too upset to eat, so that left major portions of lunch for Camden and me. We ate at the dining room table and listened to the growing list of grievances.

Reg picked at his plate. "This Sheila person is totally unphotogenic. I mean, those ghastly teeth! She's like some kind of Beaver Woman from Hell."

Ellin's own teeth were on edge. "Her appearance is the least of our worries, Reg."

"How long are we supposed to put up with this Oracle nonsense? Do we know if she has a shred of talent? She's going to scare people away. We need an exorcist."

"I say let her do what she wants, hope the whole thing falls apart, and corporate lets me pick up the pieces." She took a little bite of lasagna. "This is really good, Cam. I'm sorry my appetite isn't what it should be."

"That's okay," he said. "We like leftovers around here."

"Reg and I needed to get away from the studio for a while." She took a sip of tea. "There is one interesting development, though. Sheila is so over the top, I've noticed some of the audience laugh at her pronouncements."

"That's good, isn't it?"

"Not really. I don't want 'Ready to Believe' to be considered a comedy show. But if Sheila sees she's not being taken seriously, maybe she'll stop, or at least pull back a little. Is there any bread left?"

From where he was sitting, Reg could see himself in the mirror over the fireplace. He stopped admiring his fake tan long enough to pass Ellin the breadbasket. "Ellin, if you'd just listen to me, I have dozens of great ideas for programs."

"Reg, we've been through this."

"How's this for an ideal concept?" He held up his hands as if presenting a newspaper headline. "'New Age News'! News from all parallel dimensions. Latest UFO and Bigfoot sightings. Alien Abductee of the Week. It's exactly what our network needs."

With Reg as anchorman, I'm sure. "New Age News" didn't sound any screwier than the other segments of "Ready To Believe," but if something isn't Ellin's idea, it doesn't stand a chance. Make that a ghost of a chance to keep the theme going here.

"I don't think so."

"At least give it a try!" He looked around the table for support. "What do you guys think?"

"It sounds interesting, Reg," Camden said.

Ellin sighed. "We have barely enough money for our existing programs, which is why we have to appease the Kirks. Take it up with our new head of advertising."

"Oh, my God," Reg said. "That would be Dirk Kirk, King of the Neanderthals."

"Can we get through this crisis first, and then talk about 'New Age News'?"

He brightened. "You'll consider it?"

"Honestly, anything would be better than dealing with the Kirks. Is there any butter?"

I passed her the butter dish. "Have you been actively hunting more sponsors?"

"We're always hunting more sponsors. In fact, when we finish lunch, Reg and I are going by Leaf Express, Gremlin Cleaners, and Box-It. Leaf Express is a jewelry store that specializes in necklaces and earrings made of real leaves. They bronze them or something. Box-It has boxes for any size package, all colors."

"I'm not sure you'll have much luck with Box-It. The owner's my latest client."

"Yes, Cam told me about that. He and his brother are magicians, right? Like Dirk?"

"Considerably better than Dirk, but yes."

"I asked Dirk if he'd ever been to the Magic Club. He said he auditioned there. I'm sure it will shock you to learn they didn't appreciate his considerable talent."

"Did he happen to say when he went?"

"Saturday."

This corresponded with what Fancy had told me. "Thanks."

"You know his mother wants to put him on the program."

"More comedy. How long is a typical season for the PSN?"

"'Ready to Believe' is quite popular, so we usually tape forty to fifty shows and then repeat them. But Phil Kirk has paid for an additional twenty-five."

Reg shuddered. "Seventy-five days of Sheila. My God, Cam, can't you look into the future and see when this will end?"

"Sorry," he said. "I'm so close to Ellie, it's like trying to see my own future."

"Well, you're not close to me." He reached across the table and put his hand on Camden's. "Tell me my future."

After a few seconds, Camden grinned. "You've got to stop running after younger women."

Reg withdrew his hand as if scalded.

"You asked for it," I said.

Ellin checked her wristwatch. "The Oracle is dispensing wisdom this afternoon. Cam, I know you don't like coming to the studio, but it really helps to have you there."

"Okay."

His answer took Ellin by surprise. "Oh, well, then. Thanks."

Reg thanked Camden for the lasagna and apologized for his lack of appetite. Ellin gave Camden a quick kiss on the cheek.

"See you later."

I helped Camden carry the dishes to the sink. "You actually volunteered to go over there?"

"Well, she's not asking me to be on the program. She needs backup."

"You just want to mess with Sheila's aura." I put some foil over the leftover lasagna. My phone rang. It was Kary.

"David, I called Omar today, and we're meeting at the Magic Club this afternoon. I guess he wants to see if I can hand him the right thing at the right time."

"When's your audition? I might stop by."

"Five o'clock."

"Okay. While you're there, see if Jilly will talk to you. I know WizBoy will."

"I am on the case."

"Speaking of cases, what's the deal with Baby Love? Have you uncovered anything shady?"

"I went by their office and picked up some brochures. I checked the names of the owners on the Internet, but so far, nothing's jumped out."

Whew.

"However..."

Uh, oh. I'd whewed too soon.

"I did speak to a woman in the parking lot who told me she'd heard some things about the company. We're going to meet for coffee at Perkie's, and I hope she's got some useful information. Check with you later."

"Okay. See you at the Magic Club." I hung up. "Kary's got an audition with the Ring Master and a lead on the adoption site. She sounded very excited about both possibilities."

"And you sounded remarkably calm."

"Like I said, learning from my mistakes." I put the lasagna in the fridge. "Fancy, who, by the way, is quite fancy, remembers seeing Dirk at the Magic Club auditions on Saturday. You have to admit he's memorable. She said it was the funniest thing they'd ever seen. So I need to have a word with Dirk."

"A word of one syllable."

"Worth a try. Fancy also told me Jolly Bob covets the Finches' collection. Jolly Bob was in the club on Thursday, talking with Rahnee. According to Rahnee, Jolly Bob would like to buy the club. And he's pissed that she won't hire him to perform."

"He wouldn't kill Taft over that, would he?"

"Well, he might if he thought Rahnee was going to let Taft run the club."

"What about opportunity?"

"Rahnee, Jilly, and WizBoy all have keys to the Magic Club. Any one of them could've let Taft in on Sunday morning."

"You still don't know why he came back to the club on Sunday."

"Rahnee said he liked to get in extra practice on stage. Or someone could've called him and said, 'Come on over. I've got a neat new trick to show you.' Let's go to Box-It and make sure the Houdini box isn't there. Then we'll visit Transformation and Company and see what the Magic Bob has to say."

◇◇◇

The temporary clerk at Box-It, a small nerdy-looking teenager with a vague expression and tri-colored hair, glanced up from his motorcycle magazine.

"Welcome to Box-It. You got it, we box it."

"We're just looking, thanks," I said.

When I was certain the clerk was involved with his magazine, I directed Camden to the storage closet. Then I strolled up to the counter to keep the clerk entertained.

He pulled his gaze from the pictures. "Help you with something?"

"Actually, I'm here on business. I'm investigating the death of Lucas Finch's brother, Taft."

A gleam of interest lit the dull young face. "Really? You're like a detective?"

"I'm exactly like a detective. How long have you been working here? How well do you know the Finch brothers?"

All of a sudden, he was eager to help. He set his magazine aside. "I've been working for Lucas Finch about a year now. He's great to work for, gives me time off when I need it. I don't know a lot about what happened, but Mister Finch was really upset.

When he called me to come mind the store on Monday, I could hardly understand him. The cops came by here and everything. They asked me all kinds of questions, like, when did I see Taft Finch last, and when did I see Mister Finch last, and did they get along, was he a good boss. Stuff like that."

I could tell he was thrilled by the real life drama. "Had you seen Taft Finch lately?"

"No, I hadn't seen him. He doesn't come around much. He's got another job somewhere. Mister Finch I saw Saturday."

"As far as you know, did the brothers get along?"

"Yeah, like, they were both really into magic, you know. Any time I saw them together, they were talking about the tricks they wanted to do."

"Did you ever hear them mention a locked trunk act?"

"Oh, yeah, they were pretty excited about that. They were big Houdini fans. Mister Finch has got a lot of books and things about Houdini. They always wanted to try an escape act." For a moment, his face registered an expression almost like sympathy. "Didn't work out too well for them, did it?"

"How often do you work here?"

"Most afternoons after school, some weekends."

Maybe he recalled Lucas having to deal with an angry customer, or quarreling with a fellow magician. "You ever have a problem with dissatisfied customers? Somebody not happy with their boxes?"

"Nah. People come in, buy a box, go out. Except for this murder, it's pretty calm in here."

"What about the special box the Finches had for their Vanishing Ruby trick?"

"It's not in the shop anymore. He took it to his club."

"Did he ever show it to you?"

"Just once. He was real proud of it. It was okay, if you like that kind of thing. I mean, can anybody really prove it belonged to Houdini? He and his brother have tons of old stuff."

"You're not interested in the old stuff?"

"Well, some of it's kinda cool. Like there's a trick to opening that box, but Lucas wouldn't show me. He said it would be more fun if I figured it out myself, but I never did. He said nobody would ever guess. We magicians do that. We like to see if we can fool each other."

"Did you ever see him show the box to anyone here in the store? Anyone ask about this kind of box?"

"He and Jolly Bob talked a lot about it. I heard him tell Jolly Bob he'd never figure out how to open that box."

Maybe Jolly Bob took this challenge to the extreme. "When was the last time Jolly Bob was in Box-It?"

"Oh, he's in here about every couple of days. He and Lucas got kind of a friendly rivalry going on. But Jolly Bob's a great guy. He's helping me with an act. You wanna see it?"

"Sure." It wouldn't hurt to give Camden a little more time to look around.

The clerk hopped up and dug around in a stack of boxes and cans of spray paint. He then placed three boxes on the counter. "They're still a little sticky. I painted them gold and red because that looks better. Gold and red are my colors. I'm going to be the Amazing Flash."

I watched with an interested expression as he made the red boxes turn gold and the gold boxes turn red. "Not bad."

"Can you tell how I do it?"

"Haven't a clue."

"It's a good trick, though, isn't it?"

"I've never seen anything like it."

He puffed up with pride. "Thanks." And because he was so proud, he had to tell me more. "I don't want to give away the whole secret, but there's this special two-sided paper you can use. But you have to know how to use it exactly right."

"Pretty cool."

"Yeah. Anything else I can help you with?"

"No, thank you. I appreciate the information."

"Anytime. Must be neat to be a detective, huh?"

"Almost as neat as being a magician."

Camden wandered up and gave me a slight shake of his head. The Houdini box wasn't here.

"Help you with something?" the clerk asked.

"I'd like to see your magic trick."

"You got it!" He went through his routine once more, turning the boxes from red to gold and back again.

"That's really good," Camden said.

"Thanks." He put the boxes away. "I don't think I'll ever be as good as the Finches, though. Ever see their act? Man, they could make the cards do anything. I guess Lucas will have to have a solo act now."

Camden's gaze was intense. "I think if you keep practicing, he might take you on as a partner."

"Are you kidding me? That would be great, but that's not going to happen."

"Your trick is changing the colors on boxes. Mine is telling the future. Give me your hand for a minute."

"You're putting me on."

"Worth a try, isn't it?"

The clerk hesitated and then held out his hand. "Okay, what the hell. You read palms or something?"

"Or something."

After a long moment, the clerk asked nervously, "Aren't you going to turn it over and look?"

"Oh, I'm looking." He let go and smiled. "Good news, Richard. You keep working and you'll be a fine magician. Give Lucas some time and then ask him to take you on as his apprentice. It's going to help both of you."

"Are you serious? How'd you do that? How'd you know my name?"

"A good magician never reveals his secrets."

"Well, that was a damn good trick."

"That was a damn good trick," I said as we left the bemused clerk and went back to my car. "And what was it all about?"

"I thought I'd make sure he didn't know anything about the box, and he doesn't. The other stuff came through on its own."

"Are you up for another performance? Let's see if Jolly Bob has any secrets."

Chapter Thirteen

Mr. Magic

Transformation and Company was a large shop next to the Commerce Circle Mall. We went inside, and I whistled softly in admiration. If I'd been ten years old, I'd have been in Fool Your Friends Heaven. Here were racks of fake blood, fake flies in ice cubes, arrows through heads, fake scars, disappearing ink, fake fangs, shrunken heads, and rubber mice, everything you needed to be the most popular boy in school.

"Hello," a voice called. "Welcome to Transformation and Company. The real stuff's back here."

"Depends on what you mean by real," I said to Camden.

We threaded our way past rings, scarves, hats, and balls to the back of the store. The walls were filled with very expensive-looking framed posters featuring names such as Kellar, Carter, Thurston, and Blackstone. Against the walls were gleaming cases in shiny colors and glass. Capes, Half Price read a sign on top of a rack of clothes. The cases under the cash register were filled with coins, cards, and things I didn't recognize. Music played overhead, an old rock song called "Abracadabra."

The owner of the voice was a stout man with a beaming face, black curly hair and a beard. "Don't tell me. Let me guess. The Amazing Frederick—no, no, he's not as tall. Durham the Daring—no, wait, he has red hair."

"My name's David Randall."

The man looked disappointed. "That's not a very catchy name. You need something like Randall of the Dark Arts."

"I was thinking of the Remarkable Randall."

He rubbed his hands together. "You need some help planning an act? You've come to the right place." He looked at Camden. "What about you, pal?"

"Something in a mind reading act," he said.

"You mean mentalism?"

"Mentalism?"

"Pretend ESP. Seen a lot of good teams in my time. Yeah, I can do that." He shook hands with me and Camden. "I'm Jolly Bob, the Crown Prince of Magic. I can get both of you started right away."

"I'd like to see something in a box illusion," I said.

"Dozens of those, no problem. Let me show you."

Jolly Bob showed us boxes big enough for assistants to fit inside, smaller boxes for animals, and boxes that could vanish on command.

"These are great, but they're too big for what I have in mind."

"You want something for a box trick, then."

"Didn't I say that?"

He smiled indulgently. "You said box illusion. If you want a big effect, say with people or large animals, that's an illusion. Effects with smaller objects are called tricks."

"Thanks. I didn't know that."

He took a large coin out of his pocket and started rolling it across his knuckles. *Showing off for the beginner,* I thought. "So is this a trick or an illusion?"

"A trick. I'd like to get a really special box, one like Lucas Finch has."

Jolly Bob dropped the coin. He bent to pick it up, so I couldn't see his expression. "What kind of box?"

"About the size of a shoebox. It's made of polished wood with an 'H' on top. Lucas said it once belonged to Houdini, but I'm not sure I believe that."

Jolly Bob straightened. He put the coin back in his pocket. "You're right to be cautious. I don't know how many people have brought me 'magical artifacts' that once belonged to Houdini. He did have quite a collection, of course, but most of it's in museums. He had over five thousand books now safely stored in the Library of Congress, but don't think I wouldn't love to get my hands on them."

Giving me all this info on Houdini seemed to settle him. He went right back to the box. "Does this box have stars and hoops on top?"

"Yes."

He made a dismissive gesture. "I've seen hundreds like it."

But you'd still like to have this one, I'll bet. "I'd like to use one in the act. Any idea how it works?"

"There's a secret panel. You have to press on the stars on the lid in a certain way to get it to open."

"Anything inside?"

"You could put whatever you liked inside." He paused. "Lucas Finch, did you say? When did he show you this box?"

"Couple of weeks ago."

This time, his shoulders definitely relaxed. "I've seen that one. He and his brother were planning some kind of act. Did you know his brother, Taft, was found dead at the Magic Club recently?"

"I heard about that. Was Taft a friend of yours?"

"Yes, all of us in the magic community know each other. The Finch brothers didn't come in here often, though. I think they were offended by all the cheap stuff up front, but I have to make a living, and the kids love it. Occasionally they'd come buy some cards. How did you meet Lucas?"

"I stopped by the Magic Club one day, and, like you, he was kind enough to answer some questions. I never met Taft."

"This accident at the club was a very tragic thing. The few times I saw Taft perform, I thought he was excellent."

"Cards were his specialty?"

"He had perfected a double-back shuffle that was a pleasure to watch. He was quite good with animation tricks, too."

"Animation?"

"You are new at this, aren't you? Don't tell me you've never seen the dancing handkerchief."

Thank goodness I watch too much TV. "Oh, yeah, I know what you mean."

"That's an example of animation. Taft could do it with cards. Any idea what happened to him?"

"I heard he may have been murdered."

Jolly Bob looked startled. "Murdered? My God, who'd do such a thing?"

"Maybe someone who didn't like his act."

"As far as I know, Taft didn't have any enemies. We're a fairly close little community."

"What about a group called WAM? Would they have any reason to kill him?"

All it took was the mention of the rival group to bring a sneer to his face. "They wouldn't have the brains. Amateurs."

Someone called for assistance at the front of the shop. While Jolly Bob helped the two teenage boys purchase some shrunken heads and rubber knives, Camden and I looked at the strange metal pans, the strings of different colored scarves, and the collapsible hats and canes.

"Bob wasn't so jolly when I mentioned Lucas Finch," I said.

"Definitely tense."

"But if he had the Houdini box, how did he carry it out of the Magic Club? And as smug as he is, if he had the box, he would've shown it to us."

"He's trying very hard to show us he doesn't care."

Jolly Bob came back, all smiles. "I'm always happy to help new magicians get started." He looked at Camden. "Now, what was it you said? Mind reading? You'll need an assistant, someone who can feed you some clues. I've got some excellent microphones. Practically invisible."

"I don't think I'll need microphones."

"Well, of course you're not really going to read minds. This is magic, remember? Tricks? Illusions?"

Camden had shaken the man's hand, so I knew he'd received some sort of impression. He put his hands to his temples and closed his eyes. "Let me try to read your mind."

Jolly Bob glanced at me and shrugged. "Go for it."

"Think of something I wouldn't know. We've never met, right?"

"Right."

"Your middle name is Milton."

Jolly Bob laughed in surprise. "That's right! But don't tell anyone."

"Try something else," I said.

Camden kept up the act, frowning as if concentrating. "Something you really want. Something about a challenge? A bet, maybe?"

Jolly Bob's expression changed. He looked startled. "You're off the track now. I'm not a betting man."

But he'd bet Lucas he could open the box. And he'd bet Fancy that Rahnee wouldn't hire her.

Camden opened his eyes. "No? Well, I'm still working on it."

Jolly Bob laughed again, but this laugh was forced. "Still, a good effort. You had me going for a minute. You keep practicing." He reached over to the counter and scattered a stack of business cards. "Damn slippery things." He picked up two and handed them to us. "Email me, and I'll put you on my mailing list. I have terrific sales. We can get you two set up in no time."

"Thanks," I said.

He made an attempt to straighten the cards. "You boys aren't planning to try out anytime soon, are you? I hear auditions are closed at the Magic Club."

I put the card in my pocket. "I've spoken with the owner. She seems reasonable. Very attractive, too."

He lowered his voice. "Let me give you a little advice. You'd do well to try your luck somewhere else. I hate to say this, but

Rahnee Nevis is ruining that club. Those auditions were a joke! You should have seen some of the amateurs. Pitiful."

"Did you try out?"

"Me? I don't have to audition. I'm an established artist."

"When did she have auditions?"

"Last Saturday. She asked me to stop by for a minute or two, but I couldn't stay. They were so awful. No style, no sense of drama."

"Are you a regular at the Magic Club?"

"I perform whenever I can, and only as a favor to Rahnee. I simply don't have much time. The store's more important. Only one like it in Parkland." He gazed proudly at the displays. "If I were you, I'd try the Bombay Club. They're always looking for good talent."

"Thanks. You've been a lot of help."

He clapped Camden on the shoulder. "You get yourself a good set of microphones and there'll be no stopping you, kid. You look up my name before you stopped in?"

"Yeah, you got me."

"Pretty damn clever. That's the kind of research that'll take you a long way."

He went to assist another customer, and Camden and I left the store.

"Wow, is he nervous," Camden said. "He really wants that box."

"Okay, so he gets the box and gets it open. Then what? Lucas lets him pick what he likes from the cabinet. What's the big deal about that? Unless there's something in the cabinet that's very valuable."

"Maybe there's one thing Lucas doesn't want to give up."

"I wonder if Taft liked the idea of his magic stuff being up for grabs." I took out my phone. Lucas wasn't home, so I left my questions on his answering machine. "I'll try to catch him later. On to the studio?"

"Yeah, I want to make sure Ellie's okay."

"And I want to talk to Dirk."

Chapter Fourteen

Black Magic Woman

We arrived at the TV studio right before Reg began his warm-up. Camden went over to speak to Ellin, and I went in search of Dirk Kirk. He was easy to find. He'd cornered some hapless stagehand and was making him pick a card.

"Here, I'll pick one," I said. Relieved, the stagehand fled, and Dirk fanned out the gaudy deck. A few cards fluttered to the floor, but Dirk ignored them. I picked a card, the Jack of Diamonds, and put it back in the deck.

With his tongue firmly in one corner of his mouth, Dirk searched through the cards and held up the ten of clubs.

"That's it," I said. "You're amazing."

"Thanks. Pick another card."

"Sure." I picked another. This time the card was the three of hearts. I put it back in the deck. "You know, this is a great act. You ought to be on stage somewhere, maybe playing in a club."

His dull expression grew even duller. "Tried that."

"You did? Where?"

"That Magic Club. They said they didn't want me." He shuffled the cards and pulled out the six of spades. "Is this your card?"

"I don't know how you do it."

"Pick another."

Yeah, I'll stand here all day if I have to. "Why didn't they want you?"

"I don't know. I was loads better than this woman who threw knives and balls around. What kind of magic is that? I thought those people were unprofessional, especially that red-haired woman. She thought I had a comic act. Do I look like a comic act?"

No safe answer for that one. I picked another card. King of Hearts.

"I've been over there lots of days to give them another chance to hire me, but they won't."

I remembered WizBoy mentioning someone who came to the club almost every other day, someone who wouldn't take no for an answer.

"When was the last time you went over there?"

"Last time I went was on Saturday. That red-haired woman was there."

"She's the owner."

"Yeah, and some skinny guy and a fat guy with a beard."

WizBoy and Jolly Bob.

Dirk Kirk was intensely interested in the deck. "Is this your card?"

Five of diamonds. "Wow. I can't believe they didn't hire you."

Dirk looked as smug as Jolly Bob. "That's okay."

"Why is it okay?"

Sheila chose this moment to call to him. "Dirk! We're about to start! Get over here."

Dirk patted his deck of cards back into shape. "It's okay because I'm a TV star. I don't need that stupid club to be famous. They're the ones who'll be sorry."

I asked him what he meant by that, but he lumbered over to his mother. I'd have to wait until after the taping to ask him any more questions, although I couldn't imagine him being slick enough to steal the box. He'd have to have known about the cinder block hiding place. Maybe he'd seen someone take it.

I joined the other audience members finding their seats and sat down beside Camden in the second row. He was talking to some people behind us, two women and a man, who shook his hand and greeted him like they were all old pals.

"Randall, these are some folks from church. Celia Huffman, Lloyd Johnson, and Mabel Greene."

Celia Huffman was a large woman in a bright floral dress. "Did you know we got picked to be on the show today? We're so excited. We're getting to peek into the future."

Lloyd Johnson tried to downplay his interest, but his eyes were full of curiosity. "The ladies are excited, but not me. I'm going along to be a good sport."

"I can't wait to see what she says."

The other woman, Mabel Greene, was also a hefty size, dressed in a shiny yellow pantsuit. "Oh, you'll love it, Lloyd. I can't wait to hear what she says."

"We can't wait, either," I said.

"Is she as good as you, Cam?"

"She's different."

Reg completed his warm-up and introduced the guests. "And now we'd like to welcome to our program three lucky audience members who'll each be given a special reading by our own Oracle of Truth, Sheila Kirk."

Huffman, Johnson, and Greene made their way to the set. Reg showed them to their seats, and Sheila invited Celia Huffman to go first.

"You may ask me anything you like."

Mrs. Huffman sat on the edge of her chair, her hands twisting together nervously. "I have to ask about my husband. I feel responsible for his death somehow. I must know if he's happy. Is he all right? Did he go to heaven?"

I glanced at Camden. "Isn't this a little heavy for the PSN?"

"Mrs. Huffman accidentally gave her husband the wrong medicine. No one blames her, but she's been struggling with guilt."

Sheila dismissed the woman's concerns with an airy wave of her fat hand. "Of course, he's happy. Who wouldn't be? Quit carrying such a load of guilt. It wasn't your fault. Lighten up. He's having a ball."

Camden sat up, tense. "What's she saying? That's not true."

"What? He's not having a ball?"

"Why is she telling that poor woman it wasn't her fault? It was her fault. She has to deal with it."

His anxious whisper was attracting attention. I motioned for him to settle down. "We'll talk to her after the show."

I could tell he wanted to leap onto the set and confront Sheila right then. Then Mabel Green asked about her health.

Shelia closed her eyes and made a series of faces to indicate contact with the spirits. "I see that your sugar level is fine. Eat whatever you want."

This time, I had to grab Camden's arm to keep him in his seat. "Later. We'll get her later."

"Randall, this is insane. Mabel's a borderline diabetic."

"Take it easy."

It was Lloyd Johnson's turn. "I'd very much like to know about my health, too, Miss Sheila. I have a heart condition."

Again, Sheila went through the motions, this time swaying in her chair before opening her eyes and giving him her wide toothy smile. "And you're going to be perfectly fine. It's going to clear up like magic, wait and see."

Camden sat back as if stunned. "Please tell me I didn't hear that."

I saw Ellin cue Sheila for a commercial break. "It's over."

As soon as Reg started his spiel for Candle De-Light, Camden hurried down to Ellin. "Ellie, you've got to do something. She's all wrong."

"Of course she's all wrong. What do you think I've been saying?"

"I mean, she's telling everyone wrong information. Those people are from my church. I know them. There has to be something you can do."

"I don't know what I can do right now. We're in the middle of taping."

"I know what I can do."

I wanted to see this. Although squat and square, the Deadly Sheila was several inches taller and probably a hundred pounds heavier than Camden. He was just about eye-level with her imposing bosom.

"I need to talk to you," he said.

"I'll be happy to solve any problem you may have."

"You told three people completely wrong answers, potentially dangerous answers."

She was unconcerned. "I haven't the slightest idea what you're talking about."

"You told Mrs. Huffman her husband's death wasn't her fault. You told Mister Johnson his heart condition would clear up. He's going to die."

"You'd have me tell the man that on TV?"

"He needs to know. He needs to prepare. His children are going to attack each other if he doesn't leave a will. And you told Mrs. Greene that sugar was okay. Are you aware she's borderline diabetic?"

Sheila spoke across his head to Ellin. "What is all this? Why is this man talking to me? Does he have anything to do with my show? I don't think so."

Ellin had been watching the confrontation with a mixture of hope and dread. "Perhaps you should revise some of your predictions."

"Perhaps you should get him off my set."

Reg signaled frantically. "Commercial's over."

Sheila put her hands on her hips and loomed over Camden. "Get off my set."

He wasn't intimidated. "Stop telling people lies."

"I don't have to take this from you or anyone. My husband pays your girlfriend's salary."

"Camden." Ellin's voice held a note of warning.

He reluctantly left the set, his best go-to-hell look wasted as Sheila turned back to the camera. I couldn't hear what Ellin said to him offstage, but judging from her arm waving and his glowering expression, it was a pretty fierce argument.

He came back to me. "I've got to do some serious damage control."

"You'll get your chance."

He paused. "Hang on. What did she just say?"

We turned our attention to the Deadly Sheila. She held her arms up and out in the overly dramatic gesture my actor friends call "milking the giant cow."

"That's right! Not only will I heal your souls, but also your bodies. Greater things are coming! Be sure to watch the PSN for more news about this exciting psychic event. Until next time: I'll be watching the stars for you."

As soon as Reg finished with the commercials, Camden went to his church friends.

"Celia, I hope you won't take what Sheila said seriously. It was only for entertainment. You know everyone understands what happened."

She patted his hand. "Cam, dear, I know you have the same gift, but Sheila told me my husband is happy, and that's what I wanted to hear."

He turned to Mabel Greene. "You know you can't eat anything you want."

"I know," she said. "I was curious to see what she'd say."

"And Lloyd, if you don't leave a will, your family is going to tear apart. Please reconsider."

Of the three, Johnson seemed shaken by Sheila's prediction. "That's my business, and I'll thank you to keep out of it. Ladies, are you ready to go?"

"We'll see you Sunday, Cam," Mabel said, and they left.

Sheila came off the set toward Camden like a runaway train. "All right, you little jerk. What do you mean by undermining my authority?"

He stood his ground. "What authority? You're wrong and you know it."

"I saw you talking to those people. You have no right to interfere. This is my show."

Ellin found herself in the unlikely position of peacekeeper. "Sheila, Cam was only trying to help."

"He can help by leaving."

Camden wasn't through. "What do you mean by healing bodies as well as souls? You're not planning some psychic surgery, are you?"

"It's none of your business what I'm planning, and unless you want all of these people fired, you'll get out right now."

Faced with Ellin's pleading eyes, Camden let Sheila win this round. "I'll see you later then, Ellie."

We went out to the car and Camden vented some anger by kicking the tires. "I can't believe she told people those things." He'd almost used up his voice, so he sounded like a squeaky toy.

"I can't believe she's immune to your boyish charm."

"She'd like to kill me."

"I don't have to be psychic to see that. I also don't have to be psychic to see she's going to make life harder for Ellin if you interfere. I'm going to ask Dirk a few more questions. You'd better stay here."

"Yeah, I'd better save what little voice I have. I'm sure Ellie will be coming by the house later."

Back inside the studio, I found Dirk sitting in the first row of empty seats in the audience. He looked kind of lost. I knew he couldn't be lost in thought. Maybe he was planning his next magical illusion. I sat down beside him.

"What's up, big guy? How about showing me another trick?"

"Yeah, sure." He pulled his pack of tacky cards from his pocket.

"You said you auditioned Saturday at the Magic Club. Are you sure that's the last time you were there?"

Like WizBoy, Dirk had to scrunch up his face in order to squeeze out a memory. "No, I went back another day. Didn't do any good. That woman still wouldn't hire me."

"When did you go back?"

As he clumsily shuffled the cards, several fell to the floor. He picked them up. "Sunday. No, Monday. They were closed on Sunday."

"Monday morning?" I would've remembered seeing him.

"First thing when they opened. Nine, nine thirty."

So he was gone by the time I arrived. "You tried out, got turned down, and left? You didn't hang around?" It was too much to hope he'd seen something useful.

"There was no need to hang around."

"Do you remember who else was there?"

"The skinny guy and that red-haired woman, and she was in a real bad mood. She looked mad enough to kill somebody. I even asked her what was wrong, trying to be nice, and she told me to get out."

Was it possible Rahnee had killed Taft and all her tears were part of an act?

"After I tried out, I stopped by the bar to get me a drink, and this guy came in with his bird act. I don't like birds, and his dog was real mean, so I left."

"Those were the only people you saw? What about the bartender?"

"Nobody was there. I helped myself to a drink. They owed me, you know?"

I'm not sure how he figured that. "Okay."

"Yeah, I'm not going there again," Dirk said. "I've got a better trick in mind."

I looked interested, but he wasn't going to tell me. "It's gonna be a secret. It's gonna fool everybody."

"Well, good luck with that," I said.

Chapter Fifteen

Magic Man

By the time Camden and I arrived at the Magic Club, Kary and Omar the Ring Master were already on stage. We sat down at the bar and watched as Omar went through his act step by step, pausing to show Kary which ring or hoop he wanted and how to hand it to him.

"And present each item to the audience first, like this, and turn it so they can see it's a real hoop without any breaks or slots. Yes, that's it. Excellent. You have lovely stage presence, Kary. I can tell you're used to finding the light."

"All those pageants had better be good for something," she said.

The lights on stage were not the special colored lights, but even so, Omar looked regal and handsome and Kary, of course, glowed.

Jilly came up behind us. "Drinks for you guys?"

"No, thanks," I said. "We're here to watch the audition."

She heaved a wounded sigh. "I don't know why he didn't ask me to be his assistant. I'm way better than that girl."

I could tell that "girl" was not the word she wanted to use. "Omar's not a headliner, though, is he? I'd hold out for a star attraction if I were you."

She gave Kary another look and went back to the bar.

"I'm surprised she has the energy to be jealous," Camden said.

"Oh, she's still smarting because her dad used to be a magician but gave it up before the two of them could take the magic world by storm."

"He quit? Any idea why?"

"The Lord told him to."

"Oh, 'Let no one be found among you who practices divination or sorcery.'"

"See, I knew you'd have just the right verse."

"Deuteronomy 18:10."

"I knew that, too."

"I don't think the Lord was talking about card tricks."

On stage, Omar showed Kary a few simple dance steps, which she had no trouble picking up. "And then hand me each silk. With a little flourish, if you please."

What Omar called silks were multicolored scarves with tiny gold threads and beads that sparkled in the light.

"That's a nice effect," Camden said.

"Yeah, it's the light that does it. I've been noticing that."

Kary must have done exactly what Omar wanted because when he finished, he thanked her and shook her hand. "I'll give you a call this evening." He packed up his hoops and rings and scarves, gave us a wave, and left. Kary came to the bar, all smiles.

"Wasn't that fun? I think I've got the job."

"You looked great," Camden said. "Very professional."

She glanced at Jilly, who'd moved even further down the bar. "And I think I may have ruffled a few feathers."

"Don't worry about her," I said. "She's not happy with anybody."

"I tried to talk to her, but she said she was busy. WizBoy's not here, and neither is Rahnee."

"No problem. Let's go. Where are you parked?"

"In the next block."

"Learn anything from your Baby Love informant?" I asked as we walked her to her bright green Festiva.

"I told her I was looking for parents for my baby. There's a Baby Love meeting tonight, and she said I could come along with her. It will be a good way to get some inside information."

Camden took her hand and held it for a long moment. He and I have an odd telepathic link that he doesn't have with Kary, but he can usually tell if something drastic was going to happen in her future.

"This meeting's okay."

"Thanks, Cam. You know I'm going anyway."

"Yep. This was for Randall."

She gave me a grin. "Don't wait up, David."

"You know I will."

◇◇◇

At 302 Grace, I recognized the old blue Toyota in front of the house. As soon as I parked the Fury, Bart got out minus Binky and his Baffling Birds.

"Randall, I thought of something that might help you."

"Great. Come on in." I introduced Camden and explained about his laryngitis.

"You got any lemon and honey? That'll fix it up," Bart said.

Camden shook his head and whispered, "Coke."

"Great. I could use a shot myself."

We went inside, and I showed Bart where to hang his coat on the halltree. We gathered around the kitchen counter. Camden took three Cokes out of the fridge and handed them around.

"So what's up?" I asked.

Bart took a drink. "Well, I've heard that the box is dangerous. In the wrong hands, it could be deadly."

"What exactly are you talking about?"

"You ask the Finch boys where they got it? How they got it?"

"No."

"From another group of magicians. The Willow Creek Brothers of the Sacred Arts. It was a going-out-of-business sale." Camden and I must have both looked skeptical. "I'm telling you so you'll find out what happened to Taft. I used to belong to the Willow Creek Brothers. I saw what the box did to them. When I tried to tell Lucas, he cried sacrilege. He said I couldn't talk that way about something that belonged to Houdini. Houdini! Just because the box has got an 'H' on it doesn't mean it belonged to Houdini."

"Tell me why this box is dangerous."

"Hard to explain. It's got powers. With the right people, it can work miracles. The wrong people handle it, you've got disaster."

Camden and I looked at each other. "I don't believe that," I said.

"You don't have to. People believe it, so it works. Don't you know that's the basic principle of magic? Deep down, people want to believe in magic, even if their brains tell them it's only a trick. People are ready to believe. They want to believe."

"Then, deep down, they must want to be swindled, too."

"You and old Harry Houdini would've gotten along fine. You know he spent the last years of his life exposing fake mediums and frauds."

"Any idea who'd want to steal the box?"

"That box belongs in a museum. Safest place for it."

"What can you tell me about a magician named Jolly Bob?"

"Does a comic act for the kids, pulls balloons out of their ears, stuff like that. Used to be a headliner, but now he mainly fills in. That store of his takes most of his time. Collects stuff, so he'd probably be interested in the box. I sure as hell don't want it. I think I've made that plain." He turned to Camden. "You got another Coke?"

Camden got up to get it when Ellin came into the kitchen.

"If you're drinking, get one for me," she said. "It took me forever to calm Sheila down."

"Sorry, honey." He popped the top of a can of soda and handed it to her.

"Thanks. As much as I love having you at the studio, you'd better stay away until she's gone."

"And have her ruin peoples' lives? I don't think so."

"Cam, please. I'll do what I can, okay? And your voice sounds awful. Have you been to the doctor?"

"Yes."

"What did he say?"

"I'm not supposed to talk."

"Well, then, let me do the talking and let me handle Sheila." She glanced at Bart, who'd been listening avidly. "And you are?"

He got up and bowed. "Bart of Bart, Binky, and His Baffling Birds, at your service, ma'am, should you need a real magician."

She was not impressed. "I've got all the magicians I need, thank you. I've even got things disappearing."

"Disappearing?" I said.

"Some items have been stolen from peoples' desks. We think somebody's sneaking in during filming. That's all I need. As soon as I finish my drink, I've got to get back."

"You can hire me to solve the mystery."

"Maybe later, Randall. Sheila's the main issue right now."

Camden managed to crank out another sentence in his raspy voice. "And tell Sheila to stop giving bad psychic advice."

"Look, I don't like this any more than you do, but I can't risk losing the PSN. You know what the network means to me."

"Start a new network," I said.

"With what? Beans? I just have to put up with her nonsense for this season."

"Seventy-five shows, Reg said. Sheila can do a lot of damage in seventy-five shows."

"Maybe she'll get tired of it. Maybe she'll find a new hobby. I can't think of anything else to do right now." She took one more drink and set the can on the counter. She gave Camden a kiss. "I never thought I'd say this, Cam, but don't come to the studio. Let me take care of this."

"I won't if you promise you'll make her stop."

"You heard what she said. She's moving on to psychic healing. That can't be any worse."

Camden just looked at her.

"Or maybe it can," she said. "At any rate, it's my problem. Stay here and take care of your voice. In fact, you ought to go upstairs right now and get some rest. Come on."

She took his arm and herded him up the stairs. After a few minutes, she came back down and out she went.

Bart whistled. "That's one fierce little woman."

"You're too kind."

"That's the last we'll see of her, then."

"Oh, no. She likes to make you think she's gone."

"Misdirection."

At first, I thought he was giving Ellin a title. "Miss Direction?"

"The central principal in the art of magic. It's not what you see, it's what you think you see. Observe." He took a handkerchief from his pocket and fluttered it. "If I want you to look in a particular direction, I look in that direction. If I look you in the eye, you'll meet my gaze, and if something happens that is more intense, you'll automatically look at that. A large movement always draws attention from a smaller movement." He made a sudden gesture with the handkerchief, and by the time I'd glanced over and back, a red ball appeared in his other hand. "Look at the wrong thing at the right time, that's the key."

Fancy had done the same thing. Now I was so intent on the red ball, I missed his next move. Two red balls appeared in his other hand. "Very good, but still, it's all sleight-of-hand. It's not really magic."

"It can be whatever you want it to be." He put the balls in his pockets. "Well, I'd better be going. You've got my card, right? Let me know if you find the box."

"Where would I find the Willow Creek Brothers if I need to talk to them?"

"They have a temple in Piney Woods off Route Sixteen."

Bart let himself out and I went to my office. I looked at my list. Rahnee Nevis, WizBoy, Jilly, Lucas Finch, Jolly Bob, and now Bart, who seemed way too interested in the box, cursed or not, plus I needed to go to Charlotte and talk to the Wizards and Amazing Mages. I could be going off in hundreds of misdirections.

I called Rahnee and asked if Jolly Bob had helped with auditions on Saturday.

"Did he say that?" she said. "No, he didn't help. I don't need his help."

"He also said he performed at the club."

"No, he knows I don't care for his clown act."

"Clown act?"

"Goofy stuff that wouldn't fool a child."

"So he wasn't there?"

"He stopped by on Saturday to give me the usual grief about selling the club. I told him my usual answer and asked him to leave."

"I thought the store was his life."

"He hates that store. He hates dealing with the kids. He wanted to buy the club from the original owners, but I outbid him."

"Well, no wonder he warned me away from you."

"Did he tell you I'm ruining the club by letting everyone perform and ignoring the real talent?"

"That's it. Sounds like he's got a real grudge."

"You mean bad enough to start killing off my acts? My God, I'd hate to think that!"

"Well, how angry was he when you outbid him?"

"Pretty angry, but he's been perfectly civil since then. Besides, he liked Taft, and he and Lucas are good friends."

"Would you say they're competitive? Maybe trying to outdo each other?"

"Yes, they do that all the time. What are you getting at?"

"This bet Lucas had. I'm pretty sure it relates to Taft's death. Did you ever hear either of them say anything about that?"

"No, but when Jolly Bob came to the club, they were always at the bar. Jilly might have heard something."

"I'll stop in tomorrow and ask her, thanks. Oh, one more thing, please. What's the deal with WAM?"

Rahnee finally told me the Dark Secret. "It's sheer foolishness. Every year in Atlanta, we attend a convention. One year, things got a little out of hand, as things tend to do, and a member of WAM accused a WOW magician of stealing his illusion. It was

Jolly Bob, actually, and even though he's been known to 'borrow' tricks from other magicians, he went ballistic. He told the entire magic community how the illusion was done, so now it was useless in the WAM member's act. The worst thing a magician can do is reveal another magician's secret."

"So it's unlikely Taft would have gone to Charlotte."

"Yes, but I couldn't say for certain."

"Who would know?"

"The main club is called Ali's Cavern. You could check with them."

I called Ali's Cavern. A recorded message accompanied by "I Put a Spell on You" informed me the club was open Thursday through Sunday for lunch, and Friday and Saturday for lunch and supper. For all other inquiries I supposed the magicians of WAM communicated telepathically.

Chapter Sixteen

Night Time Magic

When I went to the kitchen to make a sandwich, Angie lumbered into the dining room, several dresses draped over one huge arm. She spread her sewing projects out on the dining room table. In a few minutes, Rufus and Camden came downstairs and took their jackets from the halltree. Camden wrapped his muffler around his neck. Rufus pulled his baseball cap down on his scruffy hair.

Angie took some pins out of her mouth. "Where do you think you're going?"

Camden gestured to the door, and Rufus said, "We're going out. Going to drown our sorrows."

"The hell you are. Cam don't need to go out in the cold, and he sure as hell don't need a beer."

Rufus ignored her. "Come on, Cam."

"All right, fine," she said. "Go on. See if I care."

The next sound was the roar of the bigfoot truck and the screech of tires. I sat down at the counter to eat. Angie did something with scissors and brown tissue paper. Silence reigned for about twenty minutes, and then damned if Ellin didn't come back. She has this truly frightening habit of reversing herself, sometimes in mid-sentence. She stepped in and shut the door behind her.

"Oh, hello, Angie. I'm going to go up and check on Cam."

"He isn't here," Angie said. "He went out with Rufus. Couple of dopes."

"Went out? He was supposed to rest."

"They couldn't wait to guzzle a couple of six-packs."

"Well, of all the stupid things."

Ellin stood in typical pissed position, arms folded, mouth tight. She and Angie don't get along that well, but for the moment, the bizarre behavior of their boyfriends allied them.

Then Ellin turned on me. "You could have stopped him, Randall."

"He certainly could've," Angie agreed.

"Excuse me," I said. "The last time I looked, Camden was the same age as me."

"You know he shouldn't drink."

"Delbert only serves him Coke."

I wasn't sure her lips could get any tighter. I was wrong. "And he should be home taking care of that sore throat."

"He's a grown man."

I got the full glare. "In case you haven't noticed, I've had things on my mind. And now I'm supposed to tell a grown man, as you just pointed out, to take some cough syrup and go to bed, the same grown man who has decided to go out to a bar tonight and get bombed on whatever he can get his hands on? I call that running away from the problem."

"You tell him, girl," Angie said. "That's exactly what my big fool is doing."

"It's Wednesday night," I said. All I got from Ellin was a blank look. "Choir practice. This is the first time he's missed in years."

"Oh, for goodness sake. He shouldn't be so worried. His voice will come back."

"I'm just saying."

She gave an exasperated sigh and left. I looked at Angie, who shrugged. I finished my sandwich and went back to the safety of my office. My phone rang. I'm always glad to hear a woman's voice, but this was Julia Wright, Barbara's older sister. I knew right away why she was calling.

"David, we haven't heard from you. You're coming to the reunion, aren't you?"

"Thanks for the invitation, Julia, but I'm swamped with work. I've got several cases going."

Julia's a big blonde woman who likes to mother everyone. I'm sure she envisioned me sitting at home, alone and friendless. "Well, you could leave them for one evening, anyway, couldn't you, and come to the cookout? It's on Upper Lake, only a couple of hours from where you are."

"Thanks, but I can't make it."

"I really think you and Barbara should get back together. It's been how many years now?" Here it came. "I think it's about time you got over it."

Why do people feel compelled to say that? "It's not something you get over, Julia."

"You need to get on with your lives, and I really think it would help if you did that together. You know how the other one is feeling. You could console each other."

Actually, I had no idea what Barbara was feeling. I knew she hated me. I knew she blamed me. Anything else was up for grabs. Did she want to be consoled? Did she want another child? Was she able to look at Lindsey's picture without that horrible stab of grief and regret?

"I appreciate your concern, but I'm pretty sure Barbara doesn't want me there."

"I think she'd feel differently once she sees you."

I think she'd heave the nearest bowl of potato salad at my head. "Well, I've got to go."

"Are you still living in that big house with all those weird people?"

"I fit right in, trust me."

"If you change your mind, call me."

"I will, thanks."

I hung up and sat for a moment, looking at the phone. Why hadn't I married Julia instead of her sister? Of course, Barbara had started out as a cheerful, fun-loving person, too. Nothing like a little car accident to change the mood.

I really didn't want to dwell on that, so I finished reading the notes on Houdini Kary had compiled and compared the information with the book I'd borrowed from Lucas Finch. There was more to Houdini than magic tricks. He was into aviation and had been one of the first to make a controlled power flight over Australia in 1910. He'd had a movie career, even running his own studio before deciding it was too expensive. His silent films included such riveting titles as *Terror Island* and *The Grim Game*. I had to laugh, though, when I found out the Society of American Magicians was also known as SAM. SAM, WAM, and WOW.

Houdini was also an author, and his book, *A Magician Among the Spirits*, cost him his friendship with, of all people, Arthur Conan Doyle. Houdini's book was all about his successful attempts to debunk spiritualists, and Doyle, being a believer in spiritualism, was furious with him. Two reasonably intelligent people at war over ghosts. Sounded like something that would go on in our house.

When I heard Kary come in, I didn't leap up. She stopped by my office door, all smiles. "I got the job, and wait till you see my outfit."

"I hope it includes spangly tights."

"I'm going to let it be a surprise." She came in and sat down. "Omar is a riot. His real name is Horace, and he works for Arrow Insurance. He's married and has three grown children. He's been doing his act since he was thirteen, and he says he doesn't really care if he makes money or not. He loves performing. Oh, and he said I was the perfect distraction."

"I've been saying that for years. Now what about your meeting?"

"Couldn't have gone better. I'm all signed up, and soon prospective parents will be beating down the door."

"Really?"

"Not exactly. I listened and learned. Baby Love makes thousands of dollars a year, but where does that money go? No one seemed to have a good answer. I want to have a look at their financial records."

"That might be tricky."

"The head of Baby Love also keeps track of all the money. I've got her name and address."

"Well, unless you've got her bank account numbers, you can't find out anything, and please don't tell me you're going to break into First National."

"I'll think of something." She indicated my notes. "Any help?"

"Yes, thanks. I've learned that in addition to his escape skills, Houdini was a pilot, a movie star, and a ghostbuster. This case is coming along slowly, though. Yet another magician showed up today. I guess they'll be popping up everywhere, like magic."

"What did this one want?"

"He tried to scare me with some story about the Houdini box being dangerous and ruining lives and told me I needed to find it before it destroyed the world."

"Really? Sounds like he wants the box."

"Yep. Even told me where to look. The Willow Creek Brothers of the Scared Arts."

"Ooo, spooky. Who is this guy?"

"Bart of Bart, Binky, and His Baffling Birds. He scoffs at the notion the box actually belonged to Houdini, however," I pulled a page from the notes Kary had given me, "I found something interesting in your research. Seems according to Houdini's will, all his special effects were to be burned and destroyed, but his brother didn't do that. He sold a lot of stuff to one of Houdini's fans, a Sidney Hollis Radner. Mr. Radner displayed everything in The Houdini Magical Hall of Fame in Niagara Falls, Ontario, but in 1995, a fire destroyed the museum. This is the interesting part. Many of the props survived and were auctioned off in 1999 and 2008."

"So this box could have been one of those props."

"Or it could just be a box with an 'H' on it. 'H' for handkerchiefs or harmonicas."

"Or handcuffs. Wasn't Houdini the handcuff king?" She took the paper and read the information again. "If this box is the real thing, it could be very valuable. Maybe I can find out some information from Omar. He knows a lot about the history of magic."

"Sounds good. Now there's just one other thing."

She leaned forward. "Yes?"

"Marry me. Right now. Right this minute."

She laughed and sat back. "Not today."

"Tomorrow, then."

"I think we still have a few things to work out."

I got as far as "Kary, I—" when my phone rang. I was going to ignore it, but she said, "I've got to have something to eat. I'm starving," and left.

Damn. It was Delbert, bartender at the Crow Bar.

"Cam says come get him and Rufus."

I didn't hear any opera singing in the background, so Camden wasn't drunk. Of course, he wouldn't be able to sing anything tonight. "What's the trouble?"

"Rufus is tanked, and Cam can't drive that bigfoot truck of his."

I looked at my watch. It wasn't even eight o'clock. Rufus must have been guzzling the beers down. "Tell him I'll be there in a minute."

"No rush."

Well, I wasn't doing anything else, was I?

◇◇◇

At the Crow Bar, I crossed the crowded, smoke-filled room to the back. Rufus was draped across a table. Camden sat sideways in a booth, feet up, drinking what looked like his tenth Coke.

"He didn't have no beer," Delbert told me.

"Thanks, Del."

Camden saw me and raised his bottle in greeting.

"You got the keys?" I asked.

He tossed them to me.

"You think the two of us can haul Rufus out?"

He pointed to a large tattooed man at the next table.

"Carl," I said, "give us a hand with Rufus."

Carl heaved up and came over. We hauled Rufus off the table and dragged him through the bar out to his truck, where we folded him into the back. Camden climbed into the passenger's seat. I got behind the wheel and admired the view.

"I can see our house from here."

The truck started with a roar. The huge tires gripped the street and gave us a smooth if elevated ride.

"You two get it out of your system?"

Camden shrugged.

"Ellin came by. She and Angie had a heart to heart."

He kept looking out the window.

"What do you think? Is the PNS too important to her, or will she do the right thing?"

His lack of interest made me wonder if he'd given up on Ellin. Ellin and I have our moments, but oddly enough, I didn't feel a sense of triumph.

"I need to check out Ali's Cavern in Charlotte," I said. "You know what this means."

Camden looked cheerful for the first time that evening.

"That's right, pal. Road trip."

Chapter Seventeen

You Can Do Magic

The prospect of escape gave breakfast a festive air. Camden's voice was a little better. Must have been all the cola. We had more Coke for the road as well as a big bag of nutrition-less snacks.

I made the turn onto I-85 toward Charlotte. "We will finally gaze upon the mysterious Ali's Cavern. I was beginning to believe it existed in another realm."

Camden was already into the chips. "Are you sure they're open on Thursdays?"

"According to their website they're open Thursday through Saturday for lunch."

"I get lunch, too?"

"You're going to take part in a little deception. I want you to pretend you can read minds."

"Okay."

"Try to look mysterious and otherworldly."

"That'll be extra."

I passed a couple of slow-moving trucks and swung back into the right-hand lane. "Let me try out my theories on you. Rahnee Nevis and Jolly Bob were rivals for the Magic Club. She thinks he's a loser. He thinks she's too ambitious. WizBoy lied to me about the box, so he may have lied about other things.

Bartender Jilly would do anything to be on stage, and I'm not sure what Bart's game is."

"All this over a box that may or may not have belonged to Houdini."

"Here's something about the Finches' box. Houdini's personal props were in a museum that burned in the mid-90s. Quite a few of these props survived and were sold. I'm thinking if the box was one of those items rescued from the fire, then it's the real deal."

"And filled with evil power."

"Only if you believe Bart, which I don't. For some reason, he's misdirecting us."

Camden tipped the bag so I could get a handful of chips. "If he wants the box, why doesn't he go talk to the Sacred Willow Brothers, or whoever they are?"

"If they even exist. I say we storm the temple later today."

"I'm all for it. I haven't stormed anything in a while." He cleared his throat. He was keeping his voice to a whisper. "Anything else about Houdini?"

"Now there was a man who had no problem with self-esteem. He practically willed himself to succeed. He flew airplanes and starred in his own silent films, and he was married to the same woman for over thirty years. Can you see you and Ellin managing that?"

"Could be a challenge."

"Here's something really interesting. He and Arthur Conan Doyle were big pals."

"The man who wrote the Sherlock Holmes stories?"

"Same guy. They had a falling out over spiritualism. Doyle believed. Houdini didn't."

"That's odd. Sherlock's such a logical character."

"Well, apparently, Doyle was convinced by someone probably like the Deadly Sheila that his departed loved ones, his brother and son, communicated from the Great Beyond, what the medium called 'The Summerland.' Houdini couldn't believe his otherwise intelligent friend was such a sucker."

"Houdini didn't believe at all, then?"

"He wanted to. He'd tried to reach his mother, and when he couldn't, he declared war on all mediums, fortune-tellers, so-called psychics. You would've been on his hit list." I watched as a string of cars shot around the Fury like bullets. I was going sixty-five, but apparently, this was too slow. "He was even on a *Scientific American* committee that offered two thousand dollars for an actual spirit photograph and twenty-five hundred dollars to any medium who could show them real results. He was serious about it."

"Did he and Doyle ever reconcile their differences?"

"Nope. Doyle was one of those people mediums called 'shut eyes.' He couldn't be disillusioned or turned from his belief no matter what."

"Exactly like Sheila."

"Houdini spent his entire farewell vaudeville tour exposing spiritualists. There's even a theory he was poisoned by them— that'd be a great mystery—but most of the research said he was suffering from appendicitis and died when someone punched him in the stomach too hard."

"That's weird."

"And he died on Halloween."

"Now you're scaring me." Camden observed the scenery for a while and then said, "He was married for over thirty years, huh?"

"He left a message for his wife. 'Rosabelle, believe.' If she ever heard a psychic say that, she'd know it was really him."

"I take it she never heard this message."

"Nope."

"Maybe she did, but didn't want to admit it."

"This from someone who gets messages all day long."

"Oh, I've gotten messages, all right, loud and clear. I just didn't want to hear them."

I had to slow down for a driver who'd never gotten the message on How to Merge. "We're talking about Ellin now, right?"

"Well, I really hope she'll be able to do something about Sheila."

"What if she can't? What if it's 'Ready To Believe' at any cost?"

"I'll have to think of something."

"You know, there's a whole city full of women. You're bound to find someone else who can be the one."

"Nope. Ellie's the one. Always has been."

"Can you explain that to me? Why Ellin? You've had dozens of girlfriends. Why her?"

"Can you explain why you love Kary? She and Ellie are both beautiful blonde women who are independent, ambitious, and downright stubborn when it comes to getting their way. Why one and not the other?"

I didn't know how to explain it. It wasn't just her beauty. Something in Kary reached out to me, to the inner me, the me I was always telling to shut up. It was as if she could see the person I was supposed to be, the better self, while I wanted to be this other better David Randall for her.

"My reason is heavy with psychological significance," I said.

"Mine is completely selfish. I need looking after, and I know Ellie will take care of me."

I had indeed seen evidence of this. "You also know she's all about money and power."

"I can pull her from the dark side."

"Think so? You've got your work cut out for you."

"She's worth it."

I turned on my signal for our exit. "Well, I've got another job for you. Pretend to be a mentalist, so I can solve this case."

◇◇◇

WAM was doing a lot better than WOW. Ali's Cavern was a huge flashy club, all black and white, with touches of red and gold, impressive and elegant all at the same time. The large stage had a computerized lighting system and red velvet curtains. An ornate chandelier hung over the dining area. No glitter balls for this crowd.

At noon, the club was quiet, with a few people eating sandwiches and a few more painting some scenery. "This Magic Moment" was the background music.

"You know, Camden, I never realized how many songs there are that have to do with magic. I'll bet I've heard a dozen this week."

"It's in the air."

A trim young woman in a tuxedo greeted us. "Good afternoon, gentlemen. Welcome to Ali's Cavern. Two for lunch?"

"No, thank you," I said. "We heard you were looking for outstanding acts. This is Camden. I'm sure you've heard of him."

The woman looked slightly confused. "I don't believe so."

"The mentalist? We've been on a twelve-city tour, opened for Penn and Teller in Vegas. He's the finest ESP act you're likely to see."

She looked at Camden again, taking in the faded jeans, worn sneakers, and general dishabille. "Really? And you are?"

"John Fisher, Camden's agent and manager. Give her a sample, Camden. She doesn't seem convinced."

Camden took her hand. "Nice to meet you, Donna." His faint voice made him sound even more mysterious. "You'd rather be skiing Beech Mountain, I see."

She stared and then began to laugh. "My boss put you up to this, didn't he? That's very good. You really had me going."

"You recently lost your mother. She told you to look after your sister. 'Look after Annie,' she said. You promised you would."

The laugh stopped in her throat. She pulled her hand away. "H-how could you know that? No one was there but me when my mother—"

Camden gave me a look that said he'd had enough. "I'm sorry," he said to the woman. "Sometimes I get a very strong impression. You must have loved your mother very much."

She straightened her jacket. "Mister Fisher, I don't think our customers would want that much information revealed in front of everyone."

"We can tone it down, no problem."

"I'm afraid we're booked at present, and truthfully, no matter how good, we don't get much call for mentalists."

"Can you suggest another club, then? If not here, then, say, Greensboro? Parkland?"

"The only clubs in Parkland I could recommend are the Magic Club and the Bombay Club."

"So you hire magicians from those clubs?"

"On occasion. If they're exceptionally good."

Camden closed his eyes and put his hands to his temples. "I see the initials 'T. F.' I'm getting a strong impression of a magician. Tom, perhaps? No, Taft."

"Taft Finch?" Donna looked at him askance. "I know Taft Finch."

"He performed here Friday—no, Saturday night."

I wasn't sure how much he was guessing or if he'd picked up something. Either way, it worked.

"Saturday night," Donna said.

"Are you aware he died Sunday morning while apparently attempting an escape act?" I asked.

"Yes, I heard about that. A horrible thing to happen. He was a great guy. He always bought a round for everyone and kept us up late telling about his adventures. I liked him well enough to book him several times. Do they know what happened?"

"There's a possibility he was murdered."

"Good lord."

"Anyone here at Ali's Cavern have a grudge against him? Maybe they weren't happy that someone from Wizards of Wonder was working this club."

She hesitated. "No, we're over that."

Camden closed his eyes. "I see some sort of conflict. A secret revealed. A split with no hope of reconciliation."

Reconciliation. He'd been saving that one up. Donna looked uncomfortable. "All right, so maybe some of them aren't over it."

"Then why would a member of WOW be allowed here?" I asked.

"From what I understand, Taft knew the parties involved, and he smoothed things over. Because of that, he was the only member of WOW who could perform in the club."

Hmm, maybe a matter of contention between the Finch brothers? Lucas had said it was hard to find work, yet Taft could perform in the war zone. And exactly how much money was a considerable amount? Had Taft sold some of the Finches' special collection?

"Donna, do you happen to know the name of the WAM magician whose trick was revealed?"

Her eyes narrowed. "What's with all the questions? I thought you wanted an audition."

Camden moved his hands as if feeling invisible walls. "The vibrations here are strong. There may be a way to solve this mystery, a connection to the feud. Perhaps if we could speak with this magician, we could know what happened to Taft."

She took a step away from him. "I don't know. He wasn't with WAM for very long. He wasn't quite as accomplished as our usual magicians, but he did a good job with the rings."

"Rings? Silver rings?"

"Yes, and sometimes scarves."

"I see his name," Camden said in his best far away voice, which sounded really spooky thanks to his laryngitis. "Omar the Ring Master."

"Oh, wow," she said. "That's it. You are really good. That's what he called himself."

Now that we had her attention, I said, "Just a few more questions, please. When did Taft leave here Saturday night?"

"He performed from midnight until one a.m. As usual, everyone sat around talked, had a few drinks. Then he got a phone call and said he had to go."

I glanced at Camden, who went back into his act. "A phone call. From his brother? I hear a man's voice—no, a woman's."

"I didn't hear who called, and he didn't say," Donna said. "It must have been a voice-mail message. He said, 'I've had some good news, Donna. See you later,' and hurried out." A group of people came into the club behind us. "You'll have to excuse me."

"You're sure you can't grant us an audition?" I asked.

Camden pulled on my sleeve. "That's all right, John. I feel the spirits calling me to move on."

"Very well. Thank you for your time, Miss Donna."

She'd kept her eyes on Camden. "You're welcome."

◇◇◇

We got back in the Fury. "Well, that's interesting," I said. "When Taft finished his act at the Magic Club, he hurried out to get to Charlotte by midnight. Does his act here and then gets a phone call that probably lures him back to the Magic Club."

"'I've heard some good news.' Possibly about the missing box?"

"Maybe Lucas still has Taft's phone, and we can see who called him. By the way, you were quite convincing."

"I really didn't mean to depress her, though."

"I'm sure you got up this morning thinking, 'Oh, I'll go to Charlotte and upset a total stranger by repeating her mother's dying words.' And how about Omar being a former member of WAM and possibly the one who blew the whistle on Jolly Bob? I'll have to put Kary onto that part of the puzzle."

My phone rang. It was Lucas returning my call. "Sorry, Randall. I've been working to get Taft's memorial service ready. To answer your questions, I can't say Taft liked the idea of the bet. But there was no way anyone was going to figure out how to open the box."

"Well, suppose someone got impatient and broke it open to get your cabinet key. Is there something really valuable you don't want to lose?"

"I consider everything in our collection valuable."

"Yet you're willing to risk it for a bet."

"As I said, no one would be able to get the box open. And as for breaking it, no real magician would destroy that box."

"Do you have Taft's cell phone?"

"No. I suppose the police have it."

I almost asked him if he called his brother late Saturday or early Sunday to leave a voice-mail message, but I didn't. I couldn't completely rule Lucas out as a suspect. The brothers had argued about the box. More than likely Lucas knew about Taft's affair with Rahnee. If I could get Taft's phone and hear the message, maybe I could recognize the voice. If Lucas had called with good news, what else could the news be except the box was found? And since the box was still missing, did Lucas use this false message to lure Taft to the club, kill him, and then play the grieving brother?

"When is the memorial service?"

"Tonight at seven."

"I'll see you then." I closed my phone. "Lucas is positive no one can open the box. There's a memorial service for Taft tonight at seven. I may have need of your extra senses."

"You still owe me lunch."

"No problem. We will fortify ourselves and pay a visit to the Willow Creek Brothers."

Chapter Eighteen

It's Only Make Believe

The Sorcerer's Temple in Piney Woods turned out to be a cinder block building with all the warmth and charm of an old church fellowship hall. Someone had painted stars and crescent moons on the door and misspelled "Sorcerors Temple" in squiggly letters.

I knocked. A middle-aged man in a plaid flannel shirt and overalls opened the door.

"Willow Creek Brothers of the Sacred Arts. What's the password?"

I took a wild guess. "Abracadabra?"

"Enter."

Inside, the walls had been painted dark purple. A folding table and seven wooden chairs sat to one side. A large book lay open on a metal stand. Candles were everywhere.

In the midst of all this, the man looked very ordinary. "What can I do for you gentlemen?"

"I'm the Remarkable Randall, and this is Camden the Mentalist. We've come in search of a special box we understand used to belong to Houdini. It's about twelve by six inches, golden brown, 'H' on top."

"We got rid of that," he said. "Sold it to a fella name of Finch."

"Why did you sell it?"

"Well, they offered us a nice chunk of money for it."

"Do you mind telling me how much?"

"Don't mind. Twenty-five hundred dollars. Wish they'd buy some more of our magical artifacts. We got plenty." He pointed to a bookshelf on the far wall. "You can come have a look."

The magical artifacts included a battered top hat, a stack of wands with silver tips, capes with red velvet lining, several boxes, a mask, decks of cards, and a lot of books in cracked black leather bindings. Camden and I did our best to look impressed.

"That's a fine collection."

He picked up the top hat. "Now this here's the exact same hat that Theodore Toombalt wore in his act during the thirties. We got that from his nephew lives down by the mill. Got the gloves, too, around here someplace." He put the hat down and picked up one of the wands. "You don't see wands like this anymore. Genuine silver tips. Not like them silly folding ones that shoot out and poke you in the eye. Wanna hold it?"

"Thanks." I took the wand. "How often do the Brothers meet? I thought you had disbanded."

"We did for a while."

"Because of the box?"

"No." He grimaced. "Because of our wives. They didn't like us going off without them. I told mine, it's Brothers of the Sacred Arts, not Brothers and Their Wives. She said it was just another way of getting out of doing some work around the house. I told her she and her cronies got together to play bridge and yak all the time, why shouldn't I meet with my buddies and learn some new tricks? She finally saw the light. I think she got tired of me being around the house so much."

"Is there some sort of curse on the box?"

"Not that I know of."

So all this nonsense about the box destroying the Brotherhood was Bart misdirecting me. I handed the wand back to him. "I understand there's a trick to getting the box open."

"Could be. Never needed to open it, myself."

Camden held out his hand for the wand. "I'd like to see that."

"Sure, buddy. Look at anything you like. Give you a good price."

"Where did you get these things?"

"Oh, here and there. And one of the fella's had a grandpa who had a magic act."

"Is that where the box came from?"

"Can't say as I remember."

While Camden carefully picked up and examined all the items, I had a few more questions for the Willow Creek Brother.

"Did you hear what happened to Taft Finch?"

"Can't say that I did."

"There was an accident at the Magic Club. He was found dead in a large trunk."

"I'm sorry to hear that."

"Do any of the Willow Creek Brothers perform at the Club?"

"Ain't none of us good enough for that. We like to keep to ourselves." He scratched his head. "I think a few of the fellas went one time. Said the drinks were overpriced. Too bad about Finch's brother, though. What was he trying to do with the trunk?"

"An escape act."

"Didn't go too well, then, did it?" He turned to Camden. "See anything you like, buddy?"

Camden set the top hat back on the shelf. He hadn't fallen over or zoned out, so I could safely assume none of the items had a curse or evil back story. "No, thanks. It's a nice collection, though."

I thanked the man for his help. "Now why would Bart want us to believe the box was cursed?" I asked Camden as we walked back to the car.

"Maybe he thinks it is."

"You get anything from the sacred artifacts?"

"It's ordinary stuff. The hat did belong to Theodore Toombalt, but since it has his name written inside, I didn't have to go to the Other Side to figure that out."

"So now we've checked out the Willow Creek Brothers. You didn't have a chance to shake hands with Bart, did you?"

"No, but you could tell he was interested in the box."

"Everybody wants it, and where in the hell is it?"

◇◇◇

Two hours to Charlotte and two hours back, plus a lunch stop and a trip to the Sorcerer's Temple meant we got back to the house around three o'clock. We were greeted at the front door by Fred. He had on his rumpled brown jacket, his boxer shorts, and his bedroom shoes.

"I need to go to the bank."

Camden backed him into the house. "Fred, you need to put on some pants."

"Then will you take me?"

"Randall might be able to."

I pulled the mail from the box and started looking through it. "Maybe later, Fred."

"You're a damn nuisance."

"Yeah, well, so are you."

Still grumbling, Fred went up the stairs. "Camden, that old boy should be in a home."

"He is in a home."

"You know what I mean." I handed him his latest issue of *UFO Monthly.*

"How would you like it if I kicked you out?"

"At least I have all my clothes on."

I was glad to see my mail was the usual junk mail and bills. No more invitations to the reunion. I put it on my desk and then had a surprise phone call from Ellin.

"How's Cam's voice today? I know he's not supposed to talk."

"A little rough. You sound a bit calmer. How are things going?"

"As well as can be expected. Tell him I'm trying to redirect Sheila. This new act, for instance. I don't think it'll involve predictions."

"I'll tell him. Did you find out who's stealing things? I'm available."

"Thanks, but we've got it under control. The receptionist is going to make sure the side doors are locked during taping. We think that's how our thief is getting in."

"If that doesn't work, give me a call."

She thanked me and hung up. I went in search of a snack. Camden was already in the kitchen hunting for a Coke in the fridge. He tossed me one.

"Your sweetie just called. She wants you to know she's doing her best to keep Sheila from predicting."

"I hope she can."

"I've got to do some work on Sandy's case. I've run out of places to look for her bracelet. Guess I'll retrace my steps and see if I missed anything."

"I could always give it a try."

"I'll let you know." I wasn't ready to have Camden's help. Unlike tracking Taft's murderer, finding a bracelet wasn't a life or death situation. Even though it bugged me not to have solved her case, I knew Sandy would be patient.

"Oh, that's all right, David," she said when I called her. "I've been so busy with various functions lately. I did have a few phone calls, though, from people who thought they had my bracelet and wanted a reward. Of course, none of them knew about the initials, so when I asked them to describe the bracelet, they always left out that important little detail."

"Sorry you're being hassled about it."

"Well, you never know. Someone honest might find it and call me."

"How did these people know you'd lost a bracelet?"

"Oh, word's gotten around the club, and once that happens, the world knows. It's all right, really."

"Sandy, I wish all my clients were as understanding as you."

"I know you're doing everything you can."

I thanked her and hung up. Her upbeat attitude made me even more determined to find her bracelet. Was I doing everything I could? I checked off the places I'd searched: jewelry stores, pawnshops, the country club, the churches. Maybe, like all the magicians kept telling me, it was right before my eyes and I couldn't see it.

Rufus wandered into my office, looking particularly scraggly in his worn bib overalls and Harley Davidson t-shirt. I wouldn't have been surprised to see a mouse peering out from the undergrowth that was his beard. I didn't want to provoke the beast, but I had to ask.

"How's the hangover?"

"Ain't no big thing." He settled himself into the chair across from my desk and pulled out his tobacco pouch. "Want somethin' to do?"

"I've got plenty to do, thanks. What's up?"

"Your little romance with Kary's getting along pretty good, right?"

"Pretty good."

"Then you tell me what the hell I can do to fix things with Angie."

"Marry her."

"Aw, hell. That dog won't hunt."

"Translation, please."

Rufus dug a wad of tobacco from the pouch and stuffed it in one cheek. "I ain't ready for that."

"Who is?"

"Well, you, for one. Can't go anywhere in this house without stepping on your tongue."

"Are you in love with Angie?"

He squinted at me, so I figured he was thinking about it. "Yep."

"Have you told her? Maybe that's all she needs to hear right now. Come on. We can have a double wedding. No, a triple wedding, if Camden decides to man up."

Rufus shifted the wad of tobacco to his other cheek. "Think that's likely?"

"Let's all get it over with."

"I dunno. You can put your boots in the oven, but that don't make 'em biscuits."

"What? Speak English, damn it."

Rufus leaned forward. "What I mean, Yankee boy, is that it's a bigger commitment than anybody thinks, and just sayin' 'let's get married' don't cut it. You gotta have a plan. You gotta have resources."

I knew what he meant. "You're not making enough money."

He sat back with a sigh that ruffled his beard. Any mice in there needed to hang on. "Want Angie to have everything she deserves, you know?"

"I know. But if she loves you, she won't care about that."

"But I care. I want the time to be right. She's just gonna have to wait." He looked around for a place to spit.

"Not in here," I said.

"Where's your trash can?"

"Go out in the yard. But before you go, let me ask you something. The bartender at the Bombay Club told one of her employees to shape up or he'd be sorrier than a mustard-eating frog on Sunday. First of all, do frogs eat mustard, and second, why Sunday? Are there other days on which said frog would be less sorry?"

He shrugged. "Same as a jumped-up toad in a pickle barrel."

"That doesn't make any sense, either! How do these sayings get started? You have to be making these up as you go along."

"Nah. Heard 'em all my life. Part of our colorful Southern heritage. You like that? 'Heritage'?"

"I'm impressed. How about he looked like death sucking a sponge?"

"Same as death eatin' a cracker, only messier."

"Thanks for clearing that up."

He pulled himself out of the chair and went to the door where he turned for his usual parting joke. "Know what a redneck's last words are?"

"Lay it on me."

"'Hey, ya'll watch this!'" He gave a snort of laughter and left.

Yeah, watch this. Watch the Three Stooges lose the women they loved because they were too busy trying to figure out what they wanted. We would all be sorrier than mustard-eating frogs or pickle barrel toads.

I was still wondering what else I could do when Jordan called. I was a little surprised to hear from him until I realized he wanted some information.

"Randall, I'm sure you've been talking to Rahnee Nevis. What's the deal between her and Taft Finch?"

"They were having an affair. She's not a suspect, is she? I haven't been able to find a motive."

"That's what she told me. And she was not planning to sell the club to anyone."

"That's right."

"Just crossing some t's here."

"Then cross one for me. Do you know the cause of death?"

"Apparently, Taft Finch had a drink Sunday morning and either forgot and took some pills along with it, or someone had already mixed the pills in for him. One second here." I heard the click of his keyboard. "The report says 'doxylamine succinate, a short-term sedative, and traces of diphenhydramine.' It's my guess these two things should not be together."

Doxylamine was the name Nick used for Taft's blue pills. "I can't imagine he forgot. Rahnee and Lucas both told me Taft rarely used his sleep medication, and he would've known better than to wash it down with alcohol."

"That's why this is a murder investigation."

"Then someone big and strong would have to put Taft in the trunk—unless he was tricked into getting in."

"Well, of the three people who have keys to the club, only Ms. Nevis fits that description."

I didn't like the way this was going. "Are you trying to paint her as the woman scorned? I think she and Taft were genuinely friends."

"Didn't you and Cam take a little trip to Charlotte this morning?"

"Wow, your spies are everywhere."

"It's easy to spot that white whale of a car you drive. I'm guessing you spoke to the woman at Ali's Cavern."

"Again, she and Taft were friends."

Jordan gave a snort. "Maybe Rahnee Nevis didn't think so."

"Did you find Taft's cell phone?"

"No. We found his car, though, parked several blocks away from the club. The keys were still in it. The team's going over it."

Parking was always a problem on Freer Street, but if Taft had come to the club early Sunday morning, he could've parked right in front. But Monday someone would've noticed his car and wondered where he was. Someone called him to the club, killed him, and then moved his car. This person probably got rid of Taft's cell phone, too.

"Do you have access to Taft's phone records?"

"We're working on that. Notice I said 'we'?"

Jordan signed off with his usual warnings about getting in the way. I sat for a few minutes more, listening to the sounds of Kary in the kitchen opening cans—of tuna, most likely—opening packages of crackers, banging a cabinet door in search of the right baking dish. Then I went into the kitchen to see if I could help.

She said I could fix some more tea, so I pulled out the tea bags and sugar. "How was your day?"

"Dana told everyone he'd seen me at the Magic Club, so I answered questions all day about that."

"Did you tell the kids you were going to be a magician's assistant?"

"Of course. Now they're really excited." She crushed the crackers into the bowl of tuna. "How was your road trip?"

"We found out Taft performed at Ali's Cavern Saturday night and received a phone call that made him rush back to Parkland. Unfortunately, his cell phone's missing, so we don't know who made the call."

"Maybe the phone company can help you with that."

"Jordan's on it, but he might not be persuaded to share."

"Maybe I should join the police force. Then you'd have someone who would share information with you."

I was determined not to let her rattle me. "You'd look very fetching in a police uniform."

"'Fetching'?"

"Fetching, knock down dead gorgeous, amazing. The list goes on."

"We'll need some napkins, too, please."

I took some napkins from the cabinet, started to put them on the table, and had an idea. I chose a pen from the pencil holder on the counter and sat down to write. "Camden and I also visited the Willow Creek Brothers of the Sacred Arts."

"Ah, yes, the mysterious Willow Creek Brothers."

"It wasn't. A bunch of guys trying to get away from their wives. Nothing there."

Kary dumped the tuna mixture into a baking dish. "That's too bad."

"Oh, we'll find more clues, I'm sure."

"No, I meant it's too bad the guys want to get away from their wives."

"Maybe the wives have a secret club of their own."

Kary chuckled. "I'll bet they do."

"I learned a magic trick."

"Oh, really?"

"The Remarkable Randall, at your service. Pick a napkin. Any napkin."

She put the dish in the oven, wiped her hands on a dishcloth, and chose a napkin from the stack.

"Open it."

She opened the napkin and read the message I'd written. "'Will you marry me?' Great trick! How'd you do it?"

"Pick another."

She opened the second napkin and laughed. "You wrote it on all of them."

"Damn, there goes my secret."

"Well, every good magician has to start somewhere."

I set the magic napkins aside. "Speaking of that, I'd like you to ask Omar about his days as a member of WAM."

"Omar was a WAMer? He's never mentioned it."

"I think he must have been starting out, and Ali's Cavern gave him a try. If my information is correct, Jolly Bob stole one of Omar's tricks, and when Omar caught him, Jolly Bob retaliated by ruining part of Omar's act, and thus began the Great Magic Feud."

She took the silverware from the drawer. "I'll be sure to ask him about it. Does this have anything to do with Taft's murder?"

"I don't know. Stealing another magician's trick is a big deal in the magic world. According to the woman we spoke with at Ali's Cavern, Taft took care of things, which makes me wonder if he gave the WAM member a new trick, which is why Taft could perform at the Cavern despite his ties to WOW."

"Then Omar and Jolly Bob would have cause to hate each other, not Taft."

"Unless Jolly Bob hated Taft even more for going over to the other side."

"I'll find out," Kary said. She started into the dining room with the silverware.

"You never answered my napkin."

She paused. "Your napkin has been taken into consideration."

"The Remarkable Randall would appreciate an answer soon."

"The Candid Kary will get back to you."

◇◇◇

During supper, Camden indicated he had no voice left. Kary told everyone about her new job with Omar the Ring Master. Rufus talked about his latest construction job. Angie talked about a suit she was altering for someone. Fred grumbled about how no one would ever take him anywhere, and I valiantly ate tuna casserole.

After everyone had managed to eat enough, Rufus pushed back from the table and stared at Angie. "Need to talk to you about something."

She wiped her mouth and tossed the napkin on the table. "Yeah?"

"Yeah. Been thinkin' about it all day."

"Well, I think you can say it right here."

"Nope. It's private."

"Private?"

"That's what I said. Private. Just you and me."

For a moment, we saw all saw Angie's little eyes as they widened in surprise. "All right," she said.

The two of them lumbered out of the dining room and into the island.

Kary's eyes were wide, too. "Oh, my gosh. Is Rufus going to propose?"

We couldn't hear their voices, only a slight rumbling from Rufus. Camden pointed to his ring finger and frowned a question.

"I don't know if he has a ring," I said. "He talked to me earlier about wanting to wait."

Fred glared around the table. "What the hell's going on?"

Kary shushed him. "Shh, Fred. We think Rufus is asking Angie to marry him."

"What? Marry that big gal? She's so fat it takes two dogs to bark at her."

"Fred!"

Camden gestured for silence. We strained to hear and were rewarded by a loud smack that I hoped was a kiss and not a punch in the face. It must have been a kiss, because a few moments later, the beaming couple came back to the dining room. Angie held out her plump hand to show us the tiny diamond while Rufus grinned, as he would've said, "like a goat eating briars."

Kary jumped up. "Oh, Angie! Congratulations! Congratulations, Rufus!" She gave them both a hug. Camden did the same. I hugged Angie and gave Rufus a slap on the shoulder, which was like slamming my hand into a wall.

"What was all that about waiting?"

He shrugged. "Might as well bite the bullet. I had my granny's ring, so I thought, why not?" He looked at me and then at Camden. "Now, who's next?"

"Kary," I said. "I don't have a ring yet, but will you marry me?"

She laughed. "No, this is Rufus and Angie's moment."

Rufus turned to Camden. "I'll call Ellin for you if you're in the mood."

Camden shook his head.

"Nah, I don't guess this is a good time. But you'd better get a move on. I ain't gonna be palling around with two wild bachelors." He put his arm around Angie. "Well, sugar lips, we got some planning to do. What say we head out to the Crow Bar?"

"All right," she said. "And I want to call my sister."

After they'd gone, we sat back at the table, explained to Fred what had happened, and had some leftover cookies Kary had baked a few days earlier.

"Well, wasn't that a surprise?" Kary said. "A wedding! That will be fun."

"We could make it a double ceremony," I said.

"I believe Angie and I have different ideas about our special day."

"Camden, what do you say? Oh, that's right. You can't say anything. Rufus and Angie, me and Kary, you and Ellin. One big splashy magical wedding, and it's all done."

He went to the counter and got paper and pencil, scribbled a note, and passed it to me. I read it aloud. "'That would take more magic than we have.' Too true."

"Let's take this one wedding at a time," Kary said.

Fred banged his spoon on the table like an annoyed infant. "What wedding? Who's getting married? And where's my cookie?"

Chapter Nineteen

Magic Night

After all the excitement at home, it was sobering to go into the quiet of the Magic Club. About twenty people had gathered at the club for Taft's memorial service. On stage, a blue spotlight gleamed on a black stool. On top of the stool was a pack of cards and a broken wand. I came in as WizBoy was finishing his eulogy.

"Taft was a great guy and a great magician. I'll miss him."

I sat down at the bar. Jilly, dressed in black lace, sat at the far end. She didn't look my way. Bart and Fancy shared a table. Jolly Bob sat with Lucas Finch at another.

Rahnee was next on stage. The blue lights made her hair an odd purple shade. She looked as if she'd been crying.

"This club won't be the same without Taft. He was a wonderful person. Everyone loved his act, and everyone loved him."

She went on about how loved Taft was. Well, it was entirely possible somebody in this group didn't love Taft. I watched faces as people listened. Jolly Bob gave Rahnee his complete attention. Jilly sat with her head down. Fancy brushed tears from her cheeks. Bart looked uncomfortable, as if he'd rather be somewhere else. Lucas had no expression.

When Rahnee finished, she invited others to speak. Fancy went on stage.

"Taft was one of the nicest men I've ever known. He was also one of the most generous. I can't tell you how many times he helped me with a trick, or showed me how an illusion worked. I don't think I'd have much of a career if it hadn't been for Taft."

Jolly Bob was next. "I want to make certain Lucas knows everyone in the magic community is here for you, pal. If there's anything any of us can do, you just let us know."

Lucas nodded his thanks.

Afterward, everyone had a drink and wandered off in little groups. Lucas was surrounded by people offering condolences. Bart approached me.

"Any luck finding that box, Mister Randall?"

"Not yet. I did speak with a member of the Willow Creek Brothers. He had a slightly different take on the cursed box."

"I imagine he did. By the time any of them could figure it out, the curse had done its work and they'd disbanded."

"Oh, they're back together now."

"Really? That's good news."

But Bart didn't look as if he thought it was good news.

"I think you're misdirecting me, Bart," I said. "You wanted to know if the box had found its way back to the Brothers. You could've asked them yourself."

He almost pouted. "They won't talk to me."

"Why wouldn't—oh, I get it. You told me you used to be one of them. What's going on? A little professional jealousy?"

Bart turned red. "Professional? Hah! Those dolts will never be professional. I left them in the dust a long time ago."

"Before or after they acquired the box?"

"Before."

"So you sent me to find out if the box had magically found its way back to them? I oughta charge you my usual fee."

"I was only trying to help your investigation."

"Why do you want the box? What's in the Finches' cabinet that you have to have?"

"I don't want the box. I don't want anything the Finches have. Like you, I want to find out who killed Taft, and I think whoever has the box killed him."

"Then they're not likely to come forward, are they?"

Bart glared and moved on to the bar. I waited until people shifted away and then sat down at Lucas' table. "I was at Ali's Cavern earlier today. I spoke with a young woman named Donna. Taft performed at the club Saturday night around midnight. Did you know about that?"

He looked startled. "He performed at the Cavern? No, I didn't know that."

We were interrupted by a shrill scream from backstage. WizBoy came running, his face twisted in horror.

"Somebody help me! Rahnee's been stabbed!"

We ran backstage. Stabbed might have been a bit dramatic. Rahnee's shoulder was bleeding. She pointed to a large knife on the floor.

"Who the hell is throwing knives around back here?"

WizBoy dashed up with several towels from the bar. She snatched the towels from him and pressed them against her shoulder. "Damn! Of all the clumsy things!"

Lucas held up the knife. "Fancy, this is one of yours."

She was as pale as Rahnee. "That's impossible!"

"But this is your knife."

"I was going to do part of my act as a tribute to Taft. Naturally, I had the case backstage so I could get to my things. I left it there because I've always been able to leave my case backstage. Someone must have gotten into it."

"Don't you keep it locked?" I asked.

"Usually I do, but I was going to show Jilly how to juggle the hoops. Rahnee, I'm so sorry. I can't believe anyone would use one of my knives to attack you."

Rahnee's eyes were glazed with pain. "It came out of the dark. When I find out who's been playing around, they'll never work in my club again."

I turned to WizBoy. "Who else was backstage?"

"Just me."

"Can you turn on some lights? And keep people back, will you?"

WizBoy took charge, telling the curious crowd to sit down, everything was taken care of. He turned on the backstage lights, and I looked around. Fancy's case stood slightly open. The rest of the knives were in place, but whoever reached in had dislodged the colorful hoops. They lay scattered on the floor along with a small silver object. It was a tiny silver bone, exactly like the ones hanging on WizBoy's key ring.

"Everything's okay," I heard him tell the crowd. "Randall's a detective. He'll figure it out. Everybody calm down."

"Come back here a minute, Wiz," I said.

He came up to me, almost twitching with anxiety. "Yeah? You find anything?"

I held up the little bone.

WizBoy turned pale.

"I found it right over there by Fancy's case. I'd like to see your key ring."

His hands were shaking as he pulled his keys from his pocket. "I swear to you I had nothing to do with this."

One of the little bones was missing from his key ring.

WizBoy's voice was low and frightened. "I'm back here all the time! It could've caught on anything."

"Did it catch on Fancy's case when you were getting out a knife? That's what people are going to think. That's what I'm thinking."

"Randall, I swear to God I didn't throw that knife. Somebody set me up!"

"Who would do that?"

"Randall?" Lucas called. "What's going on? How long do we have to stay here? Rahnee should go to the hospital."

"Randall, don't say anything about this," WizBoy said in a frantic whisper. "Please!"

"Let's see what everyone else has to say."

Rahnee sat with her arm propped on one of the tables. Jilly came around from the bar with a glass of water. "You need to go to the hospital Rahnee. A doctor ought to look at that cut. You might need stitches."

She glared. "I'll be fine. I don't want any more bad publicity for the club." She lifted the towels. The long cut was still bleeding. "It's a scratch. It's not that deep. Randall, you're the detective here. Do something."

I appreciated the opening. "I'd like to ask everyone where they were."

"Well, Miss Fancy was sitting with me," Bart said. "And she can vouch for my whereabouts."

I turned to Jolly Bob. "What about you?"

"I was at another table with Lucas. The only one backstage with Rahnee was WizBoy."

WizBoy's reaction was understandably violent. "Don't try to pin this on me, you old fool! You're the one with a grudge against Rahnee. Ever since she outbid you for the club, you've been mad at her. You'd be really happy if something happened to her."

Jolly Bob put up both hands. "Hold on! Who's the one who wants to take over the club? You've been a greedy little bastard from day one. If Rahnee can't run the club, who's next in line? You, you punk."

Lucas stepped between them. "Please! No more of this! We should be thinking about Rahnee."

WizBoy wasn't finished. "You've always wanted this club. If you were running it, it'd go under in a week!"

Bart caught Jolly Bob's arm as he hauled back his fist. "Bob, for heaven's sake, calm down. Everyone calm down."

"Jilly, where were you?" I asked.

"Sitting at the bar."

WizBoy transferred his hostility from Jolly Bob to me. "There's no way she could've done this!"

"You were backstage, Wiz. You couldn't see out here."

"Jilly, tell Randall you didn't do anything!" He tried to put his arm around her, but she shrugged him off.

"Of course I didn't. Why would I want to hurt Rahnee?"

"None of us would," Fancy said. "No one should have been anywhere near my case."

"You didn't see anyone else backstage?" I asked.

"It's so dark back there I could barely find the side door."

Bart frowned. "So someone could've been hiding in the dark."

Jolly Bob gave him a scornful look. "And then what? Disappeared?"

"Why not? We're all magicians here."

WizBoy continued to pace. "Maybe Rahnee wasn't the target."

"Who, then? You?"

He gave me a worried gaze. "Maybe."

Jolly Bob laughed a short bark of laughter. "What makes you so special?"

"I've got people jealous of me."

"I doubt it."

If WizBoy had had a knife right then, he would've stabbed Jolly Bob. "You can't even do the simplest card trick, you washed up old hack. Taft was way better at cards than you."

"Well, he's dead, so I guess that makes me better now, doesn't it?"

Rahnee slammed her free hand on the table. "Shut up, you two! I've heard enough playground silliness."

Jolly Bob started for the door. "And I've had enough of this."

I took out my phone. "Don't go yet. I'm giving the police a call."

"What?"

"Taft's death is part of a murder investigation, and I don't think this attack on Rahnee was an accident."

There was immediate commotion from everyone. WizBoy steadied himself on the bar.

Jolly Bob got right in my face. "That's nonsense. For all we know, someone slipped in the back door from off the street and played a prank."

WizBoy rounded on him. "How stupid are you? It was somebody right here in this club. Call the police, Randall."

Rahnee held up her uninjured hand. "No, wait, please. Randall, I can't have any more bad publicity for the club. I'm all right, really. Maybe it was an accident."

WizBoy was insistent. "The police can check the knife for fingerprints."

Lucas looked ill. "I picked up the knife. My prints are all over it. But I didn't do it! You know I didn't!"

"Everybody, calm down," Fancy said. "I think we should call the police. That way we can be sure no one here is responsible."

Rahnee put her head down on her hand. "I don't want the police involved. I want everyone to go home. I need some peace and quiet."

Despite Rahnee's request, I'd already punched in Jordan's number. "Sorry, Rahnee. We need to straighten this out. Everyone, have a seat."

Lucas rubbed his face. He looked old and tired. "Rahnee, I can't believe all this is happening at the club. It makes me wonder if there really is something cursed about that box."

"Don't talk like that," she said. "We're all worn out."

WizBoy hovered over her. "Don't worry about anything, Rahnee. I got it covered." He was still pissed at me, though. "Man, there is no way Jilly could have thrown a knife at Rahnee."

"I don't know. She was all in black, and everyone had their backs to her. Fancy was going to show her something in the case. She could've helped herself."

"But why? She's not mad at Rahnee."

"How do you know? If Jilly knew about Rahnee and Taft, she might be a little ticked."

"Yeah, but mad enough to do something like that? It doesn't make sense."

"Excuse me, but how long is this going to take?" Jolly Bob asked in a peevish tone.

WizBoy turned on him with a sneer. "You got someplace special to be? The Magic Castle in Hollywood, maybe?"

I stepped between the two of them to forestall the fight. "If everyone cooperates, it shouldn't take too long."

It took two hours. Jordan and another officer arrived before the ambulance and took Rahnee's statement first so she could be taken to the hospital. Then he talked to everyone else while the officer checked every inch of the backstage area and the alley behind the club.

Wizboy kept shooting me anxious looks until finally Jordan said, "Do you need to talk to Randall about something?"

I motioned for Jordan and WizBoy to come over. "A word in private." I showed Jordan the little bone. "I found this backstage by the case. It came off WizBoy's key ring. He insists he's being set up, and frankly, I don't think he would've thrown a knife at Rahnee."

WizBoy looked so relieved I thought he might cry. "I wouldn't. I care too much about this place to jeopardize my chance to run it. Somebody's got it in for me."

"Anyone in particular?" Jordan asked.

"Jolly Bob, Bart, Lucas, any of those old guys who're jealous of my talent."

"Is there any way someone could've gotten a hold of your keys?"

"I don't know. We're all magicians here. We're all good at sleight of hand."

Jordan finished taking WizBoy's statement, and when everyone had been allowed to leave, Jordan came over to me.

"Some kind of magic trick going on here, Randall?"

"You never know what's going to happen at the Magic Club."

"What's your take on all this?"

"I don't know. WizBoy was the only one backstage unless Jilly somehow snuck back there when we weren't looking. I can't see Jilly throwing a knife that accurately, though, unless she's been taking lessons from Fancy. And was the intention to kill Rahnee or just scare her?"

"Any way the knife could've been rigged? Any of these magicians good with wires and strings?"

"Not that I know of. And as for the little bone, it could've fallen off earlier and happened to be near the case."

"Or young Mister WizBoy is doing a fine job of misdirecting us." Jordan looked around the room and scratched his stiff brush of black hair. "Well, I sure as hell don't believe in magic, so there has to be an explanation. We just haven't found it."

Chapter Twenty

Magic in Here

I didn't believe in magic, either. On my way home, my head was dizzy with mysteries. Taft Finch's murder, the missing Houdini box, and now, someone throwing a knife at Rahnee—if indeed, Rahnee was the intended target.

It was after ten, and the house was quiet. Camden was sitting on the sofa watching *Forbidden Planet*. He muted the sound, and then reached for a pad and pencil. He wrote, "Now what?"

"Someone threw one of Fancy's knives and hit Rahnee in the shoulder."

"Is she okay?" he wrote.

"The cut needs stitches, but I think she'll be all right." I sat down in the blue armchair. "These magicians are an ornery lot."

"Suspects?" was his next note.

"I found a little bone off WizBoy's key ring right by the case, but the Wiz insists he's being set up. Bart was sitting with Fancy when the incident happened. Lucas was with Jolly Bob. WizBoy was the only one backstage. That leaves Jilly and about thirteen other people."

Camden frowned. "Thirteen?" he mouthed.

"From what I can tell, everyone was out front watching the stage. If I've got thirteen more suspects, I'm going to shoot myself."

Camden wrote, "Jilly?"

"Aside from some jealousy, I don't know. She's certainly not strong enough to have folded Taft into the trunk." I put my feet up on the coffee table. "If WizBoy's playing me, I'm going to wring his scrawny little neck." I yawned. "Anything else from the happy couple?"

He wrote for a while and passed me the notepad.

"'Rufus would like for you to be a groomsman.' As a reward for all my sound advice, I'm sure. I'll be glad to."

Camden took the pad and wrote something else.

"'Sheila's excited about performing miracles.' Well, that's nice. 'Plans to unveil a secret tomorrow.' I'll bet Ellin can't wait."

He added, "A ratings bonanza."

"We'll have to be sure and watch."

◇◇◇

Friday morning, Kary was already in the kitchen when I came down for breakfast. She was buttering some toast and asked if I wanted any.

I sat down at the counter. "No, thanks."

"Angie is so excited about her wedding. She said she's going to start on her dress today."

"Have they set a date?"

"Not yet. Maybe around Christmas."

"So what would you like? Christmas wedding? Spring?"

"I'd like to know what happened last night at Taft's memorial service."

"Yes. I promised to keep you informed, and something definitely happened last night. Someone threw a knife from Fancy's case at Rahnee and hit her in the shoulder."

"Good lord. Is she okay?"

"Fortunately, she wasn't badly hurt. WizBoy swears he didn't do it, even though I found a little bone off his key ring backstage. Everyone else was out front. I didn't see Omar there, though."

She brought her toast and sat down across from me. "One of his grandchildren had a birthday party last night. I didn't get a chance to ask him about Jolly Bob and WAM."

"The next time you see him, ask him what he knows about Rahnee and Fancy. While you're at it, a little background on Jilly and on WizBoy might be useful, too."

"All right."

"Now that you've gone full tilt into the detective world, I expect results."

"You'll get them—even if I have to search every dark alley in Parkland."

The sparkle in her eyes told me she was teasing. Before she could say anything else, I leaned over the counter and kissed her.

"Now what was that all about?" she asked.

"A little fringe benefit from the Randall Detective Agency."

"The Randall and Ingram Detective Agency."

"That'll cost you more than a kiss."

◇◇◇

I left the house in a pretty good mood. When I stopped by the Magic Club, Rahnee was in her office. She looked pale, and her shoulder was bandaged.

I pulled up a chair. "How are you doing?"

"It hurts, but I'll manage."

I motioned to the huge flower arrangement on the desk, complete with tiny stars and top hats. "I see you have an admirer."

"They're from WizBoy."

"I wanted to talk to you about him. Is he capable of running the club?"

"We had a long discussion earlier in the week. He had some legitimate complaints and some good ideas for the club. I've decided to give him more responsibility. I know he looks like a useless teenager, but he's a hard worker, and he really knows his craft."

"You're sure no one else was backstage?"

"Just WizBoy."

"What about Jilly?"

"If she was backstage, I didn't see her. And why would she attack me?"

"Did Jilly know about your affair with Taft?"

"I don't see how. We were very discreet."

I know a thing or two about women. And one thing I know is that they *always* know.

Rahnee shifted her arm and winced. "Taft liked Jilly, but he felt she was too young for him."

"He told her this?"

"No, he was very careful not to get her hopes up. He'd stop by the bar and have a drink, maybe talk a little, but that's as far as it went."

That was far enough to get Jilly's hopes way up. "What about his offer to put her in his act?"

"I don't think he was serious. He liked working alone." Her gaze went to the flower arrangement. "WizBoy is desperately in love with her. If she'd give him a chance, he'd teach her all kinds of magic, make her his assistant, create illusions for her to perform. She doesn't realize what she's missing." She looked back to me. "That's the problem, isn't it? We don't realize what we're missing till it's gone. Taft was a wonderful man. I really should've tried harder to make things work. Do you know what I mean?"

We don't realize what we're missing till it's gone. I didn't want to go down that road. "How interested is Jolly Bob in the Finches' collection of magic memorabilia?"

"He was always after Lucas and Taft to sell him something or another from their collection. I know he offered to buy the box from them, but they wouldn't sell. They'd rather have this bet of theirs."

Would Jolly Bob have killed Taft to get his hands on the box? Would Bart?

"Do you have any idea who could've taken the box from the club?"

"No."

"Did you know Taft was the one who ended the WOW/WAM feud?"

This surprised her. "Where did you hear that?"

"The woman at Ali's Cavern. She said Taft had taken care of the problem. After Jolly Bob revealed how Omar's illusion was done, I think Taft gave Omar a new illusion, or gave him money to buy one."

Tears slid down her cheeks. "That sounds like something Taft would do. And he wouldn't want everyone to know about it. Omar's the one who caught Jolly Bob stealing? I didn't know that, either. No wonder they hate each other."

I got up. "I'm going to talk to a few more people. I'm glad you're okay."

"Thanks for telling me about Taft. He was always willing to help another magician."

And another magician was willing to shove him into a trunk. The more I learned about Taft, the more I wanted to catch his killer.

Before I left, Rahnee wrote me another check. I went to the bar, hoping to speak to Jilly, but she wasn't there. Since no one was in the club, I went around behind the bar. I found two interesting things. A playing card, the three of clubs, was wedged in a crack in the floor. Of course, since this was a magic club and practically everyone knew card tricks, I didn't think too much of it. There were probably cards wedged everywhere. But when I pulled it out, I saw a familiar pattern on the back, a pink and red paisley design. Dirk Kirk had indeed been here.

However, the more interesting thing was a box of something called Sneeze Ease. I reached for it.

An annoyed voice said, "Can I help you?"

I looked up and across the bar into Jilly's dark wary eyes. "Yes, you can. Is this yours?"

"Yes."

"I've never heard of Sneeze Ease. Do you have allergies?"

"Yes. Did you want something?"

"I want to know about the Houdini box. When Lucas first had the box, WizBoy says he brought it to the bar. Do you remember seeing it?"

"Yes. He thought he could get it open. Of course he couldn't."

"Then Lucas took it back, right?"

"Yes. After that, he decided to have this contest with all of us."

"Any money involved?"

"No. He only wanted to see if anyone could get it open." She crossed her arms. "Do you mind coming around from back there? I have work to do."

"Sorry." I came back around. "Did you know there was a card wedged in the floor?"

She took her place behind the bar and opened the register. "There are cards everywhere."

"Mind if I take this one?"

She gave me a look as if to say, why in the world would you want it? "No. Go ahead."

WizBoy came around the corner of the stage. "Randall, I want to talk to you."

"Sure. Excuse me, Jilly."

She nodded. WizBoy motioned for me to come to the stage. He kept his voice low. "Have you found out anything?"

"Not yet."

He wiped his palms on his jeans. "Man, I don't like this at all. You think the police are planning to arrest me?"

"Calm down. The police don't have any proof. Rahnee doesn't believe you threw a knife at her. She's the only one you have to worry about."

"Yeah, but I been wracking my brain trying to think of anybody I might've insulted, or anybody who wants my job here. If they think I'd hurt Rahnee, what's to keep them from thinking I murdered Taft? The police would like that. Solves both the crimes at once."

"Where do you keep your keys?"

He patted his back pocket. "Right here."

"You never take them out, set them down somewhere, loan them to anybody?"

"No, never."

"So somebody picked your pocket, took off one of the little bones, and then returned your keys before you noticed they were gone."

He scrunched up his face so hard I thought his features might fuse together. "Okay, when I first got the key ring, I showed it to everyone 'cause it was cool. Then maybe a couple of weeks ago, Rahnee left her keys at home and she used mine to lock up. I got them right back, though. And Jilly had to borrow them because she accidentally locked herself out Monday night."

"The Monday we found Taft?"

"Yeah, I remember now. She was really upset and crying and left her keys on the bar. She called me and I came over and let her in so she could get them." He looked disgusted. "I thought I was being helpful, you know, coming to the rescue and all that? Didn't make things any different between us."

"You let her in, right? She never had your keys?"

"Maybe for a minute or two. What the hell are you saying?"

"I'm saying everybody associated with WOW is supposedly good at sleight of hand."

"She'd have to be a genius at sleight of hand, and believe me, she's not."

WizBoy was getting riled and probably would have asked me to step outside had Rahnee not called for him. "WizBoy, could you come here a minute, please?"

His dark look disappeared. "Look, what do you charge to solve things? I'd better hire you."

"We can discuss that."

"Later. I'd better see what Rahnee wants."

I thought Jilly had gone, but I heard sounds behind the bar like very large mice having a party. I glanced over the bar. Jilly was down on her hands and knees, trying to get something from one of the lower compartments.

"Need some help?" I asked.

"No, thank you. I can manage." She rummaged around and pulled out a stack of towels. "Did you want to ask me something?"

"I understand you're pretty good at sleight of hand."

She gave me a wary look. "Sort of. Why?"

"Did you ever think of getting an act together for the club?"

"No. I'd rather be an assistant. It's more fun and the costumes are prettier." She stood and put the towels on a shelf behind her. She gave me a more thoughtful look. "You're a detective, right? But are you a magician, too?"

"The Remarkable Randall."

She gave me her full attention. "Do you need an assistant?"

"I might."

"Well, watch this." She went to the register and hit a button that made the drawer pop out. She got three quarters, put them on the bar, and proceeded to make them disappear.

"That's excellent."

The quarters reappeared in her hand. "I can do lots of other tricks, too."

"I'm surprised no one's hired you."

"Me, too," she said glumly.

"You don't want to work with WizBoy? He seems interested in you."

"All he wants to do is run the club and hang around with Rahnee, even though she's way too old for him."

"Sounds like you don't like her, either."

"Don't get me wrong. Sometimes I'm annoyed because she thinks she's so great and everything, but I like this job, so don't think I'd be hiding backstage throwing knives at her."

"Who would be?"

Jilly leaned forward on the bar. "I wouldn't put it past Fancy to have something rigged up in her case."

"And what's Fancy got against Rahnee?"

"She probably didn't tell you, but when both of them were starting out, Rahnee beat Fancy out for all the best jobs because Rahnee would do anything to get an audition."

"Are you saying she slept her way to the top of the magic world?"

Jilly gave me a lofty look. "That's the way I heard it."

"Intriguing stuff, Jilly, thanks."

"You're welcome."

Intriguing, but not necessarily true. Since Rahnee and Fancy were both very attractive women, I doubted they had to do anything extra to get hired. I'd seen Fancy in action, though, and it was possible she could make a knife do whatever she liked.

Jilly was rubbing her shoulder again. "Are you cold?"

She frowned. "No."

"Hurt your shoulder?"

Her expression said, None of your business, but she answered calmly enough. "Sometimes it itches."

"Okay. Just curious." Did you sprain it heaving Taft into the trunk? No, even on a good day, Jilly couldn't manage that.

◇◇◇

I found Fancy on stage at the Bombay Club, rehearsing her act. She stopped for a moment and came to the edge of the small stage area.

"David, I sincerely hope you're here to tell me you've caught whoever stabbed Rahnee."

"Wish I had good news for you, but nothing yet."

"I've got the stage for a few more minutes and then we can talk. Would you start the CD player? I need to time this part."

I sat down at one of the little tables, pressed play, and watched as Fancy made balls, hoops, and knives spin in dizzying circles above her head. Then she made everything disappear.

When she finished, I applauded, and she took a bow. The music changed from the lively rock theme to another song, something slower and sweeter. She looked startled, and then said, "Turn it off."

I pushed the off button. Fancy stood still for a moment. "You okay?" I asked.

She took another moment. "Yes, fine. I forgot that was on there. It was my sister's favorite song."

I wasn't sure what to say.

"Today's her birthday. She would've been thirty-nine. I would've teased her up one side and down the other." She came and sat down at the table with me. "She died four years ago of cancer. I think of her every single day."

"I know the feeling."

"Have you lost a sister, too, David?"

"My daughter."

"Oh, my God. I'm so sorry." Fancy's eyes sparkled with tears and suddenly, words burst out. "I still get so angry! How can you be here one moment and be gone the next? Something made you move and breathe and talk. Where's that something now?"

For years, I'd asked myself the same question. Oddly enough, I always thought of a program I'd seen about a woman grieving for her dog. She'd looked at the camera with the most anguished expression. "Where's the thing that made it go?" she'd asked. "Where's the thing that made it go?"

The thing. Life. Some impossible combination of blood and breath and nerves and personality.

Fancy's face was streaked with tears. "You're going to think I'm crazy, but every time I see something as insignificant as a bug, I get so frustrated. Bugs have it. Bugs and worms squirming on the sidewalk and gnats, for God's sake. Things that don't matter! It's still inside them. They still have it. They're still living. I don't understand."

"Me, either."

"Why can't we know what happens? What's the big secret? Why can't I know for certain my sister is happy and free from pain? What's with all the mystery?"

I put my hand on hers. I'd asked myself the same questions, over and over. I didn't have any answers. Not for her. Not for me.

Abruptly, she brushed the tears from her eyes. "Sorry for going on like that. You'd think I'd get over it. I mean, it's been four years."

If I live four hundred years, I'll never get over Lindsey's death. "Who says you have to get over it?"

"Everybody tells me it gets easier as time goes by, and she's in a better place, and you should get on with your life. Things like that. But I want to hear the truth, and the truth is I'm not going to 'get over it.'"

"No," I said. "You live through it."

"I'm sorry," she said again. "You wanted to ask me some questions?"

I was glad to change the subject. "How long have you and Rahnee known each other?"

She opened the player and took out the CD. "Since high school. We both moved to Parkland about the same time."

"Any trouble finding work?"

"Rahnee never had any trouble. Club owners took one look and hired her right away."

"What sort of act did she have?"

"Very sexy stuff. She'd dance around and make things appear and disappear. Scarves, mostly, and handkerchiefs. She was very good."

"No jealousy between the two of you?"

"No. Our acts were very different." Her eyes narrowed. "Did someone at the Magic Club suggest that to you?"

"You have to admit it's a possibility. Two extremely attractive magicians in the same town. Maybe a little rivalry going on?"

"I suppose so. Yes, okay, maybe I was a little jealous, but I found plenty of work. And I'm certainly not jealous enough to start flinging knives at anybody. What's my motive? If I attack Rahnee, no more jobs at the Magic Club for me. Word would get out I'm unstable, and then there are no more jobs for me anywhere. That's not something I'd risk." Her cell phone rang. She checked the number. "Speaking of jobs, excuse me a moment, please. This is a club in Greensboro."

I told her I'd see her later. I went out to the Fury, sat down, and took a few deep steadying breaths. When my phone rang, I wasn't surprised to see it was Camden. His voice faded in and out like an old radio station.

"I need pizza."

"What a coincidence. So do I."

Chapter Twenty-one

She Didn't Do Magic

I picked up Camden and we headed to Pokey's Pizza for some lunch.

Although I was sure he had picked up all the distress from my conversation with Fancy, he didn't comment on it. "What's new at the club? How's Rahnee?"

"She's okay. WizBoy insists he never let anyone use his keys, but he did let Rahnee borrow them one time, and he let Jilly in the club when she locked herself out. Both of these ladies are good at sleight of hand, so I guess either one could've taken a little bone off the key ring without WizBoy noticing."

"But why would Rahnee throw a knife at herself?"

"Exactly. And aside from a little natural jealousy, why would Jilly throw a knife at her? I talked with Fancy, too, and I can't see that she has any reason to attack Rahnee, either."

All the tables had little signs announcing that Pokey's was giving kids free pizza for every twenty tickets they brought in from a recycling center. This gave me an idea. While we were waiting for our pizza, I called Sandy's house and asked the housekeeper if Sandy did any recycling. She told me she took the recycling to the center on Marsh Road.

I thanked her and hung up. "Would you like to revisit your troubled dumpster-diving past and dig through some trash, a last ditch effort, so to speak?"

"I'd better eat two pizzas, then."

"Here's something to make you lose your appetite. I think someone made sure Taft had a mix of medications with a drink so he was completely disoriented when he attempted to escape from the trunk. Which reminds me. A little while ago, I found something called Sneeze Ease behind the bar. I didn't get a good look at the package, but the picture of the pill on the front looked a lot like Taft's pills." I used my phone to find Sneeze Ease and magnified the photo. "Looks the same to me." I let Camden have a look.

"But it's not a sleeping pill, is it?"

I read the package. Sneeze Ease was a local drug store chain's brand of Benadryl. "Listen to this. 'Compare to the ingredients in Benadryl.' It's diphenhydramine. That's one of the drugs Jordan said was found in Taft's body."

"You found this behind the bar?"

"Jilly said it was her allergy medicine, but anyone who knew the key to the trunk was behind the bar could've unlocked the trunk, spiked Taft's drink, and convinced him to get inside."

"That's extremely cold."

"I also found this." I produced the card. "Recognize the lovely pattern?"

"Yes, I do." Camden took the card and held it for a few moments. "This has Jilly's feet all over it."

"It was also behind the bar. Dirk said he helped himself to a drink." I took the card and put it back in my pocket. "I'll hang onto it just in case." I paused to listen to the muzak. "Do I hear 'Have To Believe We Are Magic'?"

Camden listened a moment. "Yep."

"Yet another magic song."

"Trying to tell you something?"

"I wish I could hear 'Who Done It.'"

◇◇◇

After lunch, we went to the recycling center on Marsh Road. I explained who I was and what I was looking for and asked if we could look through the recycle bins. We didn't find the bracelet, and Camden didn't get any helpful vibes. The center also had several large trash piles.

"While we're here, we might as well check those, too," I said.

The man in charge gave us some plastic gloves and showed us the places to avoid.

"Them stacks over there are from the housing development, and them stacks over yonder come from the hospital. If I was you, I'd look over there by the fence. That's the stuff what come from some of the richer neighborhoods in town."

Camden and I waded through the trash for about an hour. I found a pretty nice belt, and Camden found a perfectly good baseball cap, but mainly it was garbage and soggy things we didn't want to inspect too closely.

Camden peeled something sticky from his sneakers. "This really is above and beyond my duties as a sidekick."

"I thought you liked this kind of thing."

"Every now and then I touch something that gives me a real kick in the brain. You wouldn't think a disposable aluminum pan would have bad vibes, but whoever cooked that dinner was madder than hell about something."

"Why can't you be like one of those dousing rods and pinpoint the bracelet?"

"Why can't you have a better idea than this?"

"Because I've run out of ideas, and I hate to admit defeat."

Camden dug through another plastic trash bag. "Oh, look. A baseball to go with my hat." He rooted around for the ball and came up with another object. "Here's a broken cell phone. Too bad it's not Taft's."

"Yes, where the hell's his phone? He gets the call while he's in Charlotte, rushes back to the Magic Club, meets the killer, gets killed, and that's it. If he left the phone in his car, the police would've found it. If it was in his pocket, or fell out in the trunk, the police would've found it."

"What about a coat pocket?"

"I checked the coat he left in Rahnee's office."

"As cold as it's been, he would've had on another coat Saturday night, right?"

"Good question. I'll have to check."

We searched for another hour and then decided we were too cold and too smelly to continue. It's fortunate that there's more than one shower at Grace Street. When I'd finished with mine, I went down to the island. On the coffee table was a shoe box set on its side with paper figures stuck inside. Something from one of Kary's students, no doubt, a diorama, I think they call them. I'd helped Lindsey make one about dinosaurs. I remembered how each little paper tree had to be placed exactly right and how she delighted in having a real clay volcano with red lava spilling over the side.

Damn.

I thought of the DVD, and for a moment, considered watching it.

No, not yet. Maybe never. But it was almost impossible to resist. To see that shining little face…

Not yet.

Camden came in, buttoning his faded blue corduroy robe, his wet hair in spikes. He went past me into the kitchen with only the slightest hesitation. I knew he could feel my emotions like waves of heat off a hot pavement, but he always knew when I wasn't in the mood to discuss them. He came back with a large plastic cup of Coke and sat on the sofa. The blue robe had faded in stages, so the sleeves and collar were darker than the rest, and the buttons were secured with large safety pins.

"There's something else you're going to have to get rid of," I said.

"Not this. This is my favorite robe."

"Out with the garbage, pal. Trust me."

He looked down at the worn sleeves. "I won't marry her, then."

The back door slammed, and Rufus came in. I'm sure there's some bizarre southern saying that would describe how he looked, like "a deer in headlights," or "a possum on New Year's."

"Whew! There's more to this wedding business than I thought! How'd you go through it twice, Randall?"

"All I had to do was show up."

Rufus sank down on the other end of the sofa. "Well, there's pictures and flowers and invitations and a cake and I don't know what all. Angie's gone wild. You two have got to come up to snuff and propose. I ain't going through this nonsense by myself."

"Sorry," I said. "Camden's been saved by a ratty bathrobe."

"What in hell's a 'soiree'? Angie said we were gonna have one. She's makin' it up, ain't she?"

"No, it's a twenty-dollar word that means an evening party."

"Well, why didn't she just say so?" He rubbed his face, and his beard stuck out in all directions. "Maybe this ain't such a good idea."

"Don't cry off now," I said. "We'll never find your body."

"I had in mind we'd invite some friends down to the Crow Bar, have a little ceremony, beer, pretzels, a little cake, maybe, and ride off to Dollywood for the weekend."

"Oh, no. You have to understand that most women start dreaming about their wedding day in the womb and have extravagant plans for exactly how it's supposed to be."

"We can't do extravagant. She has to know that. She said she's making her dress and the dresses for the bridesmaids. We got to cut corners wherever we can."

"I'll be glad to take care of the music," Camden said, "and I'm sure Kary will help, and Randall can walk you through it. Don't panic. It'll all work out."

Rufus pointed a large tobacco-stained finger at him. "You remember that when it's your turn. Why ain't you asked Ellin, anyway?"

"There's this little problem of my voice."

"Ha, ha. If she's so hot for you, she won't care if you use sign language." He pointed to me. "And what about you?"

"I ask Kary every day. You've heard me. She keeps turning me down."

"Yeah, well, she's a smart girl." He smacked his hands on his knees and stood up. "Well, I guess there's no help for it now. The hay is in the barn."

I looked to Camden for clarification. "It's a done deal," he said.

Rufus left, still grumbling. "'Soiree.' What's wrong with just sayin' 'party' like normal people do?"

We watched him go. "Should we worry?" I asked.

"No, he'll be all right."

I glanced at the clock. "Oh, look, we're in time for the Oracle. Want to see it?"

"Might as well."

I turned on the TV in time to catch a commercial for Leaf Express. "At least they've got a new sponsor."

"Do we have Dirk to thank for that?"

"I doubt it."

The commercial ended and the camera unfortunately had to zero in on Sheila, who was looking even more insufferably pleased with herself than usual.

"Today, as promised, I have the Healing Wonder, the Delphic Secret Revealed!"

I sat back and put my feet up. "Gosh, I'm glad we didn't miss it."

"Yes, viewers and listeners of all ages, your cares are over. I can See and Know All."

"Thought that was your trick, Camden."

Sheila spread out both hands and then brought them together as if ready to pray. "Your prayers have been answered. I have heeded your calls. Today, anyone can be healed of any physical or mental distress, thanks to this remarkable treasure!" She motioned to something under a cloth on the table in front of her, something unmistakably rectangular.

By now, we were leaning forward in disbelief.

Sheila flung the cloth aside. "And here it is!"

"Camden," I said, "what are we looking at?"

He said it for both of us in his faint voice. "The Houdini box."

◇◇◇

We got dressed and rushed to the studio as Sheila was "healing" a member of the audience. Ellin had been standing by, looking bored, but when Camden and I burst in, she gave us a glare and motioned for quiet.

"Where's Dirk?" I asked.

"He's over there, but—"

Camden and I hurried to the other side of the audience where Dirk Kirk was trying to get someone to pick a card. Things started to make sense to me now. Lucas had told me when he went to check on the box on Thursday it wasn't in its hiding place behind the cinder block. What if whoever took it hid it behind the bar? Monday morning, after another failed audition, Dirk had stopped by the bar to help himself to a drink. He dropped some of his cards, as usual. When he stooped down to retrieve them, what if he saw the box and decided he was entitled to it?

Had the box been sitting under there since Thursday? Why didn't anyone look for it there? And who put it there in the first place?

"Dirk," I said, "Where'd you get that box?"

He gulped and turned a very guilty shade of red.

"Did someone give it to you?"

"No, I took it."

"You took it. You mean you stole it."

"Those people at the Magic Club kept turning me down. Said I wasn't good enough. Well, I took the box without them noticing, didn't I? They're not so smart. And Mother said it'd be perfect. It has a 'H' on it for 'healing,' so I gave it to her."

"You stole the box from the Magic Club. Was it behind the bar?"

"What does it matter? It's mine now."

Ellin had followed us. "Randall, what is going on?"

"Mister Dim Bulb here stole that box from the Magic Club."

She couldn't help a brief grin of triumph before she schooled her features into their usual businesslike expression. "I hope you can prove that. That's a serious accusation."

"When's the next commercial break? I want a word with the Oracle."

"There's one in about two minutes."

As soon as the commercial was on, Dirk ran out to the set and grabbed the box. "It's mine."

Sheila gaped at him. She'd probably never seen him move so fast. "What in the world is going on?"

"Give it here, you dope," I said. "It doesn't belong to you."

He gave me what I'm sure he thought was a sneer. "You must think I'm really stupid."

"No, I think you're beyond stupid. You are stupid squared. Stupid in three-D. A steaming stupid hunk of moron pie."

Dirk blinked. "Oh, yeah?"

Sheila was about to pop. "How dare you speak to Dirk that way!"

Reg waved frantically. "Clear the set! The commercial's almost over!"

Dirk and I got off the set. Sheila rearranged her features into something resembling affability. "Welcome back! It's time for some calls from our listeners, and then I have another special announcement."

Dirk stood with the box under his arm, still glaring. "It's my box."

Ellin faced me, hands on hips. "Randall, this had better be good."

"I think you'll enjoy it. Last Saturday, Dirk went to the Magic Club to audition and was turned down, so he went back on Monday to try again and happened to have the opportunity to take that box. It belongs to my client, Lucas Finch, so I'm taking it back to him. Oh, and by the way, it's involved with a murder investigation."

"If you can get it away from Dirk, do it. It's certainly not going to make things any easier around here."

Sheila spoke to the viewers. "I realize that not everyone is as truly gifted as I am. I plan, like the great Harry Houdini, to hunt down all the fake and fraudulent magicians, faith healers, and psychics who prey upon the unsuspecting citizens of Parkland."

"What's this?" I asked Ellin.

"Her latest crusade."

"I thought she was going to heal people."

"I think she's realized that's harder than it looks." She let out a long breath. "I want my show back but not if it's going to be like this."

This was in direct conflict with her love of money. "Are you actually having a moral dilemma?"

I'm not sure what she would've replied, but Phil Kirk arrived, looking stern. "Ellin, a word with you, please."

I saw her stiffen. "What can I do for you, Phil?"

"I understand there was a problem Wednesday after the show."

Ellin has a blank look that's perfect for situations like this. "A problem?"

"Someone in the audience was questioning Sheila's predictions, arguing with her, talking to people afterward." He glanced at Camden. "Cameron, is it?"

"Camden," he said.

"Mister Camden, your actions were quite upsetting to her. If she's hosting the show, that kind of thing shouldn't happen."

"I believe there may have been a difference of opinion."

"I don't see how that's possible when Sheila's predictions are always accurate. We can't haveg anyone questioning her." He turned back to Ellin. "I don't want this man in the studio audience again. He's a disruptive influence."

About that time, Sheila finished whatever idiotic thing she was saying and came running to her husband.

"That's him! He's not to be anywhere near me or Dirk. I wish you could've heard the horrible things he called our son."

I raised my hand. "I take credit for the horrible things."

Phil Kirk did not appreciate this. "Perhaps both of you should leave."

"We're on our way," I said. "But first, I need that box. I was hired by Lucas Finch to find it. It belongs to him."

"Are you certain this is his box?"

"Yes, and I'd rather not involve the police."

"The police? Now wait a minute."

"Dirk took the box from the Magic Club." Phil puffed up to protest, but I saw a way out for everyone. "It was only a trick, right, Dirk? To show everyone your magical talents?" For stealing. "How 'bout if I take it back and explain things to the owner? He'll be happy to have it. I doubt he'll press charges."

When I mentioned the police, Dirk looked frightened, as if the seriousness of what he'd done was finally sinking in, but he had enough sense to recognize a lifeline. "It was just a trick."

"That's what I thought. Hand it over."

Phil Kirk's anger deflated. He gave his son a long thoughtful look. "Did you take the box?"

Dirk hung his head.

Sheila put a hand to her considerable bosom. "I don't believe it. Dirk, you told me someone gave it to you."

"No," he said. "I took it."

Sheila's mouth opened and then closed. She looked at me but didn't say anything.

Phil Kirk's attitude changed completely. "I think Mr. Randall is being more than generous here." He took the box and handed it to me. "My apologies."

"No problem."

"Dirk, come with me. We need to talk. Sheila, you, too."

Amazingly, she still didn't say anything. She followed her husband and son out.

Ellin watched them go, and then turned a wide gaze to us. "Guys, what was that all about? Is Dirk a suspect in the murder case?"

"He could be," I said.

"That would be ideal. Please find some proof that Dirk is the murderer." She laughed. "'Dirk Kirk: Murderer.' It's even fun to say."

"What we're going to do first is take this box to Lucas," I said. "I want to see what's inside."

Chapter Twenty-two

Midnight Magic

When I called Lucas to tell him I'd found the box, he said, "Oh, my God, that's wonderful news."

"We'll be over there in a few minutes."

"Thank you!"

On the way, Camden held the box in his lap. The box was shiny warm brown wood with a fancy "H" on top, carved with curlicues, flowers, rabbits, hoops, and stars. I didn't see any way to open it.

"Randall, what was Houdini's message to his wife?"

"'Rosabelle, believe.'"

His hand hovered over the lid. Then he pressed down on a carved rose, then a series of stars, and back to the rose. A panel slid back, revealing a red velvet-lined drawer. It was empty.

"Uh, oh," Camden said.

"Can you tell who took it?"

He felt inside the panel. "No." He shut the little drawer.

"I know why whoever has the key hasn't come forward in triumph. That person probably had something to do with Taft's death, and they don't really care about claiming a prize from the cabinet."

◇◇◇

Lucas was waiting for us at the door. His hands trembled as he took the box.

"I don't know how to thank you."

"Well, you can open the box and let us see the key," I said.

"Of course! Come in, come in."

Once inside, Lucas made the same series of touches on the rose and stars until the drawer slid out. Lucas stared. "What the hell?" He shook the box. "But that's impossible!"

"Tell me the truth," I said. "Were you going to play fair? Did you really put the cabinet key in the box?"

"Yes! I knew no one could figure out the sequence. I knew our collection was safe."

"That's one reason you and Taft argued, isn't it? He didn't want you to risk the collection."

Lucas wearily rubbed his face. For a moment, I didn't think he was going to answer. "Yes."

"Did Taft know how to open the box? Would he have taken the key?"

"He knew the trick, but he wouldn't have taken the key out. He might have been angry with me, but we don't go back on our word. I made a legitimate bet with all the members of WOW." He turned the box in all directions, as if hoping somehow the key would fall out. "Where could it be? What's going on?"

"I think we can assume someone else figured out how to open the box."

"Then why not come to me and say, 'I've won the bet'?"

"Maybe since Taft died they wanted to wait a while."

"Jolly Bob wouldn't wait. Neither would WizBoy. They'd both be too proud of themselves. Where did you find the box? You didn't say."

"Someone had taken it for a joke. We tracked it down."

Lucas smoothed the lid of the box. "I don't suppose it matters as long as I have it back. And I am grateful to have it back, don't get me wrong. I only wish I knew what happened to the key."

So did I.

◇◇◇

On our way home, I got a call from Kary.

"David, if you want to see me in Omar's magic act, you can come to the rehearsal right now."

"Okay, where are you?"

"We're at Robertson Elementary School. The principal said we could practice in their auditorium if we did a show for the students later this month."

"We're on our way."

◇◇◇

Kary's costume was fantastic. She did have on tights, and the costume was a bit dance hall girl on top, but since Omar's act involved scarves, the short skirt was made of multicolored bits of filmy material that was really quite pretty. She waved, and Omar motioned us in.

"Come sit down front. I like having an audience."

The school auditorium had recently been remodeled, so the chairs had comfortable seats, and the stage had new curtains. Camden and I sat down next to the janitor, the cleaning ladies, and several interested-looking teachers who must have been working late and needed a break.

Kary introduced the Ring Master and handed him his first set of rings. He made them leap about, hook together and unhook, and ended with them all in a chain. Then he shook them free, and as each one bounced, Kary caught it gracefully on her arm and set them back on the table. Then she handed him a smaller set. He continued with his act, but I watched Kary. She stood in one pose while he did another trick and did a little dancing move when he needed a distraction. I could tell she was having the time of her life.

Camden leaned over. "She's doing really well."

"Think she'll run away with the circus?"

When Omar finished with the rings, Kary handed him three scarves which he turned into six scarves and then more and more until the stage was littered with them. Kary then brought him a top hat. He showed us the hat was empty. She helped him scoop all the scarves into the hat. He tapped the hat three times, and she reached in and pulled out a kitten. We applauded.

Omar bowed. "Thank you very much. I am Omar the Ring Master, and this is my lovely assistant, Kary." Kary took a bow. "Thank you for coming to our show."

There were compliments all around from the teachers, janitor, and cleaning crew.

"Great job," I told Kary.

She was still cuddling the kitten. "Thanks. That was only part of the act. We have a longer set for the Magic Club."

"It's a little early, but Camden and I would like to take you out for a victory dinner."

"Okay, let me change clothes and help Omar pack everything. And I have some information for you."

"You don't have to change clothes."

She gave a little twirl. "Oh, I think so."

◇◇◇

We took Kary to the Elms, a nice restaurant near the shopping center, and ordered their special of the day, which was fried shrimp and salad. While we waited for our order, Kary brought in her laptop and set it on the table.

"Omar knew quite a lot about Fancy, including her webpage address." Fancy's web page was elaborately decorated with stars and sparkles. "Fancy is her actual given name, and she's been a professional magician for ten years. Here are some reviews of her act and links to some of her performances on YouTube. That's where I found this."

A few more clicks and we were treated to the sight of a younger Fancy and a tall redhead performing together on what appeared to be a stage in a high school auditorium. The quality of the film wasn't the best, but I could tell the redhead was Rahnee, even though the clip was titled "Fancy Henderson and Rhonda Nevis, Tellareed High School Talent Show." She made some cards disappear, and Fancy did her trademark juggling act, only the younger Fancy used traditional clubs instead of knives.

"Looks like they worked together for a while." Kary let the clip run to the end and then took us to another page. "Here they are when they were a little older."

The young women shimmered in golden spotlights. Rahnee's hair glowed red while Fancy had opted for a shiny pink shade, and they both wore form-fitting black velvet suit jackets and black tights. I'd seen acts where the magician and his assistant magically change places, but the women put their own spin on the illusion by standing in two tubes that filled with swirls of metallic confetti. When the confetti settled, Rahnee was in Fancy's tube, and Fancy was in Rahnee's. Even viewed on the computer screen, it was a dazzling effect.

"Omar said Rahnee also went by RhoAnn, so I tried that name and this came up," Kary said. Here was a glamour shot of a younger Rahnee captioned "RhoAnn." "She modeled for a while and then took up magic again. The rest of the sites show her act, and the latest one is for the Magic Club."

"That corresponds with what I know," I said. "She and Fancy may have had a little rivalry, but nothing so serious that they'd attack each other."

The Magic Club website featured a picture of the club's grand opening. Fancy and Rahnee stood on stage together with another group of magicians, all smiles.

Kary pointed to Lucas and Taft Finch. "There are the Finch brothers. They all look so happy, don't they?"

"Well, we managed to cheer up Lucas a little. We found the box. You'll never guess who had it. Dirk Kirk."

"How in the world did he get it?"

The waitress brought our food, and after she'd gone I explained what had happened.

Kary closed her laptop and set it beside her. "But didn't Lucas look everywhere in the club?"

"I'm thinking the box wasn't there until Monday."

"Someone took it, hid it, then brought it back to the club on Monday? Why?"

"I don't know. But it was there, and when Dirk saw it, he decided the club owed it to him. Despite the fact he always dropping things, he has sticky fingers. Ellin said things were missing from the studio. From the way the Kirks reacted, I think he's stolen things before."

"Does this mean the Kirks will go away?"

"We can only hope. Good work, by the way."

"You see? There are ways to find facts."

"And you've already got a gig at the school."

"Omar says he does a lot of school performances. He'd like for more kids to take an interest in magic."

Especially if they see you standing there, I wanted to say.

Camden put another pack of sweetener in his tea. "How did he do that trick with the kitten?"

"I am sworn to secrecy." She chose a fat shrimp from the platter, and after eating it in two bites, set the tail on her plate. "Okay, here's what Omar told me when I asked him about the big WOW/WAM controversy. As you'd guessed, he was just starting out and got a chance to perform at Ali's Cavern. He'd worked hard and paid a lot of money for a special illusion called the Dancing Fire. He kept an eye on Jolly Bob because he knew Jolly Bob had a reputation for stealing other magician's tricks and passing them off as his own, only Jolly Bob would change things a little so it wasn't exactly the same trick. When he caught Jolly Bob taking a younger magician's trick, he told everyone at the Cavern. In retaliation, Jolly Bob told everyone how the Dancing Fire was done. Things were getting really heated between the two groups of magicians until Taft stepped in and gave Omar enough money to buy a new illusion."

"I knew it had to be something like that," I said.

Camden slid a shrimp through a pool of ketchup. "So a WOW magician crossed the picket line to aid someone from WAM."

"Which brought peace to the land, except for Jolly Bob, who was banned from Ali's Cavern."

I unwrapped the crackers that came with my salad. "And the Magic Club. Rahnee doesn't want him there. When I first talked to Omar about Taft, he said, 'I owe him a lot.' Now we know he wasn't talking about Taft giving him handy tips about magic tricks. Taft saved Omar's career."

"That's what it looks like." Kary wiped her fingers on her napkin. "Omar did say something else about Jolly Bob that might be interesting. Jolly Bob is a fanatical collector of magic memorabilia. Omar said he covets the Finches' collection. He's tried to buy it from them several times. Omar said one night before all the trouble started, a group of magicians had a party and Jolly Bob got a little drunk and told him the only way to have real magic was to possess things that had belonged to the famous magicians of the past."

"Like Houdini."

"Especially Houdini."

"So Jolly Bob feels if he could get his hands on the Finches' magic treasures, he'd be the greatest magician of them all?"

"That's what it sounds like."

"Would he be desperate enough to kill for those treasures? I'm not sure."

Camden signaled the waitress for more tea. "Why wasn't Omar in on the Finches' Find the Box contest?"

"He and his wife were celebrating their anniversary out of town when all that happened. He said he didn't have an interest in the box, anyway. He's not a member of WOW. He said as long as Jolly Bob is part of the group, he doesn't want to join, and I don't blame him. Jolly Bob sounds like a big loser."

He is, I thought, *but sometimes big losers have big grudges.*

◇◇◇

Omar had given Kary a smaller set of rings and some scarves. Back in the island at home, I stood in for the magician as she practiced her assistant moves. Camden sat on the sofa, drinking more Coke. Cindy hopped up next to him and curled up in his lap.

"You're good," I said. "Thinking of moving up in the magic world?"

She caught the next ring and slid it gracefully up her arm. "You never know. Try the scarves next."

"Does he pull them out one by one, or all in a string?"

"One by one."

I put the scarves in my pocket and pretended to make them magically appear. Cindy was immediately interested in the bits of shiny cloth. Her eyes moved back and forth as Kary presented each scarf.

She handed me the scarves. "Thanks. You remember you said getting a look at Baby Love's financial records might be tricky? Well, what if Omar and I do a magic show at their next meeting, and while he's dazzling them with his tricks and doing all sorts of misdirections with kittens, I could sneak around the house and maybe get into the owner's computer."

She was facing me, and behind her back Camden's eyes went wide at her suggestion and at what I might do. I'm sure he heard my first thought, which was *Have you gone completely crazy?* but I didn't say this out loud. "Aren't you a vital part of the act? Wouldn't you need to be there during the show?"

"For the first part, yes, but at parties Omar likes to do little sleight of hand tricks, like WizBoy did that night at the club. I'd ask to use the bathroom and take a quick look around. It's the perfect cover."

I grasped for any possible straw. "Is it likely the folks at Baby Love would want a magic show?"

"That part might need work. And I'll need to convince Omar. But at least I have a plan."

"You'd have to know the owner's password," Camden said in a vain attempt to dissuade her.

She gave a little wave. "There could be all kinds of evidence lying around. Checkbooks, receipts, photographs. It's worth a shot."

It's not worth you getting shot, I thought, and I know Camden picked up on that one. "Don't rush into this, okay? Make sure you know everything you can about the owner, the house, the rest of the guests."

"I will be amazingly careful."

She went upstairs, no doubt planning how to get her hands on some explosives. Camden and I looked at each other.

"Let it go," he said.

"I'm going to have to."

◇◇◇

I made several more phone calls to pawnshops and jewelry stores searching for Sandy's bracelet. Fred grumped about not being able to go to the grocery store until Camden showed him the cabinets full of food. He continued to fuss until Camden made him a sandwich. Rufus and Angie didn't come in. I wondered if Rufus had convinced his sweetie to elope, or if her demands for a soiree had been the deal breaker and the hay in the barn had gone up in flames.

Around nine o'clock, I saw Ellin's car drive up, and in a few minutes, Camden greeted her at the door.

"I thought you might like to hear the latest on the Dirk Kirk incident," she said. "It's not all good news."

As I may have mentioned before, my office is perfectly positioned for eavesdropping, and if I lean over a little, I can see most of the island.

Ellin shooed Cindy off the sofa before she sat down. "Dirk had all the missing items from the studio in the trunk of his car. Phil Kirk apologized again. He said they thought this problem was over, and if Dirk had something to occupy his time, like helping Sheila run the PSN, he wouldn't feel compelled to take things."

"What happens now?"

"Sheila wanted to stay, but Phil didn't think that was a good idea. He can't babysit Dirk. Well, let me put it this way. He won't babysit Dirk. But someone has to, or their son will end up in jail. Neither Phil nor Sheila could handle that sort of social embarrassment. Phil said he would continue to donate to the show, but he asked if I would please not say anything about Dirk's kleptomania."

"Which gave you the ideal leverage to kick Sheila out."

"No! Would you believe she had the gall to suggest she could be a special guest star? Now what I am going to do? Can one of these magicians you're dealing with make her disappear? Does Randall know how to dispose of a body?" I was surprised to hear Ellin's voice catch. "I'm never going to get rid of her."

"Well, it sounds like you need another guest star," Camden said. "Maybe somebody who's the real thing."

The silence that followed was so long, I figured Ellin had fallen over from shock. Then she said, "Do you mean it?"

"If you can wait till my voice improves, I'll come read a few people."

Another long pause. Another slightly uneven reply. "That would be great, thank you."

The sounds that followed meant a lot of thank you was going on.

I had to admire Ellin's sheer stubbornness. Her family was well-to-do, and her father could've bought the PSN, but Ellin had refused his help. She had something to prove, not only to her parents, but to her two older sisters, who had teased her all her life. Being in charge of the PSN gave her that edge, and Camden agreeing to be on the show was a huge concession—and, come to think of it, possibly part of his master plan.

"Ellie, there's something I wanted to ask you."

"Hold that thought, baby. I need to make some phone calls and get things going. I'm so excited! You'll love it, I promise, and maybe even consider being a regular."

She hurried past my office door, phone already to her ear. "Bonnie, you will never believe what happened."

She was out the front door and down the porch steps before I got to the island. Camden gave me a wry grin, and I held up my thumb and forefinger, inches apart.

"Close. So close."

◇◇◇

Much later that night, Camden and I decided to watch the Creature Feature on Channel 61. I was tired from my lack of success and from grubbing around through the trash, and I fell asleep as Gamera, the giant space turtle, careened into space.

I dreamed a moving van backed up to the house, and movers started bringing in baby beds and cribs and strollers. Then they brought in a large trunk. One mover handed me a key. "It's all yours, pal," he said. When I unlocked the trunk, it was full of babies, laughing and gurgling. And Lindsey was there in her white lace dress, her long brown curls tied with white ribbons. She picked up one of the babies and held it out to me.

"It's okay, Daddy. You can have one."

"No," I said. "I don't want another baby. I want you."

I shook myself awake. I took a deep breath and looked around. It was midnight. I was in the blue armchair in the island, and Camden was asleep on the green sofa. The only light came from the TV as Gamera swam off into the sunset.

A trunk full of babies. Good lord.

Then Camden sat up, alert. "Someone's outside."

"What?"

"Someone's at the back door."

"Didn't you lock it?"

"I thought you did."

"Let's hide and see who comes in."

We turned off the TV, crept into my office, and laid low. We heard the kitchen door open. Someone shuffled around in the kitchen and then footsteps came toward the island. When we jumped out and turned on the light, there was Jolly Bob, clutching the shoebox diorama and blinking and gulping like a toad.

"Can we help you?" I asked.

He glanced down at his prize, realized what he was holding, and almost dropped the box. "I'm awfully sorry! I thought of some useful information for your case and it couldn't wait, so I stopped by. Your door was open. I found this on the floor." He set the shoebox gently on the table. "Such a charming thing! Some child's treasured project, I'm sure."

"Camden, you have to admire this guy's nerve." I advanced on Jolly Bob. "Do you honestly think we'd leave the Houdini box on the coffee table?"

He looked around eagerly. "So you do have it?"

"No, and what makes you think we'd give it to you if we did?"

"I merely want to see it."

"Bob," I said, "let me introduce you to a wonderful new invention. It's called a telephone. You can actually stay in your own home and connect to our house and say, 'I'd like to come over and see if you have a special box.' And we'd say no, and you'd save yourself some embarrassment at one in the morning."

"Well, I'm sorry. I thought surely by now you would have found it. Didn't you go to Charlotte and speak to those ruffians at WAM?"

"Yeah, let's talk about those ruffians at WAM. Taft Finch paid them off, didn't he? You stole one of their tricks, Omar called you on it, you revealed one of his secrets, and then Taft stepped in to make sure everything was taken care of."

He spluttered for words. "What? What are you talking about?"

"You have a reputation of borrowing other magicians' tricks. You stole one off a kid, and you probably told Omar he'd never work again if he ratted on you. But Omar wasn't intimidated. When he let people know what you'd done, you turned on him and ruined his act. Taft did the honorable thing and gave Omar enough money to create a new illusion, even though Omar was working for WAM at the time. That's why Taft was welcome at Ali's Cavern, but you weren't, and that's why Omar owed Taft his career."

Jolly Bob wouldn't back down. "Don't people say that imitation is the sincerest form of flattery?"

"People also say, 'Thou shalt not steal,'" Camden said.

"And 'Thou shalt not kill,'" I said. "You were angry with Omar, but I'll bet you were even angrier with Taft."

This time, Jolly Bob blanched. "I didn't kill Taft! Paying for Omar's illusion was his idea, and didn't cost me anything. I didn't want to work at the Cavern, anyway. Bunch of amateurs. What's my motive?"

"You seem pretty anxious to get your hands on the Houdini box."

"That doesn't make me a murderer!"

"At any rate, you're too late. I'm happy to report I found the box and returned it to Lucas. So if you want to see it, go break into his house. I'm sure he'll be delighted to see you."

"You found it? Where?"

"If you'd been watching the Psychic Service Network this afternoon, you would've found it, too. A somewhat careless magician named Dirk Kirk borrowed it to prove he could make something disappear. Once I explained things to him, he wanted to return it to its rightful owner. Why? What's it to you?"

"Are you insane? It belonged to Houdini. What magician wouldn't want it?"

"Enough to break into our house?"

Jolly Bob sat down in the blue armchair, defeated. "You wouldn't understand."

"We've got all night, Bob. Actually, we've got all morning. Start talking."

I didn't think he'd say anything, but once he started talking, words poured out.

"You probably won't believe me, but I used to be an excellent magician. I could get bookings anywhere. I even caught bullets with my teeth, one of the most dangerous tricks a magician can do. And then some new upstarts came along with bigger and better illusions. Disappearing skyscrapers! Disappearing islands! Not one tiger, but a whole cage full. I couldn't compete. Then I heard about this special box. Really magic, everyone said. Survived a fire that destroyed a lot of Houdini's memorabilia. Get hold of that box, and your future as a magician was secure. So naturally, I started looking for it. I found out that the Finch brothers had it, but they didn't want to sell it. Then Lucas makes this bet. I thought, well, if I can get the box open and can have anything I want, I'm taking the box."

"But you couldn't find the box, so you decided to get rid of Taft?"

"I told you, I'm not a murderer. I might stoop to petty theft, but I'd never murder anyone. All I wanted was that box."

The hope in his voice was pathetic. "Bob," Camden said, "it's only a box. Maybe Houdini had one like it, but it's only a replica. It won't change your life or help your career."

Jolly Bob sighed. "Kid, do you have any idea what it's like to want one thing all your life?"

"I certainly do."

"Then let me have my little dream, okay? And you can't know for certain it's not a real Houdini box."

Camden knew for certain, of course, but I let that pass. "Why did you think the box was here?" I asked.

"When you came into the store the other day, you were asking about a box just like it. And last night, you were at the memorial service and WizBoy said you were a detective. I found your address in the phone book. I figured you were actively searching for the box and maybe you had some leads."

"Again, may I point out the telephone as an excellent communication device."

"I know, I know. I just thought I'd stop by. I happened to look in and see a box and, well—look, I apologize for coming in uninvited. If it's all right with you, I'll let myself out."

"Call next time, Bob."

Gathering what was left of his dignity, Jolly Bob made his exit out the kitchen door. I locked the door behind him and turned to Camden.

"Well, what do you think of that?"

"It confirms what Kary told us. Jolly Bob's a crazed collector."

"But is he a murderer? That's what I'd like to know."

Chapter Twenty-three

Magic Time

Saturday morning, Camden's boss Tamara called to ask him to watch the store for an hour, so I dropped him off at the boutique and went to the Magic Club. I'd gotten Taft's cell phone number from Lucas, and although I imagined Taft's phone was turned off or the battery needed recharging, I thought it would be worth a shot to call his number. With any luck, a little ringtone would lead me to the missing phone. I tried outside the club, at the front, and around the back. No answer. Lucas' phone was black like mine, but he'd told me Taft's phone was red. A red cell phone would have been easy to spot. If the killer ditched it outside, anyone could've found it.

Inside the club, the only sound was WizBoy sweeping the stage. When he saw me, he stopped sweeping and came over to me.

"I'm really nervous, Randall. That big policeman was here earlier. I know he thinks I had something to do with that knife. He'd probably like to get me for Taft's murder, too."

"You remember what Taft's cell phone looks like?"

"Yeah, it's red."

"Any place in here where you could hide a cell phone?"

"I can think of a few. I'll help you look."

There were some likely looking places backstage, but no cell phone.

I pointed to the rack of costumes. "What about all these costumes? Did he ever use those?"

"Not that I know of. He didn't need a coat like Bart's with all the pockets."

I checked all the pockets in all the outfits hanging on the costume rack. Nothing. Even though I knew the police had done a thorough search, WizBoy and I looked in the dressing rooms, the storage closets, and the trash cans. We looked behind cabinets and benches and all over the bar.

WizBoy gave up. "It's long gone by now. If it was thrown out, probably some kid has it and deleted everything. Or maybe the killer flushed it." He slumped down on a bar stool. "You don't think it was me, do you?"

"Well, you lied about playing the Bombay Club and you lied about the box. Maybe you lied about where you were on Sunday."

I thought he'd leap up, ready for a fight, but he just sat. "Don't look too good, does it?"

My phone rang. It was Camden calling to let me know Tamara was back and I could come pick him up. I closed my phone. "If it's any consolation, Wiz, you're one of many suspects."

◇◇◇

The faceless metallic mannequins in the window of Tamara's Boutique wore long drapes of fur and leather that I know cost an ungodly amount of money. Camden was at the register ringing up a sale for a tall lean woman, the only kind of woman who could wear Tamara's designs. The woman thanked him and clipped out of the store in her stiletto-heeled boots.

"Another exciting day at the boutique," I said.

"It's payday."

"Then you buy the pizza."

As he opened the register to take out his paycheck, I heard a buzzing sound.

Camden sighed and reached into his pocket.

"I don't believe it," I said. "Your cell phone's on?"

"I'm giving it a try." He looked at the screen. "Another voice mail from Ellie." He listened to the message. "She's heard from Phil Kirk. She says I can forward this to you. How do I do that?"

I took his phone and showed him. "Not that I need to get messages from Ellin." I handed the phone back to him. "Have you seen the happy couple today?"

"They left the house early to go to House of Pies for breakfast and a discussion. Rufus told me he thinks an outdoor country style wedding might appeal to Angie."

"Will it?"

"It might. Rufus has about sixteen cousins in Celosia, and most of them live on a very nice farm. Very picturesque."

I couldn't get over the sixteen cousins. "Do they all look like Rufus?"

"Pretty much."

"Yee-hah." I clicked on Ellin's message. Her voice sounded triumphant. "'Cam, Phil stopped by this morning to thank me for giving Sheila a chance to show her psychic talents to the world and to assure me he'd continue his support of the network. Forward this to Randall and tell him problem solved.' Well, let's hope so. Nice of her to include me in the message." Then something hit me. "Wait a minute." I stood so long, amazed by my idea, that Camden said, "What?"

"I think I know how to find Taft's killer." I punched in Lucas' number. "We need to set up a meeting at Lucas' house."

"A meeting?"

"No, even better, magic show, and invite the members of WOW, plus Fancy and Bart."

"Assemble everyone in the library and reveal the murderer?"

"Something like that."

"But how will you get them to come?"

"Everybody wants something. I'll tell Rahnee Lucas I found something special of Taft's he wants her to have. I'll tell WizBoy his name will be cleared. I'll tell Fancy there's news about her knife. I'll mention to Jolly Bob and Bart that Lucas is selling some of his collection and they might get a chance to buy the box. And I'll invite Jordan, too."

"You'd better let Kary in on this, too."

"Good idea."

"What about Jilly?"

"That's easy. I'm going to ask her to be my assistant. But first, we're going to Box-It. I want the clerk to show me how to use that two-sided paper."

◇◇◇

As I'd hoped, everyone assembled at Lucas' house around seven that evening, their expressions curious and eager. Jilly had been extremely pleased when I asked her to assist with my act.

"It starts out simple," I told her. "Camden's going to read minds. Then I will reveal a secret that will astound everyone."

She directed a baleful glance at Kary, who was sitting on the arm of the sofa. "You're sure you don't want to use her? Why is she here, anyway?"

"She's new at this. She's here to learn from the best."

Jilly assumed a superior air. "What else do you want me to do?"

I handed her my phone. "You'll see. I'll ask for that in a minute."

There was a lot of discussion about the box, which Lucas held in his lap. Fancy and Rahnee sat with him on the sofa. Jolly Bob had commandeered the best chair, while WizBoy and Bart stood somewhat awkwardly to one side.

I got everyone's attention. "Thank you for coming. I wanted all of you here for a premiere of a fine new act, featuring myself, the Remarkable Randall, and world renowned mentalist, Camden." Before anyone could protest, I added, "Before the night is over, I will have revealed what happened to Taft Finch and the key to the amazing Houdini box."

Now the expressions changed to disbelief and apprehension.

"Randall, what are you talking about?" Bart asked. "Is that why you wanted all of us here? I thought Lucas was selling his collection."

"No, I'm not," Lucas said.

Jolly Bob got up. "Well, if you're not selling anything, I'm not staying for this nonsense."

WizBoy blocked his way. "Then you must be the murderer."

His face turned red. "Don't start with me, you punk."

"Then sit down and shut up—unless you want to confess now and save us some time."

"You can't talk to me like that!"

"Fine. Go ahead, walk out. We'll all know you did it."

Jolly Bob sat down. "Oh, I'm not letting you people set me up for this."

WizBoy addressed the company. "Look. I don't know what Randall's got up his sleeve, but if he can clear me of anything, I'm going to pay attention."

"I have nothing up my sleeve," I said, which earned nervous laughs from Rahnee and Fancy.

"Go on, then," Lucas said. "I want to hear this."

"Thank you. For the first part of my act, if you will allow Camden to shake your hands, he will read your innermost thoughts."

WizBoy strode up to Camden and thrust out his hand. "I got nothing to hide."

After shaking WizBoy's hand, Camden went into his act of closing his eyes and touching his temples. He took a minute and then said, "You have a lot of anger and ambition. You want fame, and you want Jilly, but she is not the one for you."

"You're wrong there, pal."

Camden moved to Bart. "The box you seek is beyond your reach. Leave this pointless quest and find your own magical object."

"Yeah, doesn't look like Lucas is going to let go of it," Bart said.

"You can tell me the same thing," Jolly Bob said as Camden shook his hand.

"You need to give up your idea of owning the Magic Club. Sell the store and start your own club. That's one future I see for you."

Jolly Bob looked impressed. "Damn. I never thought of that."

Camden moved to Rahnee. "You must tell the truth about your relationships. There's no reason to hide your feelings."

Rahnee nodded, her eyes filling with tears.

Camden held Fancy's hand a little longer. "I'm sorry about your sister." She pulled away, startled.

He quickly moved on to Lucas. "The truth is about to be revealed."

"Well," Lucas said. "I'm ready. I think we all are."

It was my turn. "Thank you, Camden. Now if my lovely assistant, Jilly, would hand me that object, please." Jilly handed me my phone. "Thank you. As you can see, a simple black cell phone. But if I do this—" I took the phone in one hand and slid the paper across the surface as the kid at Box-It had shown me "—I now have a red cell phone. Exactly like the one that belonged to Taft Finch."

On cue, Camden said, "But that's not his phone."

"No." I changed the red phone back to black. "It doesn't have to be. What the killer didn't realize is Taft was so pleased by the message about the box, he forwarded it to Lucas. So I don't need Taft's phone. I can use his brother's. This one." I held it up. "I think everyone might like to hear that voice mail. Then we'll know exactly who lured Taft to the Magic Club."

I flipped open the phone. Everyone was leaning forward, hanging on my words. Everyone except Jilly, who snatched the phone from my hand and made a run for the door. Jordan met her in the doorway and backed her into the room. She looked around for an escape and found herself surrounded by the magicians, their faces filled with shock and disbelief.

"Here's what I think happened, Jilly," I said. "You were angry at Taft for not honoring his promises to put you in his act. You were jealous of his relationship with Rahnee. You called Taft late Saturday night and left a message saying you'd found the box and for him to meet you at the Magic Club."

Lucas was astonished. "Jilly found the box?"

"I think she knew about the hiding place in the storage room long before you discovered it. In fact, I think she's got a scraped shoulder from trying to push the cinder block back. It's kind of tough to push. Would you mind showing us your shoulder, Jilly?"

Her expression was defiant. "You don't know what you're talking about. I bumped it on the door."

"Okay, you found the box, took out the key, and took the box home. But you brought it back to the club on Sunday because you needed to show it to Taft. Then you left the box behind the bar."

"What?" It was Lucas again. "Anyone could've seen it!"

"But you'd already checked everywhere in the club, hadn't you? You wouldn't have expected the box to reappear behind the bar. And it was pushed back on the shelf. You'd have to bend down to see it. That's what happened when Dirk Kirk was at the club on Monday morning for another audition attempt. After Rahnee snubbed him, he stopped by the bar to help himself to a drink, dropped his cards, as he was constantly doing, and when he bent down to retrieve them, there was a nice shiny box he thought he needed to have. That's what you were looking for the other day, wasn't it, Jilly?"

She refused to answer.

"Well, you didn't need the box anymore. You'd already used it to lure Taft back to the club. You had his drink ready for him. A drink to celebrate. All you needed was a little piece of one of his sleeping pills and one of your Sneeze Ease, pills that look alike, so if anyone saw you with Taft's, you could say it was yours. A Screwdriver has enough orange juice to mask the taste of the pills, at least long enough for Taft to have a good drink. Before he passed out completely, you asked him to show you his latest trick. Once he got inside the trunk, you shut the lid and locked the trunk. Then you hung the key back in its place behind the bar where it was supposed to be. You moved Taft's car so no one would think he was at the club, got rid of his cell phone, and went home."

She glared at me but didn't say anything.

"Why would you do something so horrible?" Rahnee asked, her voice uneven.

"I think I know," I said. "I think Jilly feels her father betrayed her and her love of magic. She was searching for someone to fill that void, to take her on as a partner, an equal magician. Taft started out as a good father figure, but he betrayed her, too—at least in her mind." I turned to Jilly. "I'd like to see those keys you wear around your neck. I'll bet one opens the cabinet."

Glowering, she handed me her necklace. Lucas took the smaller of the two keys, placed it in the lock on the cabinet, and turned the key. The cabinet door opened.

WizBoy stared at her. "*You* opened the box?"

She turned on him. "Yes, I opened the box! None of you thought I could do any sort of magic, but not only did I find it, I figured out how it worked! No one was going to know how I did it, no one. It was going to be the best trick ever!"

"Yeah, well, congratulations," I said.

She fixed her angry gaze on the rest of the group. "None of you ever took me seriously as a magician. No one even gave me a chance, not even to assist! I could do that as well as any of those bimbos you picked!"

"So you murdered Taft and tried to kill Rahnee all because you wanted to be sawed in half?"

Her voice shook. "Taft didn't care about anyone except Rahnee. And then he started seeing that woman at Ali's Cavern! He was going to put her in his act, I know he was!"

"The day WizBoy let you in the club you took one of the bones off his key ring. Why blackmail him?"

She looked scornful. "I knew Rahnee would blame him and then he'd get fired. He's never going to amount to anything. I could've managed that club as well as anyone!"

The look on WizBoy face told me that romance was over.

"You won't be managing anything," Rahnee said. "I can't believe you did this."

"I'm curious," I said. "What did you do with Taft's phone?"

"Smashed it. I should've smashed that one, too. I never thought he'd send that message to Lucas."

"Here's the best part of my act," I said. "He didn't."

◇◇◇

Even though Camden couldn't sing in the choir, he and Kary and I went to church Sunday morning. If I was serious about getting Kary to marry me, I knew I'd have to get used to going to church. Like Camden and driving, I can do it, I just choose not to. But I like having the chance to sit beside her and fantasize during the boring parts.

Jordan had called earlier that morning to let me know that Jilly had been formally charged with the murder of Taft Finch and the attempted murder of Rahnee Nevis. Rahnee and Lucas had called to thank me. After my magic show Saturday night, the rest of the members of WOW had stayed at Lucas' to talk through what had happened. Jolly Bob and WizBoy had settled their differences. Bart and Fancy had been invited to join WOW and perform at the Magic Club on a regular basis.

It was my turn to cook lunch, so I bought everyone some Baxter's Barbecue sandwiches and fries, which we took home. Fred muttered a thank you for his sandwich. Rufus and Angie were all smiles. As Camden had predicted, Angie liked the idea of an outdoor wedding. Saturday afternoon, she and Rufus visited his cousins' farm, and the venue met with her approval. The cousins also offered to host the rehearsal dinner with a pig pickin', which I understand is exactly what it sounds like.

"So your soiree will be al fresco," I said.

"It can be whatever damn language you like," Rufus said. "It's not gonna cost us anything. Kary, you and that magician fella want to do a show at the reception? That'd be fun, and my cousins and their kids would get a kick out of it."

"Sure, I'll ask him. Or don't you need me to play for the wedding?"

"Well, since the wedding's gonna be outside, I'm gettin' the Frog Hollow Boys and Evelene to play. That gal can play the tar out of anything."

Rufus and his pals had what I called a Hillbilly Band, and Evelene played a mean hammered dulcimer. I avoided eye contact with Camden. At Christmas, we'd experienced the speed version of "Messiah." I knew he was imagining how the wedding march would sound. Rufus and Angie would be married in five minutes.

Rufus reached for another sandwich. "Cam, your voice is bound to be back to normal in time for the wedding. We want you to sing somethin' nice, like 'Stand By Your Man.'"

Angie gave Rufus' arm a smack. "That's a woman's song."

"Yeah, but I like the sentiment."

"Cam, I like that old song, what's it called? 'Perfect Love'?"

"'O, Perfect Love.' Yes, I know that one."

"And maybe 'You Light Up My Life.'"

"Sure."

Rufus chewed and swallowed. "Ain't there a song called 'When You Say Nothing At All'? I like the sound of that."

Angie gave him another smack. "Behave yourself."

We were about halfway through lunch when Ellin stopped in. She accepted a sandwich and a glass of tea. "For those of you who haven't heard the good news, Shelia's stepping down as host of 'Ready To Believe.' She said she and Phil have decided they need to take care of Dirk, and Phil's going to honor his commitment to the PSN."

Camden had another question. "What about his health?"

"He still insists Sheila can tell if anything's wrong."

"Good grief."

"You did what you could, Cam." She dipped a French fry in ketchup. "So, tomorrow morning, Bonnie and Teresa will be back where they belong, and the show will go on the way I want it to with a very special guest."

"That would be me," Camden said.

She leaned over to give him a kiss. "Yes, thank you."

"What about Reg?" I asked. "What about 'New Age News'?"

She pointed a fry at me. "Never in a million years."

Chapter Twenty-four

Could It Be Magic?

After lunch, I went into my office and sat for a while. I'd solved
the big crime, but I was stumped about Sandy's bracelet. There
had to be some place I hadn't searched. As for my desk drawer,
I kept it firmly shut. I was feeling pretty good at the moment
and didn't want to risk an emotional upheaval.

Out in the island, Angie was sitting on the green sofa, sewing
white lace onto an acre of white fabric. The TV was on, and
Marilyn Monroe was dancing around with a bunch of men and
singing, "Diamonds Are a Girl's Best Friend." I always enjoy
watching this number.

Angie picked up her plastic cup from the table. "You mind
getting me a refill?"

I took the cup. "No problem." I opened the freezer and found
another cup sitting on top of a package of frozen peas. "You've
already got one in the freezer."

"Oh, yeah? I must have had it in my hand and forgot."

"Here." As I brought her the drink, I thought, *Ice.*
Diamonds.

◇◇◇

First, I went to the Lutheran Church and asked the pastor if I
could look in the freezers. I checked every bag of chicken. No
bracelet.

"Is this all the leftover chicken?" I asked.

"I believe Mrs. Olaf took some home."

The housekeeper had said something about helping her pack the extra food. I went back to Sandy's. "Sandy, where did you store the leftover chicken for the homeless shelter?"

"In my freezer."

"Let's go see."

Sandy's idea of a freezer was a giant white chest freezer that took up almost one whole wall of her huge basement. I hoisted the lid, revealing a wealth of meat, including many plastic bags of chicken.

"Sandy, I think your bracelet fell off into one of these bags."

"Really? Let's look!"

It was in bag number twenty-five, nestled snugly and solidly against a drumstick like an incredibly expensive chicken anklet.

I wrestled the bag from the other bags and presented it to Sandy with a flourish. "Ta-dah!"

Sandy cried with joy and took the chicken upstairs to thaw. She thanked me over and over, and we sat down to share a celebratory glass of wine.

"Some lucky person would've had a very special chicken dinner," I said.

"Thank goodness they didn't! I'm generous, but this bracelet means too much to me to give away. How did you ever think of looking in the freezer?"

"Something similar happened at home—not with a diamond bracelet, however."

"I'm so grateful! I'm not sure I can repay you enough."

There was a clunk behind us. The chicken leg had given up its prize, and the bracelet lay on the counter, defrosted and de-drumsticked.

Sandy washed and dried the bracelet and put it on. "Good as new!" She beamed at me. "You know, there's something different about you, David."

"Different?"

"Oh, you're as handsome as ever, but there's such an air of confidence around you. You seem as if you can solve any mystery, I mean, figuring out where my bracelet was, it's like magic!"

For the moment, I felt as if I really could solve anything, and I stood to give her a bow. "The Remarkable Randall, at your service."

◇◇◇

And maybe I could solve the problem of getting Kary to marry me. Before Kary got home, I enlisted Cindy to help me with my next proposal. Cindy did not want to help, but I finally managed to get the ribbon with "Will you marry me?" around her neck. She wasn't a kitten, so she didn't fit into any hat, and I didn't have a scarf big enough to disguise her. I found a box in the downstairs closet that would have to do. Cindy yowled and complained.

"Be grateful you have a job in show business," I told her.

By the time I met Kary at the door with the box, Cindy had changed to a low growl.

"What's this?" Kary asked.

"Behold! Looks like an ordinary cardboard box, but presto, change-o! The magic cat appears."

And runs like hell down the hallway. I found the ribbon in the bottom of the box, well-chewed but still legible. "Look. The mystic feline has left you a message."

Kary took the ribbon and read it. "Well, I love Cindy, but I don't want to marry her."

"That message, as you well know, is from me, the Remarkable Randall."

"And have you been remarkable today?"

"Extremely remarkable. I found Sandy's diamond bracelet. It had fallen into a bag of chicken and was frozen to a leg."

"I'll bet the chicken didn't want to give it up."

"It was a struggle, but I managed to prevail." *Just as I will prevail and win you.*

She curled the ribbon around her finger. "Speaking of magic, I talked to Omar, and he likes the idea of doing a show for Rufus and Angie's reception. He's not good with the idea of playing for the Baby Love meeting, though. He said he'd think about it, and if that doesn't work out, I'm sure I'll think of something else."

I was relieved to hear her plans were on hold. "What about a country wedding at the cousins' farm? The bridesmaids could wear overalls and carry ears of corn. We could ride to the service in a hay wagon and do-si-do down the aisle."

"That sounds delightful. But no."

"What's your dream wedding, then?"

"You know, I haven't given it much thought. Something simple, traditional. Something far in the future."

"But with a tall, dark, handsome magical man like me, right?"

She stood on tiptoe to kiss my cheek. "Maybe."

That was as good as it was going to get for now.

◇◇◇

Monday I was in my office catching up on some accounts when Camden came in.

He sat down in front of my desk. "You remember Lloyd Johnson, the man with the heart condition who needed to leave a will?"

"The guy who told you to mind your own business?"

"Yes. He died yesterday, and the family wanted to talk to me. They said he changed his mind. He reconsidered what I said and had his lawyer draw up a will. The family was mad at first, but said now they see that was really the best thing because it would've torn them apart for nothing. They thanked me for making the effort. They said I could've walked away and let them fight it out, but I didn't."

"Good. Everything's settled."

"Except his daughter wanted to ask me about heaven. She kept saying, 'You're the real thing, aren't you? Is my father okay? Is he in heaven?' I couldn't answer that."

"Well, you can't know everything."

"No, I mean, I could see images, as if people were helping him cross over, helping him—I can't explain it. I don't know if that vision was real or just wishful thinking."

"Either way, it's a nice image."

"I wanted everything to be okay."

"Did you see flames and pitchforks?"

"Yep, and you right in the middle of it."

Fred came wandering in. "The bank. I got to go to the bank."

"Fred, you don't have any money there," Camden said. "We checked, remember?"

"I want to go."

I was in a good mood, and Fred wasn't going to quit. "Come on, Fred. I'll take you."

Fred put on his coat and got into the backseat of the Fury, mumbling under his breath. Camden turned around in the passenger seat. "What's at the bank?"

"Strongbox. I got a key."

Another key. "Hope it's the right one, Fred," I said.

At First Savings, Fred told the teller what he wanted, and she led us back to a row of boxes set in the wall.

"Here you are, sir."

With trembling hands, Fred put the key in the lock and turned. The box opened. He reached inside and brought out a smaller box. He fumbled with the catch and finally pushed it in my hands. "Open it."

I pried open the box and was startled by the rainbow flash of light from a gold ring. Four small emeralds surrounded by diamonds winked and sparkled. Fred's old pale eyes filled with tears.

"It was my Cora's."

I didn't know what to say. Fred had been living in Camden's house for more years than I could remember, penniless, drab, miserable. All this time, he'd had a small fortune stashed away. He could've been living in a nice place, wearing decent clothes, perhaps traveling. But looking into his sad worn face, I knew he never could've sold this ring.

Fred took the box from me and gazed at the ring for a few moments. "Cam, you take this and give it to that girl of yours so she'll marry you. She's ornery, but so was my Cora, and you deserve something for taking me in."

"Fred, no. I would've taken you in anyway."

"I know it. Don't do anyone much good sitting in a box, though, does it?" He thrust the box into Camden's hands. His voice was rougher than his usual croak. "Take it. Cora would want you to have it. You know that better than anyone." Light danced on the emeralds and diamonds gracefully set in gold.

"It's beautiful, but I can't take it. It's all you have of her."

"No, it ain't." He tapped the side of his head. "Got her right here. Always will. Nothing can take that away."

I thought of Lindsey. My memories of her, no matter how painful, would be something I'd always cherish.

"Think that noisy girlfriend of yours will like it?"

"Yes, she will."

"She'd better. It cost a lot. Just take it, boy. Take it. Don't tell her where it come from, though. She don't like me." The ring caught a ray of light and splashed colors on the wall. "Cora always did love emeralds, she did. Her eyes were green." He pulled a rumpled handkerchief from his back pocket and blew his nose. "Put it away now."

I think Camden would've stood there forever if I hadn't given him a hint.

"So it's time to pop the big question."

He put the ring back in its box. "Yes, it is."

◇◇◇

Back at the house, Camden called Ellin and asked her to stop by the house after work.

"It would be more fun if you did it on TV," I said.

He gave me a look. "No, it's not an emergency," he said into the phone. "It's important, though." He listened a moment and hung up, eyes wide. "She's coming over right now."

"Perhaps she senses something at last."

Camden paced the island until we heard Ellin's car drive up. Then he hurried to the door to let her in.

"What's all this, Cam?"

"There's something I need to ask you." He took her hand and led her to the island.

I wanted to give them some privacy, so I went into my office, but I couldn't help overhearing.

"I can stay only a few minutes."

"This will only take a few minutes."

I was pretty sure he'd gotten down on one knee. In a few moments I heard Ellin gasp, and I knew she'd been impressed by the fiery sparkles of diamond and emerald.

"Oh, Cam."

"Will you marry me, Ellie? You've always been the one. Please say yes. I'll do my best to make you happy."

I heard the odd little sounds that meant she was crying. "Cam, you couldn't make me any happier. I love you more than anything in the world."

Wow. Didn't think she had it in her. All was quiet for a while, and then she appeared at my door. She held out her hand to me. "Randall, did you see this?"

"Really nice, Ellin. Congratulations."

"I've got to call Mother."

As she hurried away to use her phone, Camden came to the door. "Whew."

"Say that again."

"No, I mean it. I wasn't sure if she'd like it."

"Can you hear yourself?"

He looked annoyed. "Well, I didn't know."

"No, can you hear yourself. Your voice is back."

"Oh, my gosh! It is."

"I'll send you my bill."

He looked at me in wonder. "Do you suppose it really was all in my mind?"

"Isn't everything?"

"Randall, you're good."

"Hey, you lose it, I find it."

He gave me one of his long considering looks. "I'll have to find some way to return the favor."

◇◇◇

Camden and Ellin went out that night to celebrate their engagement. When I came into the dining room, the dishes had been cleared. The DVD of Lindsey's dance recital lay all by itself in the center of the table.

Okay. I get the message.

I opened one more box.

I put the DVD into the player, turned on the TV, and pressed "play." I fast-forwarded through the first few numbers of chubby four-year-olds in tiny tutus, then older girls in black and gold leotards, then Lindsey's group.

There were twelve little girls in her class. They had on shiny white leotards and tights, and each girl wore a different colored skirt. Lindsey's skirt was green. She had a green ribbon in her hair. She was the only one keeping the beat, her eyes steadfastly on her teacher sitting in the orchestra pit, the only one gracefully lifting her arms at the right moment, the only one turning, one foot pointed, the other in place.

At first, I didn't recognize the music. Some easy listening tune, Barry Manilow, perhaps, and then, as the girls pirouetted in their rainbow-colored costumes, the title came to me.

"Could It Be Magic?"

Concentration shone on Lindsey's face. She was completely in the moment, circling, raising her arms above her head, then slowly bringing them down.

The dance was over. She smiled her perfect radiant smile, the smile that said, I did it exactly right. I loved every minute and can't wait to dance again.

So I pressed rewind and she danced again.

Could it be magic?

Yes.

It could.

To receive a free catalog of Poisoned Pen Press titles, please contact us in one of the following ways:

Phone: 1-800-421-3976
Facsimile: 1-480-949-1707
Email: info@poisonedpenpress.com
Website: www.poisonedpenpress.com

Poisoned Pen Press
6962 E. First Ave. Ste 103
Scottsdale, AZ 85251